Songs of Three Great South Indian Saints

Songs of Three Great South Indian Saints

William J. Jackson

DELHI
OXFORD UNIVERSITY PRESS
CALCUTTA   CHENNAI   MUMBAI
1998

Oxford University Press, Great Clarendon Street, Oxford OX2 6DP

Oxford New York
Athens Auckland Bangkok Calcutta
Cape Town Chennai Dar es Salaam Delhi
Florence Hong Kong Istanbul Karachi
Kuala Lumpur Madrid Melbourne Mexico City
Mumbai Nairobi Paris Singapore
Taipei Tokyo Toronto

and associates in

Berlin Ibadan

ISBN 0 19 564655 X

Typeset by Eleven Arts, Delhi 110 035
Printed at Pauls Press, New Delhi 110 020
and published by Manzar Khan, Oxford University Press
YMCA Library Building, Jai Singh Road, New Delhi 110 001

Dedicated to my helpers in this venture

T.S. Parthasarathy in Madras (all those days sitting side by side with Telugu lyrics while street vendors cried outside the windows . . .)

H.L. Chandrasekhara in Mysore (thanks for your hospitality at your home when I visited and for the years of discussions and correspondence)

Narayana and Yashoda Bhat in New Delhi (our many afternoons spent with the Haridasa utterances in Rohini waiting for cool monsoon rains)

And to conversation-partner friends: R. Venkataraman; Raji and Ganesan Bala; Durgu Rao; Vasudha Narayanan; Deepak Sarma; and Anand Kannan

> 'Each more melodious note I hear
> Brings this reproach to me,
> That I alone afford the ear,
> Who would the music be.'
>
> HENRY DAVID THOREAU

Contents

Introduction

Three saints' voices:
Two grandfathers and a man who rose through
the ranks

Three singers are represented in this collection. Annamacharya, the first, was the *kirtanacharya* or 'master of *kirtana*' (devotional songs) in Telugu at Tirupati in south India, and has for centuries been called the *padakavita pitamaha* or 'grandfather of *padam* (lovesong) lyrics'. The second singer, the prolific Purandaradasa, has traditionally been known as *pitamaha* or 'the grandfather of Karnatic music'. The third singer, Kanakadasa, unlike the first two was not born a brahman, but through his own irrepressible spiritual merit rose through the ranks to prominence and respect as a *bhakti* lyricist and poet. Of these three *vaggeyakaras* (composer–lyricist saints, speakers for the heart of bhakti), two spoke Kannada and one Telugu. All three lived around 1500, when the Vijayanagara empire was at its peak, and when the south saw a flourish of Hindu culture and the north experienced a wave of bhakti enthusiasm with saints like Narasimha Mehta, Kabir, Chaitanya and Vallabha. This book offers echoes of their voices, in late twentieth-century English.

All three singers were devoted to Vishnu, though they wrote occasional songs to Shiva and the Goddess Lakshmi. According to their life stories, all three were called dramatically from their humdrum lives to a transformative intensity of devotion to Vishnu. Vishnu is believed to be the divine Maintainer of the universe, preserving it from harm. Many of the stories of Vishnu show him restoring order to an unbalanced cosmos. The *mudra* or signature embedded in the last lines of each of the three singers' songs indicates the form of Vishnu which inspired their devotion. Annamacharya sang to Shri Venkateshvara, the Lord whose shrine is on Tirumala mountain. (The Lord as *Uchchiyilninran*, 'the One standing at the crest of the hill', is an old name for the deity of this sacred place, though it is not literally accurate, since the temple is not actually at the hill's highest point). The four-armed image of Venkateshvara stands with upper arms holding conch and *chakra*, while the lower right hand is in the boon-giving pose and the fingers of the lower left hand rest on his thigh, with the thumb near his waist. Devotees often understand this to mean that 'Samsara, the ocean of births and deaths, may seem deep, but devotees protected by Vishnu's grace can wade through it without being lost.' Purandaradasa sang to Purandara Vithala—Vishnu standing on a brick, with hands on hips—the form in which he appeared to devotees Pundalika and Rukmini. Kanakadasa sang to Lord Kaginele Adikeshava, Vishnu as Krishna, associated with the village where Kanakadasa built a temple with a treasure he found.

Annamacharya was the eldest of these three singer–saints, already an old man when Purandaradasa was still a youth. He belonged to the Ramanuja school of Vaishnava philosophy, *Vishisthadvaita*, which means qualified non-dualism of soul and Lord. The other two were members of the Madhvacharya branch of Vaishnava philosophy—sometimes called *dvaita,* or dualism. (Although 'dualist' is a convenient label for comparative purposes it is not the way Madhva or his followers identified themselves). These three personalities all share the south Indian Hindu spiritual ethos.

Translation as a labour of love, rife with choices

The process of translating is necessarily one of continual selection of the best from a number of possibilities; the translator is like a traveller on a constantly forking road. A sphinx is always proposing a puzzle which you must solve. If you translate literally like an automatic dictionary, then a handful of experts may add your work to the piles of hard-to-read but putatively accurate works in their domain. Such a translation will be held at a distance from everyday life—as comprising abstract intellectual matters not really connected to current events in lives today, but matters to think about aloofly, professionally. It will be data but not food for the soul.

However, if you work with the idioms in your own mother tongue and convey the universal or basic human meaning and point of the original in your translation, millions might listen and learn and assimilate something useful into their lives, while the experts quibble and sneer with disdain. It all depends on which culture you want to serve—that of the dry specialist–drones, or that of the hungry wide world. I admire the translation work of such translators as A.K. Ramanujan and David Rosenberg, for their poetry, accuracy, and ability to feed the hungry. I believe that it is valuable to have more than one translation of any given work, because there are a number of audiences and uses for translations. While one kind of translation might interest a new generation of readers another might provide the material required for the discussion of scholarly technicalities.

In selecting songs to translate from among the many compositions of the singer–saints of south India, I had the expert help and advice of Narayana Bhat and his wife Yashoda (Kannada), T.S. Parthasarathy (Telugu), and H.L. Chandrasekhara (Kannada). For the purposes of this book, I accept the texts which are commonly accepted by south Indians since I am interested in the songs which are carried on in the tradition today through performance and publication representative of Hindu values and ideals. The songs represent the organic memory, the folk mind, the collective spirituality—parts of the shared symbol system of south India's religious people. I leave to others the task of sorting and sifting involved in historical text criticism.

The poetry of bhakti, full of saint-inspired ideals found in the ethos of south India, is a rich resource. I hope, as a literary translator of that treasury into English, that my work is a kind of mirroring device, deriving from the original and evoking in the reader, the corresponding images in the songs. Just as A.K. Ramanujan used the colloquial English phrase 'for real' when the original Kannada had a similar phrase, I use the phrase 'get a life' in translating the Kanakadasa song 'Bhajisi', because it has the essence of the original wording. Language is sometimes capable of conveying with current phrasings the same ideas that centuries-old lyrics were making, and so it is absurd to assume that fidelity to earlier

literature is found only in 'thee' and 'thou' formalities. I think we are
called upon to translate into the language of the younger generation,
not the older generation. As Whitehead suggested,

> traditional ideas are never static . . . they are either fading into
> meaningless formulae, or are gaining power by the new lights
> thrown by more delicate apprehension. No generation can
> merely reproduce its ancestors . . . . You may preserve the life in
> a flux of form, or preserve the form amid an ebb of life.[1]

In this age when Shakespeare is often performed in modern dress is it
really so bold occasionally to translate with a little modern flair, to
translate 'Leader with a curled up tail (i.e. dog) who sniffs' as 'King
Snoopy'? Let the reader be ready for flexibility by becoming a little
more flexible, allowing a little play as the original texts often have a
liveliness, delighting in the fun of spoken language.

These songs are of human existential situations, sketched in *singable*
lines of verse—Vaishnava bhakti and Haridasa earnestness intent upon
digesting experience, making it into soul; secreting music for other ears
to hear. These songs form a memorable art which aims at sharing wisdom,
helping other souls to find meaning in whatever life flings at them.

A sample song from Telugu

An example of the elements of a Telugu song to be considered when
translating into English follows. It is Annamacharya's song 'Kondalalo
nelakonna' in which he mentions Ramanuja's uncle and guru:

Pallavi. Kondalalo (on the hill) nelakonna (enshrined) Konetirayudu
(presiding deity of the temple bathing pool) vadu (he) kondalanta
(mountain like) varamulu (boons) guppeduvadu (he is the giver of)

Charanam 1. Kummari dasudaina (devotee belonging to potter
community) Kuruvarati nambi (devotee's name) yimmanna (whatever
he asked to be given) varamulellan (all the boons) ichchinavadu (he was
giver) dommulu (fighting) sesinayatti (being involved in) Tondaman
chakravarti (king Tondaman) rammanna chotiki (to the place he wanted
God to appear before him) vacci (he went) namminavadu (he was the
inspirer of faith)

Charanam 2. achchapu (with obvious) vedukatoda (enthusiasm) Anantaluvariki [for Ananta alvar (who cleared the forest)] muchchili (stealthily) vettiki (unpaid drudgery) mannu (earth) mochinavadu (he was the one who carried) machchina dolaka (with much affection) Tirumalanambi toduta (uncle of Ramanuja) nichchanichcha (day after day) mataladi (conversing) nochchinavadu (he was the one who did the good act).

Charanam 3. Kanchilone (in Kanchipuram) nunde (living) Tirukkachchinambi (name of a devotee, non-brahman Vaishya guru of Ramanuja) mide (on him) garuninchi (took pity) tanayedaku (to his place) rappinchinavadu (he was the one who had him brought) yenchi nekkudaina (the great and noble) Venkateshudu (Lord) manalaku (to all of us) manchivadai (as a well-wisher) karuna (mercifully) palinchinavadu (he was protecting)

The above word-for-word translation is of the song 'Kondalalo nelakonna' by Annamacharya (SAS no. 33 p. 34). It contains more historical references than most of his songs. The lines when put in order may be translated as:

> The Lord of the temple bathing pool,
> Lord whose shrine is on the mountain
> He is the generous one—
> Giver of boons as great as mountains

1. He gave every boon asked for by Kuruvanti Nambi the devotee
   who was of the community of potters.
   And when King Tondaman Chakravarti was involved in fighting
   a war,
   and asked the Lord to appear to him, he did, and the King believed

> The Lord of the temple bathing pool,
> Lord whose shrine is on the Mountain
> He is the generous one—
> Giver of boons as great as mountains

2. He carried earth like a common labourer to help Anantalavar,
   stealthily doing drudgery without pay, with obvious enthusiasm.
   And with great affection, sympathizing with Tirumalanambi,
   he spoke lovingly with him day after day

The Lord of the temple bathing pool,
Lord whose shrine is on the Mountain
He is the generous one—
Giver of boons as great as mountains

3. When Tirukachchinambi was living in Kanchipuram, the Lord
   took pity on him, and brought him to his presence
   He protected us all, the magnanimous Lord— he's the one who has
   blessed us all, full of compassion, our Venkatesha
   Lord of the temple bathing pool . . . Giver of boons as great as
   mountains.

Translators work in a variety of ways to deal with such issues as verse form and stylistic features, drawing on different resources. The rhymes in Telugu or Kannada, the metre, the formal shape of the verses I have usually not tried to mimic very closely. My rendering is faithful to the literal meaning but is of the idiomatic English of our times showing what the refrain is, and what the verses are—that cyclical pattern which gives the content a viable rhythm. I have tried to be careful to stay close to that rhythmical thought pattern, presenting the unfolding parts of the song and the return to the deep theme of the refrain. I vary the refrains with small shifts in phrasing usually, to keep the monotony away, just as a singer in most cultures does not mechanically repeat a refrain with perfect sameness each time it comes around, but allows a little free play, just as we notice new ideas or nuances in a refrain depending on the thrust of the lines which preceded it.

Scholarship, conversation and consolidation

I am reminded of Jacques Waardenburg, the Dutch scholar who edited the book *Classical Approaches to the Study of Religion*, speaking at Harvard in 1977. Speculating on the future of research in the history of religion, he predicted that collaboration, teamwork rather than isolated research, would be more and more necessary. While researching on the singer–saint Tyagaraja of Tanjavur district a few years later, I realized the full impact of that statement. I experienced how difficult it would be for any one person to know all the languages necessary to grasp the cultural fabric of Tanjavur—Tamil, Sanskrit, Telugu, Marathi, Kannada. To do justice to the context of a single creative person's life and work there, in terms of historical, anthropological and sociological knowledge, is indeed a complex challenge.

This book in part is a result of my travelling to learn from others and gather information, from working with insightful and generous fellow students of south Indian bhakti. T.S. Parthasarathy in Madras, Rajanikanta Rao in Vijayawada and Bhadrachalam, H.L. Chandrasekhara in Mysore, Narayana and Yashoda Bhat in New Delhi all helped me to journey in the world of lyrics created by Annamacharya, Purandaradasa and Kanakadasa. Their knowledge of the original languages, and their guidance in interpretation helped orient me in this cultural landscape— their knowledge of linguistics, ethos, geography, spirituality and folklore was of tremendous help. Conversations with these friends gave me access to a world which my dictionaries, helpful and necessary as they are, could not always open up for me. (As Tagore said, 'Languages are jealous sovereigns, and passports are rarely allowed for travellers to cross their strictly guarded borders.') I am grateful for the help my guides gave me and for the many enjoyable hours spent working with these co-labourers. Encouragement from others such as Mr and Mrs Prabhakar Modur, Vasudha Narayanan and Ramesh and Lovleen Bijlani, whose hospitality I enjoyed in New Delhi, was also greatly appreciated. G.F. Shamsuddin, who helped me get around Karnataka and Andhra Pradesh, also deserves my thanks. V.A.K. Ranga Rao made many helpful suggestions in the Telugu parts of the book, and N. Geeta Rao made useful corrections in the Kannada parts. B.D. Nageshwara Rao and R. Venkatraman also read the manuscript with care.

My training in the study of bhakti is multi-stranded. At Harvard, scholars such as J.L. Mehta, John Carman, Jack Hawley, Diana Eck and visiting lecturer A.K. Ramanujan provided examples of approaches to this rich aspect of Hindu life. Annamarie Schimmel, translating Sufi verses, was also an influence. Working with Indian scholars, such as T.S. Parthasarathy and Rajanikanta Rao in my research on Tyagaraja and bhakti saints, and studying the works of one of the greatest Sanskritists of this or any other century, V. Raghavan, also shaped my understanding. The discourses of Sathya Sai Baba and twenty-five years of knowing him and his devotees, before, during and after graduate studies at Harvard, also played an integral part in my knowledge of the bhakti path of the heart which the songs gathered here seek to convey.

Notes

1. Alfred North Whitehead, cited by Felix Frankfurter in an essay 'Tradition' in *Law and Politics: Occasional Papers of Felix Frankfurter, 1913–1938,* ed. Archibald Macleish and E.F. Prichard Jr., New York: Harcourt, Brace, 1939.

Dynamic Bhakti Images in the Songs of Annamacharya, Purandaradasa and Kanakadasa

*All that a man has to say or do that can possibly concern mankind,
is in some shape or other to tell the story of his love—to sing, and if
he is fortunate and keeps alive, he will be forever in love. This alone
is to be alive to the extremities. It is a pity that this divine creature
should even suffer from cold feet; a still greater pity that the coldness
so often reaches to his heart.*[1]

HENRY DAVID THOREAU

Historical background and bhakti rules of thumb: A meander of reflections[2]

The Vijayanagara empire was founded a little before the mid-fourteenth century to retrieve Hindu south India from Muslim domination. It reached its most expansive state with Krishnadevaraya, who ruled for two decades beginning in 1509. His realm, or the area of which he was titular head and which was governed by provincial viceroys (*nayakas*), covered much of India. It stretched from Orissa in the east to Kanara in the west, and extended down to Cape Comorin in the south. Vijayanagara, the capital city, covered twenty-five square miles on the southern side of the Tungabhadra river in Karnataka. The population of the Tungabhadra heartland in Krishnadevaraya's time was about two million; 100,000 lived in the capital city, and many millions lived in other parts of the south. A number of descriptions of this flourishing kingdom exist in Sanskrit poems and in European travellers' accounts.[3]

For Europe this was an age of conquest and discovery; in the sixteenth century the term 'discovery' began to be used both in the new empirically based sciences and in the imperial exploration of new territories—for example, the 'discovery' of America. Western civilization, partially rooted in the prophetic traditions, has a linear style with brittle breaks with the past: as Abraham left Ur, so Moses, Jesus, Paul and Augustine, and Muhammad broke away too; the Protestant Reformation and the French and American Revolutions also mark sharp breaks with the past.[4] By comparison, Hinduism seems more organic and continuous, content to carry along older strata instead of denying them, preserving the old while absorbing the new. Some, like V. Raghavan, have seen this dynamic as *yogakshema* , 'keeping and getting' or maintaining and acquiring; others, like J.L. Mehta have pointed out problems with India's sometimes undiscerning 'swallowing whole' of foreign elements, which later give her indigestion.[5] In any case, perennial Hindu culture in the Vijayanagara age arrived at another culmination of its old tradition in the Sanskrit works of brothers Vidyaranya and Sayana, and in the music and vernacular lyrics of great bhakti composer saints, such as Annama-charya (1408–1507), Purandaradasa (1485–1565) and Kanakadasa (sixteenth century).[6]

In one sense, Europe prevailed in its venture of conquest and discovery; colonialism and secular science became swaying forces in the world. Yet, if one looks into modern and post-modern history, it is evident that Europe did not prevail completely and forever. The programme to modernize, rationalize, and 'civilize' had its limits. Some people today sense that though the domination of the scientific age is an obvious fact worldwide, seen in omnipresent technology and mechanistic thinking, the victors are still haunted by the presence of the vanquished. The repressed life–spirit of native peoples, the persistence of Buddhist wisdom, Vedanta's vision, the bhakti path of love, interest in the 'Tao of Physics' and chaos science may represent non-linear non-Eurocentric views one-sided moderns need for human health and survival.[7] I shall return to this later.

With its devotion to linear, literal either/or thought, modern western civilization has often tended to find comfort in conceiving apartheids[8] of human capacities, separating for example the impulses of passionate love from the pieties of spiritual devotion. On the other hand

> . . . sexuality, *eros*, passion, love, compassion, *agape* and devotion . . . constitute a kind of continuum in India. To break this up into separate insights would mean to destroy one of the most remarkable insights we could gain from the Indian traditions: that religion can manifest itself through such a continuum, instead of restricting itself to its last part.[9]

Songs of Vijayanagara poet–saint composers, arriving at new images on the path of love, help us appreciate this creative insight; holistic affirmations of bhakti help us to explore the heart's landscape. While we may not always be able to point out with absolute certainty what is unique or most specific to the bhakti lyrics of this episteme or time period, we can often say what seems to be very strong and dynamic in these compositions.

Annamacharya, Telugu poet and composer of the late fifteenth and early sixteenth century, sings of the pull of love, bhakti's all-demanding all-giving passion for the beloved, in the voice of a love–mad tribal girl, in a song beginning with the words *Kondalo koyila:*

> When I heard the call
> Of the cuckoo on the hill
> My heart was torqued,
> And, squeezed, it broke
> But when I arrived
> At your threshold
> My soul was healed
>
> When I was leaving my house
> (It makes my head spin
> To think about it now)
> My mate, tiger fierce,
> Blocked the door, snarling
> —My hairs erect with love
> Who cared what anyone said?
> I had heard the call
> Of the cuckoo on the hill[10]

Bhagavan and *bhakta*, mutually inseparable Lord and devotee, call each other into existence with irresistible affinity. It is an all-consuming relationship: What does it take? All. When will it be consummated? Now. Purandaradasa in an *Ugabhoga* emphasizes this intense urgency of bhakti, with its mood of impatient refusal to wait and procrastinate:

> What we hope with all our heart
> to get at some future time
> —let's get that today!
> What we want to have today
> —let's get it right now!
> What we can get right now
> let's enjoy this very instant!
> Let's have the loving mercy of
> Lord Purandara Vithala![11]

Bhakti gives the bhakta a caring correspondent—someone to talk to in a certain way: with love, thanks, longing, reciprocal care and awe; and with dependence in need, with hope for help in coping. The Lord is the listener of urgent pleas, the understanding helper, the parent, the beloved and the all-encompassing source and goal of existence. The bhakta needs this 'I-and-Thou' way of relating, and bhakti practices satisfy this need. Bhakti opens the way and gives continued access to the mystery of mutuality: the cosmos smiles with the dimple of antichaos, which is meaning, and the bhakta smiles back, feeling fit. The individual human being and the sacred master of the abyss are in this thing together, it seems to the bhakta, and when devoted people join together invoking and relating to the sacred presence, life on earth seems to become resonant with meaning and the harmony of well-being.

But love, as the life of a bhakti saint such as Chaitanya shows, is not always comfortable—it is being held in exquisite heartbreak's being, and letting go to flow with love. Love is like the light freed by the fireball flaring forth at the origin. Love means being made a fool of in the Holi festival of life with all its surprises. Ratiocination means rule—making a king of yourself, dictating decrees about how you want things to be. Love is the giving up, the giving over of self, not aggrandizement. Love is open, which means it is vulnerable; control means being closed, buckling down. It is a rule of thumb that to worldly people much of real bhakti seems politically inept; the devotee depends on the invisible power of God, and not on the status or the power plays of humans. Bhakti saints often seem to insult or ignore the most powerful people—kings, rich men and other elitists.

The bhakta seems unimpressed by worldly priorities. In bhakti the Lord and the devotee seem to interact, somehow sharing experiences, even if one is the master and the other the dependant. They enjoy each other in rich give-and-take *lilas* or playful pastimes of spiritual tastings, weaving a harmony of heart–hurt and bliss. Songs describing the feeling have been sung in vivid images, for example by sixteenth-century Kannada poet–composer Kanakadasa expressing his puzzlement about what's going on:

> Are you inside illusion or is illusion inside you?
> Are you inside the body or is the body inside you?
>
> Is the open space in the house, or
> is the house in the open space
>   or are both inside the eyes that behold them?
> Is the eye inside the *buddhi*, or
> Is the buddhi inside the eye, or
>   are both inside you, Lord Hari? Are you inside . . .
>
> Is the sweetness in the sugar, or
> Is the sugar in the sweetness, or
>   are both on the tasting tongue?
> Is the tongue inside the mind, or
> Is the mind inside the tongue, or
>   are both inside you, Lord Hari? Are you inside . . .
>
> Is the fragrance in the flower, or
> Is the flower in the fragrance, or
>   are both inside the sense of smell?
> Unique Lord Keshava of Kaginele,
> Life–breath is not just deep within me,
> It is deep within you, too; Are you inside illusion . . . .[12]

The bhakti life resolves such questions for the bhakta, in experiences which are lived, not just in logic which is thought, for the beloved is found as the breath of one's breath. Bhakti has often been poorly understood, only grudgingly given its place in the scheme of India's religious life, by those ashamed of its downhome qualities. True, the variety of devotees of Shiva, Vishnu, and the Goddess has confused monotheists with the display of apparent polytheism, while Upanishadic philosophy is more amenable to Protestant sensibilities. But at its best, bhakti is a purifying system of inversion and levelling—to rejoin what has been sundered, to re-win the grace of wholeness, to atone for loss of innocence, to reunite mind, feelings and will. Vijayanagara singer–saints, like other culturally creative Hindu contributors to religious life, knew that bhakti had to be simple enough to be livable, rich and varied enough to be attractive, and traditional enough to be acceptable. It had to be deep enough to be inexhaustible and always challenging, substantial enough to give meaning to all experiences, powerful enough to endow kings with legitimacy and uplift the lowest villager, with heartfelt sincerity as its trustworthy touchstone. Those are some of bhakti's 'rules of thumb'.

In humankind's quest for grace, the genuine bhakti life is a classical example of realizing the beauty, depth, exquisite sacredness and order of existence in terms of devotion to a favourite personal deity or *ishtadevata*, by means of repeating the holy name and recalling the exemplary stories told about that deity.

The rumination on the holy name is the staple of the bhakti spiritual diet.[13] It is not some trivial part of the religion on an equal footing with many others; it is a central practice. Annamacharya sang in his song 'Akativelalanalapaina' that whenever one is hungry, exhausted, in need, or lonely, in error, maligned or in terror, waylaid by creditors or locked away in prison, the only way out is through saying the Name. The prime symbol of God, the holy name, is to be always repeated, or whenever one is able to in the midst of one's busy life. This is another bhakti 'rule of thumb'.

Bhakti images of mutuality and outrageous love

Love is well known as the condition in which conventional differences and personal boundaries are dissolved and spontaneous intermingling and heightened sensibilities of union transcend individuality. Classical India had her own ethos of love—non-Platonic, non-Freudian, non-Marxian and non-Victorian. It was only with the nineteenth-century rule by colonialist England, with the intrusion of a self-styled master–race's macho self-image (and what some have rather humorously and not enviously termed 'phallocentricity') that some educated Hindus became ashamed of the emphasis on the celebration of femininity in the stories of the divine culture hero Krishna, the Lover of lovers.[14] Fearing the embarrassing revelation of an inner softness, which might seem to disclose a deep fascination with the psyche–mysterious beauty that is woman, and realizing what the British seemed to respect in terms of hypermasculinity and hyper-rationalism, they denied and buried aspects of the Hindu past. Yet if we look at Bengali memories of Chaitanya, or thousands of *shringara* lyrics of Annamacharya, or, even a few centuries later, the life of Ramakrishna Paramahamsa, we can see that it was not such a shameful or impossible dream. Through loving the unique beloved, the souls of men and women, as it were, became *gopis*, finding a union of healing within reach. To complete the soul's awakening there was a sublimation of desire, immersing the soul in sublime love, to know bhakti's deeper consciousness. The intensity depends on the personality experiencing the tantric and *sahaja bhakti* strategy of letting burning desires flame up toward the light, allowing natural psyche energy to aspire, turning base proclivities and chaotic troubles to fuel the fire of spirituality, putting passion into service of the highest goal, realization. All in life is God, Kanakadasa sings in *Tanu ninnadu*:

It's all part of You—this very body and soul
The joy and the sorrow—daily life as a whole.

Yours is sweet speech, the *Veda, Purana,* and *Shastra*
And the power with which we listen intently to your tale
And the fixed staring with great fascination
    at beautiful young girls, that gaze is you
It's all part of You . . .

The pleasure we feel anointing the body with sandalwood
    paste, *kasturi* musk and other fragrances is yours
And the tongue, Lord, which relishes food's flavours
    at a six-*rasa* feast—that joy belongs to you
It's all part of You . . .

This body of five senses caught up in the net
    of illusory bondage, O Ranga, source of all the desire
the body feels, is man his own master? Our body and soul
our very life, it's all part of you, Father of the god
of love, joys and sorrows of daily life as a whole.

The genius of seeing all in life as part of God seems able to open toward experiences of oneness where others feel only shame.[15]

Another bhakti 'rule of thumb' is that it allows for, and celebrates, the confusion of divine causes and human rights. Vijayanagara singer–saints saw loopholes of hope in such a condition: 'I've come to this earth just because of you, so why hold me responsible? O Lord, did I emerge from myself?' Kanakadasa asks in *Nandine*, asserting his dependence:

> O God, whose is the folly, yours or mine?
> For nine months I was in my mother's womb
> You were my protector, and when
> I was reluctant to leave her womb
> Vishnu, didn't you goad me out then?[16]

Kanaka goes on arguing, making an existential demand: let the one who put him here play his part. The game of casting blame and demanding satisfaction is one of the archetypal stances in the bhakti imagination. The bhakti vision reveals in Ahalya the destiny of all souls devoted to the avatar—release from *samsara*. The bhakti vision announces in Prahlada the reward of all persistent yearning devotion—rescue. The bhakti vision teaches in Gajendra the strength of the Lord's promise to protect those who cry out with full surrender. The bhakti vision encourages through Ajamila the power of the name even for worldly people. Each bhakti symbol manifests a relationship accessible to ordinary people and gives dignity to the trusting strugglers who make their way on life's rugged landscape.

In the old stories of the bhakta–Bhagavan relationship the balance of power is unequal, favouring the deity; yet the devotee can sometimes triumph over the deity, winning his boon even against the Lord's will and the usual order of things in life. The stakes are high; the heroes of bhakti play the game and take their chances, full of trust. The body is heavy but the voice of devotion can rise and the heart's feelings can fly. The bhakta's role is to surrender and offer all to the beloved great attractor.

Bhakti's liberal vision is that ordinary people, being ignorant and conditioned by karma, cannot completely control or dictate what's in them, what flows from them and therefore any intense feeling directed toward Bhagavan is liberating—the greatest fault is indifference. Bhakti traditions helped generate among all classes in Hindu society a generosity and affection toward unconventional God-obsessed people and 'fools for the Lord'—yogis, singers, mendicants, and Bengali Bauls, madcap Sufis.[17]

The aspiration toward vision in bhakti:
Mutual attraction and love's satisfaction

Bhakti's prime mood is shringara, longing, waiting, feeling separated, intently listening in expectation. The eager devotee yearns for the beloved's approach, and this leads to illumination. 'Success is immediate where effort is intense', and 'illumination is attained by devotion to Lord Ishvara', it is said in the first book of Patanjali's classic text *Yogasutra*.[18] Yoga is an experiential process, and bhakti yoga is a symbol system of transformations and purifications which precipitate realizations in consciousness; bhakti yoga drives toward experience of the beloved's presence, in a vision or a dream, in a sense of proximity and intermingling. Hence in songs of the singer–saints one encounters exclamations like: 'I saw Krishna!' or 'I saw Shiva!' or 'I saw Rama!' or 'I saw the Goddess!' The proof is in the *ananda*, the bliss of culmination, in this kind of memorable religious experience.[19]

Bhakti is usually translated as 'devotion'. 'Fealty' and 'participation' also give a sense of the deeply reciprocal relationship. Vedic sacrifice symbolized self-giving, making offerings to the loved friend. And the one who has devotion is dear to Krishna, Arjuna is told in the *Bhagavad Gita*.[20] Mutual loyalty between devotee and Lord, such as that found between wife and husband, is integral to bhakti, which teaches that the Lord responds beyond the devotee's efforts, always outdoing the devotee. Purandaradasa pictured the situation in this way:

> If you recline and sing his praise
> He will sit up, all ears; if you
> Are sitting and singing his praise
> He will stand and listen enthralled.
> If you stand and sing his praise
> He will dance with joy to hear it.
> If you dance and sing his praise
> Purandara Vithala will say
> 'Welcome to paradise'.[21]

Bhakti's rewards of bliss are sung in celebration by the poets. Would a mind enjoying spiritual nectar ever leave that for anything lower, Potana asks in the seventh book of the *Bhagavatam*. 'I have seen Lord Krishna of Udipi, the greatest lover in the whole universe—he can win anyone over!' Purandaradasa exclaims.[22] Kanakadasa in *Yelli nodi* sings, 'Wherever I look I see Rama.'

To see the beloved everywhere is to turn one's loving gaze to all living things. Thus bhakti is a one-pointedness, yet it can expansively reach inclusiveness. Some recent explorations of science and religion arrive at similar conclusions; the author of *Atoms, Snowflakes and God* considers love in this manner:

> Love is a complexified form of the simple physical bonds . . . a force which is cohesive and relatively weak . . . deepest love [attractions] are indeed the most subtle and yet somehow the most pervasive. The word inclusiveness or even all-inclusiveness expresses this quality . . . a steady inclusion . . . . In physics, the inclusive principle *par excellence* is gravity. It unifies the cosmos and is not turned off in situations wherein stronger forces dominate but operates as a steady background. It may even be that love is not complexified gravity, but the effect of gravity itself operating in complexified matter.[23]

The subtle force of love may be seen in this view as the manifestation of 'negentropy'[24]—meaning a contrary force for order amid a universe rife with decay, since entropy is disintegration. Love as negentropy is a powerful organizing consciousness—invigorating and fulfilling. Love is a drive in the psyche, a seeking of the ultimate and is dependent upon an updraft of ideal vision with beauty and meaning, pulling the soul towards wholeness. Bhakti rides on that process of affinities being enjoyed.

The Haridasas of Vijayanagara

The branch of the Haridasa tradition of which Purandaradasa and Kanakadasa are memorable examples was one composed of bhaktas who were strolling street singers, itinerant musicians singing of Vishnu's glory, preaching a spiritual life for people of all castes and communities? They held group *bhajans* in *mandapams* given to them by fellow devotees who happened to be wealthy. They coaxed and cajoled, mocked and harangued, comforted and consoled with their songs. Some other exponents of the Haridasa life wrote literature for Madhva followers only, or Sanskrit literature for the brahmanic world based on *smriti*, the orthodox Hindu ethical code; but Purandaradasa, Kanakadasa, Shripadaraya and Vadiraja were popularizers taking their broad message on the road to villagers. Using the colloquial Kannada regional language, they gave bhakti a down-to-earth flavour. The spoken tongue heightens lyrical expressions with a tone of spontaneity and sincerity, a natural heartfelt quality of soul. The songs combine this with vivid deep images. There is sometimes a living power in the singer's personality—voice, one of charismatic creativity. There is a power in good songs to turn the heart a certain way; toward repentance, regret of waste; toward restraint, spirituality; toward devotion, awe and hope. Bold and devoted souls like Purandaradasa and Kanakadasa went directly to the people with vitamins of values in their songs, which entered directly into the bloodstream of the culture, shaping the ethos, mood and world-view of the south Indian Hindus. Even the simplest villagers, who could not read and never became *dasas*, took the message to heart. This was a religious—cultural accomplishment at the time, and a legacy for Indians who came afterwards when the Vijayanagara empire had become only a dim memory. Another bhakti rule of thumb is that ordinary folk can follow its path—bhakti speaks to simple souls in their own language.

Boar and lion, dog and cow:
Images of animals, beastly and divine

The Hindu psyche, as reflected in its traditional religious symbol system, seems to be rather animal friendly—images of this truth often startle moderns. Vaishnava bhakti's two forms of surrender are depicted as 'the way of the kitten and the way of the monkey'. Hanuman, the ideal devotee and servant of Lord Rama, is a holy monkey, son of Vayu, the Vedic wind god. There are *avatars* of Vishnu who take birth in animal forms: fish, tortoise and boar. And each Hindu deity has a *vahana* or creature vehicle. Nandi the bull is associated with Shiva; the hawk Garuda with Vishnu; the lion with Goddess Durga. The peacock, known for natural beauty, is the vehicle of Murugan and its feather is a symbol of Krishna. The sage is a '*paramahamsa*', for just as a swan is said to drink the milk out of milky water, the wise can filter the eternal from time. In India the cow is venerated as a kind of motherly creature nurturing human life. Vedic Indra rides an elephant. Kundalini is a goddess of the serpentine energy in all beings, and carvings of *nagas* are found in many villages. Epic hero Yudhishthira would not enter heaven without the dog which accompanied him throughout his final sojourn. There are many images of deities and their creaturely vehicles, and sometimes the deity is part animal, like the horse-headed Hayagriva,[25] or Vishnu as Man–Lion, Narasimha. Manmatha the 'Hindu Cupid' or God of love, and his consort Rati, ride a parrot. Yamadharma, the God of death, rides a buffalo. Vishnu reclines on the serpent Adisesha coiled up as a couch (canopied by his spread hood) floating on the Milk Ocean. The Goddess of the river, Ganga, rides a crocodile, and Shani, a God who can be malevolent, rides a crow. The tenth incarnation of Vishnu, Kalki, is the future avatar pictured riding a white horse, or in some views, is even imagined as part horse, centaur-like.

It is perhaps in part because of all this animal-friendliness, this ability to be comfortable in expressing ideas with vivid images of creatures, that Hinduism has made strange impressions on non-Hindus who are overly proud of civilized abstractions and self-proclaimed monotheist superiority.

Hinduism both is and is not polytheistic; though multiplicity of the sacred is there, the One is also sung in the *Rig Veda* and the oneness of the deities is explored in the *Upanishads*, which are about the one all-pervasive divine consciousness which is the ultimate reality. Other religions may have a similar 'both/and' quality, but we see it more easily in the Hindu case. In Islam and Judaism there are angels, 'shining ones' who serve and deliver messages for God; in Christianity we find the trinity and the angels. All religions use a variety of symbols for the sacred, but Hinduism (possibly because her yogic explorers faced subconscious fears in ancient times, and her inclusive philosophers allowed many expressions and fostered *ahimsa*), has less fear of using a variety of specific vivid images of the sacred than most religions. For many centuries there have been philosophers in India who cite the Veda and expatiate on the oneness of God in many forms. There are also, of course, those who say: 'We Hindus believe in many gods'. Jews, Muslims and Christians may sometimes idolize things subconsciously: a book, a sacred place, authority, a religion. They might eschew visual images but claim that one seemingly abstract name–concept *is* God. Iconoclasm at its most conscious is an attempt to remind men that God is always beyond; yet celebrating a multitude of divine forms, none of which can fully pin down the infinite God, makes the same point. The Muslim device for prayer which consists of the 'one hundred most beautiful names of God' also shows wisdom about the necessity of keeping in mind some concepts of divine multiplicity—reality's various aspects and nuances—as well as the ultimate oneness.

The glorious boar of bothness and rescues

Animals are essential imaginative forces in the mind, symbolic images of life's energetic power; they are embodiments of life-sustaining nourishment and mysterious abilities. A serpent, for example, glides with uncanny grace, and is a natural symbol for mysterious energy.

In the Vijayanagara empire there were a number of prominent symbolic animals. The glorious boar is a prime example—it was the emblem of the Vijayanagara empire, and is associated with Vishnu as Varaha. An inscription from Pangal in Nalgonda district, Andhra Pradesh, relates how 'Prince Sharngapani-deva [was like] the great Boar in raising the earth from the calamity caused by the Turks', pointing to a mythic pattern in an historic event. 'Raising the earth' refers to the Hindu myth of the cosmic re-creation or *pratisarga*, which opens with Narayana asleep on the vast waters at the end of the long cosmic night. He awakens to give rise to Brahma, who in turn becomes just what is needed: a boar able to dive down deep into the waters, to rut the earth up on to his gracefully curved tusks and lift it above the waters. And thus he makes the levels of existence referred to in the *gayatri mantra*: earth (*bhuh*), atmosphere (*bhuvar*), heaven (*svarga*) and the *maharloka*—which are also the steps which cosmic Vishnu takes. The boar also divides up the earth into seven continents.[26] In the Vedic universe, with its triple world structure, gods offer a sacrifice of the cosmic person, so that ordered existence can begin. Later acts and other sacrifices are patterned on that paradigm. In the cycles of time, when earth is endangered, at the time of pratisarga, Brahma the boar rescues the earth, and refashions the triple world. The boar is called Yajnavaraha or Vedayajnavaraha, sacrificial boar. This sacred boar's body parts correspond to the different parts of the sacrifice: 'Your feet are the Vedas, your tusks are the stake to which the victim is bound; in your teeth are the offerings; your mouth is the altar; your tongue is the fire; the hairs of your body the sacrificial grass', as the *Vishnu Purana* describes it.[27]

In the first song of *Gita Govinda*, the Varaha incarnation of Vishnu is celebrated as rescuing earth from the sea where it was rolled up like a mat and concealed by demon Hiranyaksha, and it is pictured poetically— the earth adhering to the point of the boar's tusk like a speck of dust clinging to the bright crescent moon. This could be interpreted as the tusk being like the crescent moon, and earth being the dark phase, an image suggested by the tusk's natural arc shape, a pattern observed by people for millennia. The wild boar has been a religious symbol from ancient times. Outside India, the stone age Malekula people had a culture in which pigs and boars were of great importance[28] and in ancient Greece the boar was the sacred animal which wounds the saviour God Adonis (with similarities to Attis and Tammuz), the uninitiated male god who dies, while the Goddess goes on living. The boar is a fierce force of nature, precise and wild, 'razorback bristling and raging eyes', impressive to vulnerable human beings.

The natural power of the boar to act spontaneously may be an image of hope for divine intervention, especially against a flood of invaders. Devotion to Varaha may express a desire for aid, vigour and vitality. Eternal patterns are acted out: the affirmation of mutual existence; so that whenever the flood comes, every time chaos returns, this is the resolving answer. Varaha is a primary and suggestive enough image to be valid again and again, rather timelessly.

The boar during the time of the Vijayanagara empire was more a visual emblem (carved in stone, embossed on coins) than one sung in songs. Like the turtle (also an avatar of Vishnu), the boar is amphibious, a metaphor of both-ness and mixed-ness. (In the West the griffin as a symbol of Christ is also a mixed–media event–pattern). Reality may well be imaged as an interlacing of planes. Even the human being at his or her best is 'that great and true amphibium, whose nature is disposed to live, not only in diverse elements, but in divided and distinguished worlds'.[29] The one, who, placed between, deals with *ihaparamulu*, to use a Telugu term for 'the things of both worlds'. The Chinese character for 'human being' shows a figure between heaven and earth. This kind of connective bridge imagery militates against one-sidedness. Hinduism, in its long history, developed ways for people to experience both body and soul, in tantra and bhakti. The preserver, Vishnu, who is ever on-call in a celestial realm, or at rest on the Milk Ocean, comes to earth repeatedly to save the devotee, life and limb.

Man–lion:
God's hidden splendour and sudden fierce saving grace

> Lord Narasimha, you are cosmic existence
> the stars are your waistband
> sun and moon your eyes, sunrays your spears
> Vedas are your shaggy mane
> mountains your feet, earth your thighs
> time cycle your mouth, planets your teeth
> the whole sky is just your waist
> the seas are your nectary grace
> thunder's your roar, Venkatadri your cave[30]

Annamacharya thus described Narasimha. In the Man–lion story the need for a divine force to set things right when the demonic have sovereignty might be like a Hindu desire for the power to enter the invaders' stronghold and, amid ominous signs of catastrophe claw open the chest of the powerful ruler and rip out his entrails, to protect Hindu devotees from demonic force. The loving trust of the bhakta brings out the grace that destroys the demon threatening the survival of those relying on Vishnu the preserver. In ancient Carthage, the Goddess Tanit was depicted as a woman with a lion's head, and in the Old Testament there are statements such as 'I am the Lord . . . . I will devour them like a lion; the wild beast shall tear them', in Hosea XIV: 4–5; XI: 10; Nahum II: 12–14 and Joel I: 6. Forbidden to sculpt God as a lion, the Jews nevertheless have word–images of divine lion power in the Torah.

It was not by chance that an immense Narasimha sculpture was carved and venerated in the Vijayanagara capital during the reign of Krishnadevaraya. It expresses the desire for protection by divine power. Desire for the all-pervasive deity to descend as promised and show divine goodness and mercy to bhaktas by helping the fallen and troubled is expressed in many stories. In the stories the avatar arrives, surprises and wins, ending the reign of terror, succeeding through a trick. The highest and free-est reality leaps out fantastically from the lowest (inert matter) and densest. Many ways are blocked but the overpowering energy finds the one means by which the necessary end can be accomplished. At first the inert pillar's potential for a ferocious explosively leaping force seems ridiculously small—negligible as the presence of God in matter seen by materialist eyes. The divine takes on just the right form to change everything. Power is concealed, not seeming there on the surface, but able to burst through, emerging to take away the too powerful enemy who disturbs the world, and save the true-hearted one. And the faithful devotee can see through the eye of bhakti the whole cosmos in this twilight epiphany, the theophany of death, planets, divine beings; and meditating on this vision, the devotee becomes wise.

A reversal is enacted and so while the ruler seemed so great and the invisible Lord seemed so small, the reality turned out to be laughably and weepably otherwise. The Narasimha scenario teaches that where human and holy meet (at thresholds), God's presence overpowers little creatures: at twilight, at the moment of birth, at the moment of death, between sleep and waking, mind and soul, between breaths and thoughts, at the seams of the seasons (New Year, Holy day festivals, celebrations where the usual barriers are down). God's supremacy becomes apparent, the story asserts, and even the atheist at the moment of death meets a transcendent force he cannot deny. Though the self-centred atheist makes his soul as dry as a desert, yet in the desert the lion rages and in the end moment of mortality, the turning point of losing all, the liberating beauty of the sacred frees the tyrant from his ego and his suppression of others' hearts.

Vishnu is the sacrifice, upholder of *dharma*, expansive power of the one who holds the abyss in his pervasiveness. In Vedic vision, as is said in the first and tenth *mandalas* of the Rig Veda, Vishnu, together with Indra the divine warrior, is like a dreaded wild beast of the mountain. Vishnu is the lion of power who battled the demons. This fierce deity shows up in the ongoing cosmological context with its periodic degenerations, as the answer to the fix the devoted are in—the only way out. In Vedic imagery Vishnu took three steps[31] and helped Indra slay demons but had a greater power, more expansive than Indra's in the long run. Vishnu as sacrifice gives to first–arriving Indra his great power and glory. Vishnu is time with its inevitable re-occurrences. Because his appearance is cyclical, rhythmic, he is present in the transitional times between destruction and reconstruction, he has the potency for change with him. Devotees rely on this world-view, in their *communitas* (extraordinary experiences of sharing common bonds in devotional

practices). Vishnu's avatar power mediates amidst cosmic forces. When
the godly are imperilled he finds a loophole, and with cunning slips
through, elusive but uneludable as a thunderbolt made of foam, earth-
shaking primal power in a dark cloud. He is a much needed more fierce,
potential, able to spring out and overpower the human ego that threatens.
The antithesis of a *tamasic* sluggish, weak, hopeless victim, Narasimha
answers a deep hope for a raging energy, an uncontrollable divine
irrational overpowering; the awakening of the latent spirit with all its
energy, able to activate the hidden forces, make them patent, addressing
dangers, allaying fears.

The oppressive enemies find themselves overcome by a greater power
which they disregarded—even the materialist at death is overcome by
power beyond his control. The terrifying Narasimha is 'a Shivaesque
Vishnu';[32] his pillar is a *linga*, a sacrificial post, a centre of the universe.
In the story, the riddle of the demon king's boon to be invulnerable in
wet or dry, night or day, in or out, for man or beast, is solved by the
killer who transcends all dualities: wild Lord Narasimha.

Kanakadasa sang dramatically picturing the shocking outburst:

I saw the gods assembled in the heavens
I saw the mighty foe
    fierce and valiant Narasimha

I heard the crack of lightning rumbling in the pillar
and saw sparks fly out. The assembled onlookers
were all stunned—their stance was shaken, and they
covered their heads they were so terrified. I saw . . .

The Lord gripped his enemy's chest and tore open his abdomen;
easily he pierced it, ripped off skin this way and that.
He tore out veins and bones, the blood was spurting forth
and he garlanded himself with his foe's intestines. I saw . . .

Townspeople shrieked in shock, gods tossed a rain of flowers,
musical instruments played. 'We take refuge in you Hari!'
they chanted; child Prahlada glowed jubilantly, praising
the name of the merciful Lord Adikeshava of Kaginele. I saw . . .[33]

Such images stir the aesthetic mood (rasa) of wonder (*vibhuti*) in the
bhakta who vividly imagines them. They are exclamations of 'Ahhh!'.

Other creatures in Vijayanagara songs:
Birds, dogs, cattle

Fresh images in the songs of Vijayanagara lyricists include vividly
memorable depictions of animals. Purandaradasa, for example, gave voice
poignantly to personal grief by singing 'O Lord, the bird has flown
away, leaving just this empty cage', when his son died.[34] Abhinavagupta,
author of the Sanskrit aesthetics text *Dhvanyalokalochana*, wrote of the
importance of fresh images in literary works:

> Mind, when it becomes capable of understanding all facts
> without any temporal limit, comes to be called by the name of
> *prajna*; and this itself acquires the name of *pratibha* with an
> additional qualification, namely invention of newer and newer
> images . . . . The gift of finding out newer and newer ideas and
> things is itself pratibha. But what makes for poetry is an aspect
> of pratibha that is conducive to the composition of poetry
> suffused with thrilling emotion and aesthetic beauty.[35]

Maybe a new image involves as much creative effort as a new speciation
in nature does, as Gaston Bachelard suggested. Continuing our
exploration of animal images in songs, but turning for the moment
from the sublime to the ridiculous, we note that some Haridasas wrote
especially forceful songs about dogs. This one addressing a dog begins
Donku balada Nayakare:

> So what have you eaten today
> O leader (Nayaka) with a curled up tail?
>
> You snooped your way into a kitchen
> where a woman was trying to knead dough
> she probably whacked you with a stick
> now you're singing yelps in the *raga* of 'Kuikui!'
>
> So what else have you scarfed down today
> King Snoopy with up-curling tail?
>
> You sniffed your way to a different home
> where another sweet dish was being prepared
> and I would take a guess the housewife there
> took her ladle and bonked you good and hard
> and again you howl your 'Kuikui' raga

So what else did you scavenge or steal
to eat today, O Leader with a curled tail?

Roaming around on the big main road, sometimes
on your back rolling around in black ashes
without ever remembering Purandara Vithala
you aimlessly wander, fritter your days away

So what else did you scavenge or steal
to eat today, King Snoopy with a curled tail?

This irreverent cartooning of the nayaka–dog, which is attributed to
both Purandaradasa and Kanakadasa, connects two levels—the lowly
scavenger and the high class leader of the feudal segmented state. Such
lampooning makes us wonder if there were upstart nayakas who bolstered
their egos and insecurities by self-aggrandizing moves to appease their
base hungers. 'Nayaka' in the time of Purandaradasa was a title of a new
supralocal military class. Though such leaders could be important, their
standing in society did not insure them respectability. While a misspent
life can be an object of ridicule in Haridasa songs, there were other lives
which were positively menacing, like the actions of mad dogs:

Some kind of dog is trotting this way, my brother,
Here, let's play it safe and move off the road.

This is not your ordinary dog—
    it's the fallen state of man
        the lowest form of human existence

This dog never gives back money he borrowed
This kind of dog doesn't keep his promised word
This dog barks with vehement pride and ego
After he claws and climbs to the top of the heap

When this dog gives gifts his rancour seethes with regret
This dog teases and taunts you after donating food
This weird dog, born of a quite good mother's womb
Grows up to commit gruesomer acts than any dog would do

This is a cur who abandons the wife he married
This is a cur who sniffs out poor abandoned wives
This is the weird dog who's now trotting this way
He never stops to remember Lord Purandara Vithala

Some kind of dog is trotting this way, my brother!
Let's play it safe and move off the road.[36]

Such a song serves as a warning—a way of pointing out the sickness of
an inauspicious fool, and urging listeners to never forget Purandara
Vithala. In the value system of the Haridasa, it is important who is
considered to be the fool. It is the worldling, the hypocrite, one forgetful
of God; he is the source of societal chaos, a loser without serious
spirituality. Animals play an important part in the rich symbolism of
the religious mind.

The water buffalo is another animal Purandara sang about to teach
people lessons of self-control, bhakti's yogic discipline:

> Tether the rebellious buffalo cow
> then you may enjoy her milk,
> milk her as much as you like
> enjoy any amount, savour the flavour
>
> Your feeling of pride is the buffalo
> chanting the Name is the rope
> and the goad to control the ego
> milk this buffalo and offer some to Brahma daily
>
> Grind your mischievousness into cattle feed
> transforming your stubbornness into grain
> turn your harsh behaviour into a bundle of grass
> then milk the name of Panduranga
> and enjoy in your heart the milk . . . Tether . . .
>
> Care well for your buffalo, removing illusion
> in your consciousness
> This buffalo which few can know
> is found at the farmhouse
> of Lord Purandara Vithala . . . Tether . . .[37]

Kanakadasa uniquely put religious matters by using the symbolism
herding:

We are the Kuruba shepherd folk, our God is valiant Birayya
The whole herd of sheep (humanity) is protected by Grandpa Aja

There are eight well-fed rams, and the goat named 'Drishtijivatma'
and there's a sacrificial sheep called 'Famous in the cosmos',
Our grandfather goads these animals with his stick, ties them up.

Our grandfather takes care of the sheep-herding watchdogs named
'Veda', 'Shastra', 'Purana', who work in the midst of the herds.
When we lose our way, crying out, famished and thirsty, at last
just falling down prostrate, grandfather comes and takes
good care of us, giving us gruel to drink. We . . .

Little lambs named 'Enlightenment' frisk about in the herd, and
when the herds get absent-minded a wolf named 'Death' sneaks in.
Death blocks our way in the dark, a marauder attacking us
mercilessly. And even though Grandpa knows all about this, he
seems to look the other way, and not see what's happening. We . . .

There is no beginning to births, no end to death after death,
but our Grandpa knows the way beyond birth and death. Our Grandpa
prepares so much refreshing gruel to feed so many poor creatures
and our Grandpa feeds us all so much our bellies swell quite full.

Grandpa is the chief of the *Kaliyuga*, he's the companion,
and he is the chief minister (*mantri*). He is also the son,
and he has forgotten about many Kaliyugas already. After
pleasing the lotus-eyed Kaginele Adikeshava, this mad shepherd
is the one who is worshipping him. We are the Kuruba shepherds.[38]

Of man, *manis* (jewels), and money

Another area of rich symbolism in Vijayanagara era bhakti lyrics is that
of money, precious objects and related items. In a Kanakadasa song
celebrating the abundance of transactions at the temple of Tirupati, the
Lord is playfully spoken of as a merchant:

> O Money-lender, we have come, O Govinda Shetti
>
> We have come, hearing about the *tirtha* water
> and trays full of *prasad* sweets, waiting for us,
>   so we have come
>
> The many dishes given to devotees—*appu* sweets,
> *atirasa*, rice, ghee, milk with sugar and cardamom,
> heaps and stacks of these rare dishes made available
> for sale by you, Govinda Merchant—a variety of
> sweet dishes for the fifty-six provinces of this land

You took a broken pot made of red clay, and you pounded it
to make powder for vermilion marks, and you're offering
that dust for sale, and from whatever surplus rice there is
like a miser you turn a neat profit to buy ornaments with

You're living in Seshagiri, and you're known all over
the country as 'Shetti'. You're receiving compound interest
on every little coin, so you're known as Adikeshava Tirupati
Tima Shetti—O money-lender, we've come, Govinda Shetti.[39]

In Tamil Nadu Lord Venkateshvara is sometimes called Tandal Nayakan,
'Collector of revenues', and a name of Lord Murugan is 'the One who
listens to the daily recital of accounts of vows and offerings, blessings
received, debts paid', celebrating the many transactions between God
and the devotees. The Vaishnava saint Vadiraja, who lived after
Purandaradasa and Kanakadasa, wrote an uproarious song mocking
devotion to money:

O Money, how can I ever describe·
your marvellous worth?
Why a man without wealth
is nothing but a corpse!

The worthless becomes precious all because of you;
Wherever you happen to be everything runs to you.
You turn the lowest types into men of high calibre
And even outcastes are welcome in restricted homes.

O Money how can I ever hope
to describe your miraculous force?
Any man who doesn't have you
Might as well be called a corpse!

You allow men to enjoy the company of desirable women;
You procure jewellery and luxuries of pleasure.
Thanks to you even a monkey can become a cupid;
If he has you a blind man finds a fine bride.

O Money how can I ever reveal
your paramount importance?
Without you a man is simply a cadaver
and not really a living person!

You remove beforehand the danger of probable mishaps
With you anybody can become the best of men.
You are empowered to make the ignorant learned
You cause people to forget the horse-necked Lord

O Money how can I ever describe
your marvellous magical force?
Why, any man who is without you
is really merely a creepy corpse![40]

World-renouncing Haridasas, people on the margins of society, practising non-attachment, could speak boldly and satirically without fear of audiences taking their remarks too personally and attacking them.[41]

The metaphor of the businessman was not always negative in the works of Vijayanagara singers. The industrious spiritual activities of the Haridasas could be troped well with the vigorous work of the busy and productive merchant class.

We've gone into business—it's a service industry
dedicated to the lotus feet and this business keeps us busy.

The mercy of Shri Hari has become the shirt I wear
the compassion of the guru has become my turban.
What do I wear beneath my feet? The worst sinner called Kali
and treading on the chests of evil-souled people
has become our commerce here—we've gone into business

The heart is like white paper, the tongue's a pen
the mouth is the pen holder, the stories of the names
of Lakshmi-enamoured Vishnu form our narratives, and we
gladly give this offering to the Lord after composing it—
that has become our commerce—we've gone into business . . .

The hardship and hassles of future lives—that fear is gone
forever. I've settled my accounts; the accumulated burden
of my deeds, my debts—I've paid them off, torn up the IOU
and hey now I'm out of debt, paid off, completely debt-free!

For every word tears of joy are shed and we feel the thrill.
That's reward enough—when your hand is inside the moneybag!
He gave me an irrevocable document, authorizing the payment
of my salary in the form of *sadhana* leading to salvation . . .

I didn't prostrate shameless at the feet of all and sundry,
whenever I would meet them. The Lord Purandara Vithala
let me fall at his feet, blessed me, welcoming me, offering
hospitality, areca nut and betel leaf, and he
    showed his regard for me
We're glad we went into business, it's a service industry
dedicated to the lotus feet; this business keeps us busy.[42]

Diamonds, pearls and precious gems of various sorts, seen in the empire
and capturing imagination, shine in many lyrics of the period (in the
north the blind singer–saint Surdas sang of Rama-*ratna*, the jewel of
Rama, being different from ordinary wealth, and Mirabai sang of a gem
worth more than everything else). Annamacharya sang a sparkling little
song, *Muddugare yashoda*, about the variety of precious qualities which
different people saw in Krishna:

The son of Devaki, child of ineffable glory
he is a pearl to beautiful Yashoda.

He is a ruby in the palms of the gopis' hands
He is *vajra*, diamond hard to obstinate Kamsa.
His lustre is like emerald beads
to those who love him in the three worlds
This little Krishna so near and so dear to all.
The son of Devaki . . .

His red lips are like coral to Rukmini, who enjoys
His sweet loveplay, to Govardhana hill he's the gem
of four colours
In between the conch and the chakra he shines
bright as lapis lazuli,
The lotus-eyed one who saves when we take refuge in him,
The son of Devaki . . .

He is pure topaz for Kalinga the serpent
on whose head he dances
He is the sapphire reigning atop Venkata hill, he is
the divine gem remaining forever in the ocean of milk
The Lord Padmanabha who roams around like a little boy

The son of Devaki, child of untellable glory
he is a pearl to Yashoda of great beauty.[43]

Kanakadasa also made use of gem imagery in songs about Krishna:

> A precious pearl has come to our lane
> Listen, people, listen
> Tie up this pearl in the corner of your *sari*
> If you have real devotion
>
> This lustrous pearl, this lotus-eyed pearl
> It destroys a mountain of sin
> The sacred pearl with the name Bala Rama
> brother of Krishna
> The pearl protects those who love and worship
> cutting away all sins.
> A precious pearl has come to our lane
> Listen, people, listen!
>
> This pearl strikes terror in the men
> who are usually the fearless ones
> This pearl wipes out for good
> all varieties of sins
> This pearl enshrined in the heart
> of your dear devotee, Hanuman
> This pearl which Brahma and other gods
> carry on their heads
> A precious pearl has come to our lane . . .
>
> This pearl you can string together with
> the cord of spiritual knowledge
> This pearl shining in the minds of the enlightened
> This pearl which befits the mind
> of Lord Madhvacharya
> this pearl called the treasure of Lakshmi
> Adikeshava of Kaginele
> A precious pearl has arrived in our lane
> Listen, people, listen
> If you have devotion you will be able
> to tie this pearl in the corner of your sari.[44]

Purandaradasa sang this song in the voice of the pearl salesman:

> Pearls for sale! Come one and all, buy your pearls here!
> The best pearl of all is one called Being–Awareness–Bliss!
> This divine pearl is strung
> on the thread of spiritual knowledge
> You can possess it by becoming wise—why even
> the poorest devotee can easily afford it
> once he's become enlightened
>
> Pearls for sale! Come one and all, buy pearls . . .
>
> You can't wear this pearl on your nose
> You can't use it for a status symbol
> and to evil people this pearl is completely invisible!
> This holy pearl is also known as Krishna—Pearls for sale!
>
> You can't grab this intangible pearl, and yet
> it is truly a precious priceless gem!
> This genuine pearl known as the great
> Lord Purandara Vithala, Lord of the universe
>
> Pearls for sale! Come one, come all, buy pearls.
> The very best pearl is here right now—
> The Self of Being–Awareness–Bliss![45]

Purandaradasa also sings of receiving a diamond necklace designed around the jewel name of Rama.[46] A treasury of songs using precious stones as metaphors comes down to us from Vijayanagara singers depicting beauty, value, fascination and glory. They are among the bhakti legacy's valuables.

The question of Haridasa pessimism

> Life lasts only a couple of days
> Nobody knows what it means
> Wise up, be bright and kind
> be good, do acts of charity
>
> Feed the hungry who come to you
> feed the child with butter and milk
> give to the worthy man arable land
> don't lie to people when you converse

Don't steal just to eke out a living
don't listen and wander unemployed
In an assembly don't try acting sneaky
don't gloat saying 'I have lots of gold'.
Don't speak meanly if you get power
don't show off when riches come along
be happy, take refuge at the feet
of the truly rich Lord Adikeshava

Life is only a two-day affair
the meaning of which is never too clear.[47]

In this song Kanakadasa sings of life's ephemeral uncertainties. Some people who listen to the songs of the Haridasas emphasize the criticisms of worldly life and the urges toward renunciation. One does not have to search far to find such evidence. This aspect of bhakti carries on the critical tradition found in early texts of Buddhism[48] and other expressions of world-renouncers. Take for example these lines from Purandaradasa's song *Madi madi yendu* about 'Holier than thou' hypocrites: 'A bag of bones, you happily stand in a pit of urine and excrement—are you enjoying it? Beggar, you fell into this body of nine exits, so where do you get this *madi* or ritually pure cloth you always talk about?' It would be possible to cite passages celebrating health and well-being. For example: 'For a householder who hasn't dug himself deeply into debt, worldly life is a feast; and the body that's sound, free from diseases, also is truly a festival'.[49] But there are also others which harshly speak of living with inlaws as a misery.[50] Some lyrics seem to be the conscience of the preacher warning the worldly, others the celebrant enthusiastic with the beauties of devotion to Krishna. Either way the lyrics of the Haridasas are the voice of the soul uttering for all to hear what it feels it wants.

The Haridasa stance is articulated by Purandaradasa in a song: 'The Haridasa should learn to be in the world but not of the world'.[51] It is like the Buddhist philosophy expressed in the *Avatamsakasutra*, that enlightened people are able to provoke deep faith by being in the world yet unaffected by it, just as the lotus grows in mud and water yet neither mud nor water adheres to the pure lotus petals. The Haridasa songs show an impatience with the degradation of religion, an outrage at inflation, deception, hypocrisy and an insistence on sincerity, true sacrifice, genuine religious sentiments and actions. The dasas sang in

south India about the same time that Luther in Europe criticized
corruption and hypocrisy in the church of Rome. Unlike the court poets
whose status and prosperity could shelter them from the grim facts of
life, the wandering singers saw life's harsh realities, and their philosophy
entailed addressing those realities, rather than skirting them. They critiqued
the society which allowed them to thrive as long as it was alive. When it
was struck by the united Muslim leaders from the regions to the north,
the society broke up, and so did the Haridasas. In 1565 the capital of
Vijayanagara was looted and ruined. Purandaradasa sang out:

> Yo, Boatman, Boatman!
> I'm counting on you—
> Lord of mother earth
> My trust is in you!
>
> Yo Boatman, the boat rocks
> In the flooding river;
> Boatman this is a boat
> with nine holes in it
> O Boatman please steer
> carefully this frail craft
> guide it with fervour
> always mindful of the goal—Yo Boatman!
>
> The river's overflowing!
> See how full it is?
> Karma's current runs—
> It's so swift, and it's so deep!
> I'm caught, I'm drowning
> I'm down in this whirlpool!
> Pull me from this treachery!
> Boatman rescue me please!—Yo Boatman!
>
> Boatman, look there, see
> the six waves are coming!
> They rise up, higher
> and higher—am I a goner?
> Boatman there is no one else
> to help me overcome them—
> Only you, my Boatman,
> are able to take me across. Yo Boatman . . .

Now the sun has set, O Boatman,
Now the five senses dim . . .
Go—row full force—now.
This is the time to take me!
No, Boatman, don't linger!
Don't wait, this is my chance!
Take me all the way over
to the realm of the ultimate! O Boatman . . .

Row, Boatman, row, with
your oars of supramental bhakti
We'll wend our way
along the path of righteousness.
Take me, O Boatman
right to the *mantapa* of *mukti*
granted by the grace of
Lord Purandara Vithala—O Boatman . . .[52]

Bhakti lyric images are archetypes, proven to be *sattvic* (the strand of nature characterized by harmony), known to purify, to open up fulfilling experiences of bhakti in the soul. For listeners in the Vijayanagara empire, dwelling mentally on bhakti images was a way to experience uniquely in their own lives what the songs describe so vividly: relationships connecting deity and devotee. While singing one enters into a flow of energy empatterning the mind and nerves with moods of rhythm and sound, as one's feelings are voiced. After one has sung, one's ears ring with silence, the imagination is sensitized, and one is able to listen more intently for the presence of the beloved. Singing with devotion has this refining effect on the psyche, bhaktas would say.

A final bhakti 'rule of thumb' relates that the bhakti path is an exchange system using tokens of love for spiritual transactions between the soul and God. By the same token, love is the finest expression of the survival instinct, found burning in the heart of the sun and the atom, a story of affinities and interdependencies, attractions and harmonies. The ideal net-effect of bhakti is: one develops love, cultivates and deepens the life of love, and one's life radiates that love to others. Love is the barrier-leaping, levels-connecting plasma which like the aurora borealis is a reflected radiance in the atmosphere, a vibrant subtle brightness. 'You're mine because I adore you'—this is the simple trust and logic of bhakti: the rights of all-consuming love. The Vijayanagara singer–saints expressed anew all these perennial Hindu impulses in their bhakti songs.

The metaphors in their bhakti songs show how this path combines fiercest love with the most docile dependence and yielding. The reasonableness of bhakti is to combine love and *jnana*, feeling and wisdom. To the conventional world, with its systems of rewards, bhakti often appears as a category similar to madness or foolishness, a kind of irrational frenzy or chaos. Bhakti may seem an inconsequential throwback to the hyper-rational modern man, yet a sense of dependence and the need to love and serve are essential in human life, and bhakti deals with these depths. In bhakti, intuition is the connectivity in knowing, love the connectivity in feeling and surrender the connectivity. in volition. 'I'm a little nobody, you're the Supreme Lord, your glory alone shall always prevail', as Annamacharya sang in his song *Dinudanenu*. Devotees come to perceive the deity through their participation in devotional love, experiencing a spiritual presence, responding wholeheartedly to what is felt to be divine action in their lives. The concept of karma in isolation is apt to polarize people, spelling doom for the lowly, and justification for the high and mighty. But a sense of oneness, compassion and love in the concept of bhakti, spread freely throughout creation, nurtures a sense of equality. The Haridasas of Vijayanagara were members of bhakti's 'institution of the dear comrades'.[53] It was a somewhat fluid society, yet, to the singer of love, it was more stable and full of meaning than more official public organizations often pretend to be. While governments may come and go, the bhakti heart, with its vivid love-inspired imagination, beats on and on, enjoying the rasa, the nectar of bliss.

Bhakti may lack prestige for academic theorists and might seem confining and childish to them, since it is neither bold like Marxism, nor overly proud of human-centred systems and accomplishments. In fact, bhakti criticizes such arrogance (only in the dedications of their books do dry scholars seem able to admit that love is an authentic mode of being, knowing and relating). Yet some very intense thinkers are able to see bhakti, an image of which is the gopis hearing Krishna's flute in the night, as something essential in significance. James Hillman, who also writes of psychological healthiness in terms of polytheism (which recognizes multiple aspects of the psyche) stated that the goal of therapy was service and devotion.[54] J.L. Mehta, an Indian philosopher thoroughly conversant with rigorous modern philosophical thought, an authority on Heidegger, capable of navigating and innovating in the most sophisticated thinking, in his maturity wrote:

> Bhakti . . . implies the generation of a wholeness in our total being and as such is a total response of the reality disclosed by the experience of *rasa*[55] . . . . Contrary to modern, Western, subjectivistic and man-centred philosophies of life, feeling . . . must be understood . . . as a mode of man's relationship to Being . . . . Feeling has its own sight, that through it a disclosure of *what is* takes place . . . in which truth, reality and value are no longer separable . . . . Understood in this metaphysical, non-psychological sense of feeling, bhakti represents man's primordial relationship to being . . . . The ultimate refuge in his search for wholeness.[56]

So when the illusions of individualism become an insufferable nightmare of alienation, there is bhakti, inseparable from jnana and karma; bhakti, relating the self to others, acknowledging dependence; bhakti, offering reverence and thanks, humbly dedicating one's efforts, providing a sweetly consoling path inward and onward toward healing oneness. These functions are some of the beauties of bhakti, still viable and valuable, charming and salvific, long after the Vijayanagara empire poets sang.

Notes

1. Henry David Thoreau, *Thoreau on Man and Nature*, Mount Vernon: Peter Pauper Press, 1960, p. 40.

2. In this essay my approach is to look at the traditions of bhakti with an eye appreciating their relevance, as well as to offer some new observations to help re-focus some issues of importance to East-West understandings; to translate is to enter sympathetically into the whole system being conveyed and to try to show as well as one can the reasonableness it may entail.

3. See, for example, Robert Sewell's *A Forgotten Empire*, New Delhi: Asian Publishing Services, 1982, p. 58.

4. Jane I. Smith in a lecture at Harvard in 1975 suggested this quality of Western traditions—Judaism, Christianity and Islam. Marilyn Wald wrote about the power derived from disjunctions—especially in Islam.

5. V. Raghavan's essay 'India: Tradition and Non-Conformism', *The Eastern Anthropologist*, 29: 2, pp.189–200, and J.L. Mehta's essay on bhakti in

Philosophy and Religion: Essays in Interpretation (New Delhi: Indian Council of Philosophical Research, 1990, pp. 204–14) usefully explore this.

6. In this essay I have translated Purandaradasa and Kanakadasa lyrics with the help of Narayana and Yashoda Bhat, and have translated Annamacharya lyrics with the help of T.S. Parthasarathy. I wish to thank these scholars of Kannada and Telugu, respectively, for their assistance, insights and suggestions.

7. The vanquishing was not always as obvious as genocide, but consisted of various forms of culturecide, eldercide and other-worldviewcide, as well as undermining, dismantling, and suppressing old ways so colonialism and capitalism could thrive. See, Robert Bly, *The Sibling Society*, Reading: Addison-Wesley Publishing Company, 1996, pp. 160–4. Having colonized himself modern man is now in need of healing, and the cosmos' blessings, so bhakti, meditation, and study of whole living systems are correctives.

8. Octavio Paz noted that Europe did not have the yin–yang both/and symbol of inclusion, but more exclusive separatist concepts of either or: native Amerindians were killed or put on reservations, not included by the European-born settlers who took over the land.

9. Friedhelm Hardy, *The Religious Culture of India: Power, Love and Wisdom*, Cambridge: Cambridge University Press, 1994, p. 205.

10. I have versified this song on the basis of B. Rajanikanta Rao's 'Some Raga Patterns of the 15th Century and their Setting in Annamacharya's Lyrics', in *The Journal of the Madras Music Academy*, Vol. LIV, 1983, p. 185.

11. S.K. Ramachandra Rao, ed., *Purandara Sahitya Darshana* (four vols.), Bangalore: The Directorate of Kannada and Culture, Government of Karnataka,1985, IV, p. 326 (Referred to in this volume as PSD).

12. Kanakadasa, *Jana Priya Kanaka Samputa*, Bangalore: Department of Kannada and Culture, 1988-9, p. 24.

13. Just, for example, as *dhikr* or remembrance, is the main practice of Sufism, in Muslim spirituality.

14. What could be sweeter (or more *yin,* to use a Chinese term) than the gopis? Always submissive, passive, or at most passive–aggressive, ever gratefully receptive, they are powerlessly drawn to Krishna. Vulnerably defensive, charmingly eccentric, their minds are on Krishna, the beloved Attractor, their lives are love-deranged. They are allowed by their given roles in life to be sweet, sweeter or sweetest. They want to be at play with Krishna—whatever else they do their hearts are not really in it.

15. A disciple of Ramakrishna Paramahamsa recalled: 'Once someone asked the master, "How can I get rid of lust?" The master replied, "Why should

it be gotten rid of? Turn it in another direction . . .". He said the same thing about anger, greed, infatuation, and other passions. These words of the master inspired the young disciple . . . . "Wherever there is extreme longing, God reveals himself more".' Swami Chetanananda, *Ramakrishna as We Saw him*, St Louis: Vedanta Society of St Louis, 1990, p. 78.

16. Kanakadasa, *Jana Priya Kanaka Samputa*, p. 74.

17. See June McDaniels' work for more on this theme.

18. Patanjali, 'Yogasutras', in *The Yoga Aphorisms*, translated by Swami Vivekananda, Mayavati, Almora: Advaita Ashram, 4th edn, 1923.

19. I have written about this elsewhere, in my studies of Tyagaraja, and in *Vijayanagara Voices*, about the singer–saints.

20. *Bhagavad Gita*, ch. XII.

21. PSD Vol. IV, p. 320. In the Muslim text *Key to Salvation* by Ahmad Ibn 'Ata' Allah there is a similar depiction of God outdoing the soul in mutual responses: 'If he approaches me walking I come to him running.' A spiritual saying in both East and West is 'For every step you take toward God, God takes three (or ten) to you'.

22. PSD Vol. I, p. 224.

23. John L. Hitchcock, *Atoms, Snowflakes and God*, Wheaton: Theosophical Publishing House, 1986, p. 157. See also Brian Swimme, *The Universe is a Green Dragon*, Santa Fe: Bear & Co., 1984, for a discussion of basic allurements in the universe as forces of love.

24. I did not invent this term; it is used by Gregory Bateson (in *A Sacred Unity*, p. 201) and others.

25. Tumburu is a horse-headed *gandharva*, celestial musician.

26. Deborah Soifer, *The Myths of Narasimha and Vamana: Two Avatars in Cosmological Perspective*, Albany: State University of New York, 1991, p. 47.

27. Ibid., p. 64.

28. John Layard, *The Stone Age Men of Malekula*, London: Chatto and Windus, 1942.

29. Arthur Koestler, *The Act of Creation*, rev. Danube edn, London: Pan Books, 1970, p. 367.

30. R. Anantakrishna Sarma and U. Srinivasacharya, ed., *Annamacarya Adhyatma Samkirtanalu*, Vol. 7, Tirupati: TTD, 1952, p. 56.

31. In later myth, told in the puranas for example, Vishnu takes three steps as a dwarf brahman, and banishes king Bali to the netherworld.

32. Deborah Soifer, *The Myths of Narasimha and Vamana* . . ., p. 107.

33. Kanakadasa, *Jana Priya Kanaka Samputa*, p. 45.

34. PSD Vol. I, p. 180.

35. Krishnamoorthy, *Essays in Sanskrit Criticism*, Dharwar: Karnataka University, 1974, p. 183.

36. PSD Vol. III, p. 328.

37. Ibid., p. 325.

38. Kanakadasa, *Jana Priya Kanaka Samputa*, p. 30.

39. Ibid., p. 49.

40. Shyamsunder Bidarakundi, *Isabeku iddu Jaisabeku: An Anthology of Kannada Kirtanas by Various Dasas*, Gadag: Alochana Prakashana, 1989, p. 53.

41. The theme of money's glories is found in other cultures as well. In American folklore there is a 'Burlesque Prayer' to the 'Almighty Dollar' which was first published in 1894. It contains the lines 'Almighty dollar, thy shining face,/Bespeaks thy wondrous power,/In our pockets make thy resting place,/ We need thee every hour'. There is also the song 'Money, Money' from the musical drama 'Cabaret' which says 'Money makes the world go round', and describes money's other powers and wonders.

42. PSD Vol. I, p. 111.

43. P. Venugopala Rao, *Sri Annamacarya Sankirtanalu*, Madras: N.V. Gopal and Co. , 1993 p. 8.

44. Kanakadasa, *Jana Priya Kanaka Samputa*, p. 86.

45. Ibid., p. 86.

46. PSD Vol. II, p. 289.

47. Kanakadasa, *Jana Priya Kanaka Samputa*, p. 65.

48. The oldest Buddhist manuscript in existence, birch bark dating from the end of the first century AD or beginning of the second, held by the British Library, written in Kharosthi language, states: 'People keep you company and serve you with ulterior motives; real friends are hard to find these days. People are insincere, clever in pursuing their own ends. You should wander alone like a rhinoceros.' Disillusionment with the world is the starting point for much spiritual teaching.

49. PSD Vol. I, p. 240.

50. *Mumana* by Kanakadasa: 'Will intelligent folk lodge in the father-in-law's house?' for example.

51. PSD Vol. III, p. 85.

52. PSD Vol. II, p. 403.

53. I have borrowed this phrase from Walt Whitman to suggest congenial camaraderie in English.

54. James Hillman and Michael Ventura, *We've Had a Hundred Years of Psychology and the World's Getting Worse*, San Francisco: HarperSanFrancisco, 1993, pp. 35–6. Even Freud, who saw religion as an illusion, when asked what was necessary for a life of meaning said 'love and work'. Hillman writes: 'If the soul is a chord only the ear can reveal it. The ear is the feminine part of the head; it is consciousness offering maximum attention with a minimum of intention. We receive another through the ear, through the feminine part of ourselves, conceiving and gestating a new solution to his problem only after we have been full penetrated by it, felt its impact, and let it settle in silence . . . . Love, as agape, means 'to receive', 'to welcome', 'to embrace'. Perhaps the perfection of love begins through faith in and work on the feminine within us, man or woman, since the feminine ground is the embracing container, receiving, holding and carrying. It gives birth and nourishes and it encourages us to believe. This ground welcomes us home to ourselves just as we are.' James Hillman, *Insearch: Psychology and Religion*, New York: Charles Scribner and Sons, 1967, pp. 22, 126. W.H. Auden wrote: '. . . the first criterion of success in any human activity, the necessary preliminary, whether to scientific discovery or to artistic vision, is intensity of attention or, less pompously, love.'

55. The rasa concept gives bhakti the framework for its programme of culturally creative artistry—the soul making blissful beauty for God—and its metaphysics—the soul realizing God as the bliss of beauty. The sacred attractor in this whole spiritual process is beautiful bliss.

56. J.L. Mehta, *Philosophy and Religion*, . . . pp. 213–14.

Annamacharya's Life

A nnamacharya's parents were *smarta* brahmans of the Nandavarika community living in Tallapaka village, in what is now Rajampet taluk, Cuddapah district in Andhra Pradesh, south India. Annamayya was born in 1408. Even as a child he was devoted to Venkateshvara, Vishnu as Lord of Tirumala Hills,[1] singing jingles to him, eating prasad (offerings to God) as his food, demanding that his mother sing lullabies about Venkateshvara, and preoccupied to the point of constantly disappointing his parents and elders when they asked him to perform everyday chores around the house.

While still a youth he had a dream of the Lord of the Hills: 'I saw Lord Venkateshvara, father of the cosmos, gazing on me', he later sang.[2] He further recalled, 'When I was young you came to me in a dream, and you gave your command, honouring my tongue with the chance to sing songs of praise to you. I became so happy I coasted along, floating in pure bliss.'[3]

Probably when he was around sixteen years old,[4] Annamayya, desiring a more complete immersion in the bhakti way of life, left his village and set out for holy Tirumala Hill. In one version he 'threw down his plough' and joined a group of passing pilgrims already.*en route* to Tirupati.[5]

Climbing up the series of hills, as pilgrims still do today, the tired boy rested on a level stone ledge in a bamboo grove, still wearing the sandals he had on when he left home. When he dozed off there in the cool shade, it is said, he saw the Goddess Alamelumangamma, her presence glowing in his consciousness, manifest from his soul's depths.

The Goddess told him to remove his sandals, saying that if he had climbed the rough path without them he would not have grown tired, or needed to rest. She gave him prasad from the temple, promising that he would be blessed by her consort, Lord Venkateshvara. On the spot Annamaya composed a *shatakam*—one hundred verses of praise, to express his devotion to her.

According to the legend, the excited boy hurried up the path, and at last arrived at the temple on top of the mountain to receive the Lord's *darshan*. Gazing upon the image of the Lord whose hands indicate a protective and gift-giving gesture, the boy sang spontaneously, with a heart thrilled and filled with bliss, a song of rapt devotion. Next day when the inner sanctum doors were shut because of the temple schedule, he sang a *shatakam* (one hundred verses of praise) to Venkateshvara, which he had just composed, and the doors spontaneously opened up for him.

Annamayya felt a special affinity to Tirupati and continued living there in the atmosphere of holiness. He became a disciple of a Vaishnava sage named Shathakopayati, was initiated into the Shrivaishnava path, having the emblems of Vishnu (conch, chakra, etc.) branded on to his skin to proclaim his identity as a devotee of Vishnu. He was a member of the same Vaishnava *sampradaya* or teaching tradition as Vedanta Deshika.

Annamayya's practice was to compose one or more songs after taking his daily bath at the holy pool on Tirumala hill or at a waterfall; as the sun and the breeze played upon his drying clothes, his creative imagination played in melody and verse, organizing a song to the Lord. Then he would dress and stroll to the shrine and sing the new praise. Over the next eight decades the steady and varied reiteration of this routine of daily creativity led to the accumulation of a massive number of songs.

Annamacharya is thought to have studied deeply with Shathakopa (d. 1458), a socially active saint, and to have derived his depth of Vaishnava understanding from his guidance. As is often the case in saints' lives, at first there was some tension between his parents' desires for their child and his spiritual urges. His sense of destiny was in conflict with their plans.

After the boy had been away from home for some time Annamayya's mother journeyed from Tallapaka to find her son, and and when she found him, requested him to return with her, so that he could be properly married as the family had planned. The youth resisted but his mother insisted. The guru ended the stand-off by telling Annamayya to return with his mother, and the youth complied with his teacher's wishes.[6]

His parents celebrated a double wedding for their son, marrying him to two women, Timmakka and Akkalamma. Some suggest this double bond was their way to doubly ensure that he not wander off and become a renunciant; they hoped the two knots would twice as firmly secure him to family life and dissuade him from the single-pointed life of spiritual detachment toward which he had shown a natural inclination.

The young man accepted his duties, and as a householder with two wives, learned all about the feelings of women, to love the feminine view and to sing it. (By 'feminine view' I mean the gopi-like perspective on life as seen through the eyes of mothers, sisters, daughters, wives. In this view and its religious symbolism the soul is the female and God is the male. This allows the devotee to enjoy the poetry depicting the relationship of Venkateshvara with his consort, the Goddess.) Many bhakti songs in *nayika* moods were to flow from his soul decade after decade. But the feminine feelings of love called for the balance of a more spiritually abstracted masculine consciousness, and so, Annamayya sang songs not only in the srngara mood of longing love, yearning and burning, but also *adhyatma* songs of philosophy, cool wisdom and vision. Annamayya's life with his two wives shares a similarity with other figures in his culture at ascending levels. Krishnadevaraya, the great Vijayanagara empire ruler had two main wives (Statues of the threesome are still on display at Tirupati). Altogether he married twelve wives, and was often surrounded by women, an auspicious sign of his kingdom's vitality. Krishna, the incarnation of Vishnu as the embodiment of love, is sometimes pictured with two favourites from among the many milkmaids and sixteen thousand princesses who loved him.[7]

Even after his marriage Annamayya continued to study the sacred texts with Shathakopa, who had established *mathas* at Ahobilam and at Tirupati. Annamacharya composed a song honouring his guru:

> Gaze upon this venerable sage, approachable by all
> Lord Hari is his guide, and his only refuge
>
> He is the golden road to ultimate bliss
> He knows the meaning of the scriptures
> He's pure-hearted, sinless, a boat to cross
> Vitaja river, to win Vaikuntha with. Gaze . . .

He is the holy wisdom lamp, lighting up
    The many worlds of existence
The one who frees from sins, the raft by which
    strivers may reach the shore beyond samsara. Gaze . . .

He is an ocean of compassion, the devotee
    of the Lord residing in Shri Rangam
In Venkatagiri, in Ahobilam, he is the sage
    Shathakopa—he is the prince of yogis. Gaze . . .[8]

During Annamacharya's lifetime the Sangama dynasty ended. There were intrigues in the Vijayanagara court, with Sangama family members killing each other: prince killing king, and brother killing brother. Then Narasimha was crowned and reigned for three years, 1487–90, beginning the Saluva dynasty. According to the composer's grandson and biographer Chinnanna, Saluva Narasimha once heard Annamacharya sing a *shringara pada* addressed to Lord Venkateshvara, and was so impressed that he requested the composer to write one in his honour.[9] Annamacharya, who strongly felt that true bhakti meant an unwavering attachment to God, a passionate longing for spiritual union which excludes all lesser interests, answered: 'My tongue has no knowledge of praising a man like yourself; it is only skilled in praising Lord Hari.'

This honesty and grounded God-centredness in the face of external power was taken as insolence, and displeased the king greatly. According to the legend the wounded royal ego ordered that Annamayya be punished for insulting him, and so his soldiers put the disobedient singer in a prison cell. While locked up, the composer sang with intensity a song about the power inherent in saying the name of Hari and discovered that he had miraculously been released from his chains. Reliance on the holy name and staunch refusal to sing of the king are traits which, according to their hagiographies[10] mark the lives of a number of singer–saints, signalling that they were truly devoted to the ultimate and not to the temporal powers.

Another famous Annamacharya song regards the loss of the sacred images used for worship in his home. In some stories an invading king's soldiers took Annamayya's images. The simple refrain goes like this:

    Please bring the consort of Lakshmi, now
    It's time for me to worship him, it's been a long time

But for those who believe the story of the lost images the words would mean loss and longing, like this:

> Please bring back Lakshmi's consort—he's vanished from my sight
> it's far too long since I've worshipped the Lord here in my shrine.[11]

In other oral traditions about the saint it is said that when Annamayya offered a mango to the image of the Lord in Mandemu village, he at first did not realize that it was sour. However, on learning that the mango was sour, he begged the Lord's forgiveness and asked the tree to yield only sweet fruits thereafter, which is believed to have happened (according to the people of that village who continue to tell visitors the story).

Annamayya composed thirty-two thousand songs with the mudra Venkateshvara, and his son Peda Tirumalacharya had them inscribed on rectangular copper plates. He originated, from his humble homely heartfelt practice of singing a little song of praise each day, the major tradition of devotional *sankirtanas* in Telugu. Reiterating his praise anew each day, a mighty corpus of songs grew. There had been Shaivite *vachanas*, colloquial Kannada poems for recital, before his time in south India, and the musicologist Bharata had long ago described the *padanirukta* form which Annamacharya used—Annamaya called his works padas. Shripadaraya, who was his elder, on a much less prolific scale wrote songs in Kannada, expressing Vishnu bhakti for his region's folks.

Annamacharya was put in charge of sankirtana singing programmes at the Tirupati temple, where many pilgrims worshipped each day. As one biographer puts it, Annamayya, like Perialvar, became the 'father-in-law' of Lord Venkateshvara, arranging the *Kalyanotsava* (marriage celebration) for the deity, as well as the *Shukravara Abhisheka* (ritual anointing). Because he established the *sankirtanabhandara*, performance of songs of praise in the temple, he was given the title 'master of devotional songs' *sankirtanacharya*. He was also given the title Padakavitapitamaha or Grandfather—poet of the pada genre because he originated the Telugu tradition of bhakti songs in the kirtana form. The temple padas which Annamayya composed consisted of lyrics following specific poetic rules such as the similar sounding first syllables of couplets, and later Telugu lyricist melodists echoed and furthered this art form. One example of a later master of this form, who reiterated time-tested patterns and improved on them with unique creativity, is the Telugu composer Kshetrayya.[12]

Annamacharya wrote other works of poetry, including the Sanskrit *Venkatachala–mahatmya; Shringara manjari*, a poem of a nayika's love for Venkateshvara; a Telugu *Ramayana*, twelve *shatakas*, and a treatise in Sanskrit on music: *Sankirtana Lakshanam*, which is lost, though a translation in Telugu written by his grandson Chinnanna exists.[13] Annamacharya died in 1503 but his son and grandson, who had grown up sharing in his devotional practices and musical artistry, carried on the tradition in the family. They preserved his songs, added to them, and gave endowments, ensuring that the songs were sung at certain temples.[14] They were also musicians in their own right, theorists and composers.

Ramanuja, the smarta brahman of the twelfth century who had become Vaishnava, like Yamunacharya his guru, dedicated his life to synthesizing 'a rational and natural mingling of the rapturous devotion of the *alvars* with the Upanishadic quest of the ontological and unifying ground of the changing world of the many.'[15] So too, Annamacharya, a smarta convert to Vaishnavism in the school of Ramanuja, composed songs which played lyrically and melodically in those two interminglable realms—devotion and wisdom. As the Tenkalai teachers of Vaishnavism made the viewpoints of the *darshanas* available to people who did not know Sanskrit (and some scholars consider this democratization their chief contribution), so Annamacharya made philosophical views singable in memorable songs. Thus he further spread this Vaishnava path among the religious pilgrims, including women and children. Such pilgrims, though illiterate, could be intrigued by cadence and melody to learn a complex lesson, and reiterate it later, in their own homes.

The songs in the following chapter are a sample of Annamacharya's lyrics, selected from the thousands of available songs.

Notes

1. The Tirumalai Hills comprise a range with seven principal peaks which are thought to resemble a coiling serpent. Near one peak named Seshacalam (mountain of Sesha the cosmic serpent on whom Vishnu reclines) is the Tirumala temple dedicated to Shri Venkateshvara. They are southwest of Madras between the 13th and 14th degrees latitude North and 79 degrees longitude East.

2. H.L. Chandrasekhara, *Sri Annamacharya: A Philosophical Study,* Mysore: Vidya Shankara Prakashana, 1990, p. 8.

3. Ibid. The references to his early life are found in the song 'Ayyo poyembrayamu'.

4. S. Subrahmanya Sastry and V. Viaraghavacharya, eds, Shri Tirumalai-Tirupati Devasthanam Epigraphical Series (6 vols), Vol. 3, Madras: Tirupati Sri Mahant's Press, 1931–8, p. 226. Although the *Annamacharya Charitra,* his biography, says this happened at the age of eight, the year of thread investiture for brahmans; in other tellings he was sixteen. See, Tallapaka Chinnanna, *Annamacharya-charitramu,* Veturi Prabhakara Sastri, ed., Tirupati: TTD Press, 1949.

5. N.C. Indira Devi, 'From Tallapaka Composers to Purandaradasa: Studies in the Music of the Period', PhD Thesis unpublished, University of Delhi, Faculty of Music and Arts, p. 168.

6. Adapa Ramakrishna Rao, *Annamacharya,* New Delhi: 1987. See also, V.A.K. Ranga Rao, 'Sri Thallapaka Annamacharya', *Nayaki,* June 1978.

7. Radha the gopi, Satyabhama his favourite wife, and Rukmini are among the favourites of Krishna, out of the multitudes who loved him.

8. *Chudu dindaraku* by Annamacharya.

9. See, *AC,* pp. 38–9.

10. See, W. J. Jackson, *Tyagaraja—Life and Lyrics* (Madras: Oxford University Press, 1991), for more on this theme.

11. *Indiraramanu dechchi* is the song being referred to here.

12. Matthew Allen, *The Tamil Padam: A Dance Music Genre of South India,* PhD thesis, Wesleyan University (forthcoming). For prosody patterns see Jackson, *Tyagaraya.* . . . Rajani Kanta Rao writes about both Annamacharya and Kshetrayya in his biographies (Telugu) of lyricist–composers, *Andhra Vaggeyakara Caritramu,* Vijayawada: Visalandhra Publishing, 1975. *Muvvagopala Padavali: Amours of the Divine Cowherd with Jingling Bells* (Vijayawada: Rajani Publications, 1994) is a translation by B. Rajanikanta Rao, consisting of 160 Kshetrayya lyrics with comments.

13. *Sankirtana Lakshanamu by Tallapaka Chinna Tirumalacarya,* trans. and comm. Salva Krishnamurthy, Madras: Institute of Asian Studies, 1990; V. Vijayaraghavacharya and G. Adinarayana Naidu, eds, *Sankirtana Lakshana, The Minor Works of Tallapakam Poets,* Madras: Sri Mahant's Devasthanam Press, 1935.

14. Chinna Tirumalayya arranged for the performance of Annamacharya's sankirtanas at the Narasimha Svami temple in Mangalagiri, in what is now Guntur district, Andhra Pradesh, according to an inscription on the temple wall there. And in Simhachalam, located near Waltair, Annamacharya songs are regularly sung during the Adhyayanotsava festival, before singing the *Divya Prabandham*.

15. *Sri Ramanuja, His Life, Religion, Philosophy,* Madras: Sri Ramakrishna Math, 1990, p. 34.

Annamacharya's Songs

Akativelalanalapaina (SAS no. 57, p. 59)

Whenever you're hungry, whenever you're tired
Repeat the holy name, there is no other way

In moments of want, or when you're all alone
If someone captures you and you're locked up
The blessed name of Hari is the only support
If you're forgetful and make mistakes in life

Whenever you're hungry, whenever you're tired
Repeat the holy name, there is no other way

When danger threatens, or you're scandalized
In times of sin, whenever you are in terror
The power of Hari's name is your true comfort
Search until dusk falls; you'll find no other way

Whenever you're hungry, whenever you're tired
Repeat the holy name, there is no other way

If you're bound in chains, condemned to death
When you're waylaid on the road by creditors
The name of Venkata is the only way of release
Idiot mind, search as you wish, no other way exists

Whenever you're hungry, whenever you're tired
Repeat the holy name, the only way to go higher

Anni mantramulu (AK no. 8, p. 10)

I am saying every mantra when I repeat this one
For I have received the mantra of Venkatesha

Narada recited the Narayana mantra
Young Prahlada had his Narasimha mantra
Strong-willed Vibishana received the Rama mantra
I got a different one—the Venkatesha mantra
    and I am saying every mantra when I repeat this one
    For I have received the mantra of Venkatesha

Dhruva recited the bright Vasudeva mantra
Arjuna repeated his Krishna mantra
Shuka spelled out the Vishnu mantra early on
and I received the beautiful Venkatesha mantra

    I am saying every mantra when I go on saying this one
    For I have received the encompassing mantra of Venkatesha

The goal of all these mantras is the Lord Vishnu
And this is the mantra which reveals the ultimate
To save me my guru gave me this very mantra
This moon-bright mantra of Shri Venkatesha

    I am saying all the mantras when I revolve this one
    For I have received the total mantra of Venkatesha

Bhavamulona bahyamunandunu   (SVBPM no. 3)

Keep on singing 'Govinda, Govinda'
inwardly and out loud, O mind

All of the gods are avatars of Hari
all the universes are inside Hari
all the mantras are just names of Hari
so go on repeating 'Hari Hari Hari Hari'

The fixed duties are the glory of Vishnu
the Vedas are just the praises of Vishnu
Vishnu is the spirit pervading the cosmos
So keep on searching for Vishnu, Vishnu

Seek him singing 'Govinda Govinda'
inwardly and out loud, O mind of mine

This Achyuta is beginning and end
and this Achyuta is killer of demons
this Achyuta resides atop Venkatadri Hill
so take refuge in Achyuta, Achyuta, mind

And keep on singing 'Govinda, Govinda'
inwardly and out loud, O mind

Chanda mama   (AK no. 20, p. 22; also in SVBPM)

Uncle moon, come to me
moon come here to me
bring with you
a cup of gold
filled with buttermilk

Bring it for our darling boy
who is the timeless
father of Brahma,
he who resides in the Vedas,
our father, blue-coloured Lord
who rules the entire cosmos;
bring it to beautiful Lakshmi's consort
the great Lord, who existed
before Brahma, Vishnu, Shiva
bring to our sweet boy a drink—

Uncle moon come here to me
bring a golden cup of milk

Bring it for the glorious boy
with lovely lotus eyes, the child
whose speech is sweet, the child
lovingly embraced in his mother's arms
for the child replete with excellences
the child who lifted up
his entire clan, the attractive one
pervading the creation,
the good-natured Lord whose very sight
bestows on us nine kinds of wealth—

Uncle moon come along, with a cup
of gold filled up with buttermilk

Bring it for the hero who rides on Garuda,
the deity who protects the other gods,
to the father of the love-god
whose bow is made of flowers,
bring it for the Lord
who takes thousands of forms,
bring it for our Shri Venkateshvara
overflowing with auspiciousness
full of all knowledge and perfect wisdom

Uncle moon, come to me,
moon come here to me
bring with you
a golden cup
filled all the way up
with butter milk
for our darling boy

Chudu dindaraku (AS no. 40, p. 41)

Gaze upon this venerable sage, approachable by all
Lord Hari is his guide, and his only refuge

He is the golden road to ultimate bliss
he knows the meaning of the scriptures
He's pure-hearted, sinless, a boat to cross
Viraja river, to win Vaikunta with

Gaze upon this venerable sage, so accessible to all
Lord Hari is his guide, and his only refuge

He is the holy wisdom lamp, lighting up
the many worlds of existence
The one who frees from sins, the raft by which
strivers may reach the shore beyond samsara

Gaze upon this venerable sage, approachable by all
Lord Hari is his guide, and his only refuge

He is an ocean of compassion, the devotee
of the Lord residing in Shri Rangam
In Venkatagiri, in Ahobilam, he is the sage
Shathakopa—he is the prince of yogis

Gaze upon this venerable sage, approachable by all
Lord Hari is his guide, and his only refuge

Devadevambhaje (SVBPM no. 7)

I worship the Lord of Lords full of divine glory
Rama who defeated the demon Ravana in war

King of kings, moon of the solar race
Long armed one with body like blue clouds
Lord who took a vow to protect with mighty bow
Rama, Ramachandra, the lotus-eyed one

I worship the Lord of Lords full of divine glory
Rama who defeated the demon Ravana in war

Lord with a body like a dark blue cloud
Big-chested, pure lotus-navelled, destroyer of
The seven sala trees, establisher of dharma
Sita's Lord, the one reclining on the cosmic serpent

I worship the Lord of Lords full of divine glory
Rama who defeated the demon Ravana in war

Supreme Narayana worshipped by Brahma
Breaker of the bow Janaka received from Shiva
Protector of Vibishana, dessicator of Lanka
Worshipped by saints and wise folk—Venkatesha

I worship the Lord of Lords full of divine glory
Rama who defeated the demon Ravana in war

Devesaganaradhita (BR p. 22)

Shri Venkatagiri Nayaka
Lord whose feet are worshipped
by Indra the king of the gods
and by other deities
is arriving

The Lord whose form enchants
Alamelumanga
The Lord who removes the sins
of the people of the Kali yuga
The Lord praised in beautiful songs
is arriving

The Lord who saved Brahma
who created the world
The Lord who makes possible
crossing the ocean
to the auspicious shore
The Lord is arriving

The Lord who plays in the forest
of sandalwood trees and
vakula flowers,
expert in protecting
all the scriptures
The Lord is arriving

O Narayana, Lord
who protects mankind
Killer of demons
like Naraka
Lord who destroyed
Ravana's pride
The brave Lord is arriving

Shri Keshava, Narayana
Govinda, Murare
Shri Madhava
Madusudana
Damodara
Saure

Your abode is
Tirumala, Lord
decorated with gems
You conquer anger
and other vices
The Lord partial to saints
is arriving

O Lord wearing the garland
Killer of demon leaders
who prowl the night
Protector of Brindavan
Vijaya Gopala
is arriving

Dinudanenu (SAS no. 10, p. 10; ARR p. 34)

I'm a little nobody, you're the supreme Lord
Your glory alone shall always prevail

How can I know the enigma of birth
Or figure out the mystery of death
Can I ever really understand you?
Lord, you gave birth to me in this world
so you must also give me your saving grace

I'm a little nobody, you're the supreme Lord
Your glory alone shall always prevail

I can't understand sin, can't grasp virtue
How can I understand you with my mind
You are the dweller in my heart
And so I cry—please cleanse me
Of sins—Lord you must protect me

For I'm a little nobody, you're supreme Lord
Ultimately all that prevails is your glory

I'm fallen, unclean, a failure, despised
How can I hope to be worthy of your grace
Yet, supreme Lord Venkateshvara,
You can't forsake me—until the
Final end—you have to protect me

For I'm a little nobody, you're supreme Lord
Ultimately all that prevails is your glory

Dolayam (SVBPM no. 5)

Swing, Hari, swing
and swing again
Fish avatar, tortoise, boar
Narasimha avatar
Foe of demons. full of virtues
One who holds the world
Father of the love-god
Swing, Hari, swing
      and swing again

Vamana, Parasurama, Shri Rama,
And supreme Krishna avatar
Cloud-coloured Lord
Ranganatha, Protector
Of elephant Gajendra, Killer
Of demon Mura
Swing, Hari, swing
      and swing again

Buddha and Kalki the terrifying
You are all ten incarnations
As Krishna you are the cowherd
You're Balarama holding the plough
Lord of the Seven Hills
of Tirupati
Swing, Hari, swing
      and swing again

Ekkadi manusha janmamu (WTP Vol. II, p. 29)

It doesn't much matter—the place
where a person may come to be born
what's the use of being born anywhere
I have always trusted in you, I leave
the outcome of all this to your grace

I don't forget to eat when hungry
I don't forget to enjoy family life
I don't forget to satisfy my senses
O God this is all your illusion
Can I forget deep wisdom
Can I forget eternal truth
Can I forget my Guru and God
O God all this is your illusion

I can't leave off committing sins
I can't stop doing good things either
I can't give up my strong desires
All this, God, is your illusion
I shall leave the 'six actions of householders'
I shall eventually leave *vairagya* too
I shall leave my 'conduct' finally
O Vishnu all this is your *maya*

I'll get stuck, hung up in the knots
of useless harassments
but I won't even try to hook my mind
up with the path of liberation
You revealed yourself, Shri Venkateshvara
as the all-pervasive
It's strange, since you care for me
that I must stay troubled by illusions

It doesn't much matter—the place
where a person may come to be born
what's the use of being born anywhere
I have always trusted in you, I leave
the outcome of all this to your grace

Ekulajudemi (AK no. 29, p. 29; also ARR pp. 78–9)

What if he's this, what if he's that
    doesn't much matter what caste he's born into
      whoever he is—all alone
        he comes to know Lord Hari at last

Only one known as being devoted to truth
(not one indulging in doing harm to others
but one who thinks of others as himself)
he is the one with sympathy for all beings
and what if he's born as this or that
    doesn't much matter what his caste
        whoever he is—all alone
            he comes to know Lord Hari at last

Whoever has a pure heart, develops self-control,
he has his intellect absorbed in dharma
he does not forsake the path of appointed karma
he will not forget the secret of Hari bhakti
so what if he's born this or that
    doesn't really matter what class
        whoever he is—all alone
            he comes to know Lord Hari at last

Whoever does the right thing for others' good in this world
whoever lives without animosity in his mind
whoever lives with courage in his or her soul
that one knows—rightfully so—he serves the Lord
Venkatesha—and what if he's this or that
    doesn't really matter about his caste
        whoever he is—all alone
            he comes to know Lord Hari at last

Indiraramanu dechchi (AK no. 9, p. 11)

Please bring the Consort of Lakshmi
It's time for me to worship him now

When demonic terrorist Mahiravana kidnapped Rama
O Hanuman you brought him back, brilliant son of Anjaneya;
O Garuda, king of birds, with skilful caring mercy
You released Rama when he was bound by serpent arrows

So please bring the Consort of Lakshmi
It's time for me to worship him now

Prahlada your devotion made Narasimha spring from the pillar
For all the gods to see (and to help calm him down)
Arjuna you caused Krishna to sit in the driver's seat
Of your chariot and to reveal his cosmic form in all its glory

Please bring the Consort of Lakshmi
It's time for me to worship him now

O Adisesha you performed those countless services
On Tirumala Hill for Lord Shrinivasa, you made him belong to you
O Kartyavira Arjuna, King of the Haihayas
With your thousand arms and your chariot of gold
You desired to rule wisely, and attained the Lord's presence

Please help me find the Consort of Lakshmi
It's time for me to worship him now

Jaya Janakiramana (BR p. 16)

Hail Rama, beloved of Janaki
Lord who gave refuge to Vibishana
Victory to you, Lord with lotus feet
full of compassion for the poor

Hail refuge of the world
compassionate to devotees
Victory to you, Lord of great beauty
goodness of the world

Hail omnipresent resident
Lord living in Ayodhya
Victory to you, Lord served by
devotees without blemish
Lord with smiling lotus face

Hail Lord, whom Shuka worshipped
whose life gives auspiciousness
Victory to you, Lord with *makara* ear-rings
Lord blue-cloud hued

Hail Lord with beautiful crown
Lord adorned with the Kaustabha gem
Victory to you, lotus-eyed Raghuvira
sporting with Lakshmi Kamalavihara

Hail Lord victorious in war with foes
always full of good qualities and mystery
Victory to you, Lord in spotless hearts
Lord who removes all troubles

Hail more beautiful than the love-god
Hero with delicious qualities
Son of king Dasharatha
Victory to you, remover of earth's burdens

Hail Dispeller of all sins
foe of ten-headed Ravana
Victory to you, Consort of tender Lakshmi
Lord who sports with Sita

Kondalo koyila (SRP)

When I heard the call
of the *koyil* bird on the hill
my heart was torqued
squeezed, it broke
but when I arrived
at your threshold
my soul was healed

When I was leaving the house
(it makes my head spin
to think of it now)
my mate, like a tiger
blocked the door, snarling
—my hairs erect with love
who cared what anyone said

Kondalalo nelakonna (SAS no. 33, p. 34)

The Lord of the temple bathing pool, Lord whose shrine is on the Mountain
He is the generous one—giver of boons as great as mountains

He gave every boon asked for by Kuruvarati Nambi the devotee
who was of the community of potters.
And when King Tondaman Chakravarti was involved in fighting a war,
and asked the Lord to appear to him, he did, and the King believed

The Lord of the temple bathing pool, Lord whose shrine is on the Mountain
He is the generous one—giver of boons as great as mountains

He carried earth like a common labourer to help Anantalvar,
stealthily doing drudgery without pay, with obvious enthusiasm.
And with great affection, sympathizing with Tirumalanambi,
he spoke lovingly with him day after day

The Lord of the temple bathing pool, Lord whose shrine is on the Mountain
He is the generous one—giver of boons as great as mountains

When Tirukachchinambi was living in Kanchipuram, the Lord
took pity on him, and brought him to his presence
He protected us all, the magnanimous Lord—he's the one who has
blessed us all, full of compassion, our Venkatesha
Lord of the temple pool . . . giver of boons as great as mountains

Kshirabdhi Kanyakaku (SVBPM no. 4; also AS no.53, p. 58)

Here is the camphor flame offering to Shri Maha Lakshmi
Daughter of the Milk Ocean, sitting enthroned in the lotus

I offer this white flaming camphor
to the lotus-eyed goddess, to her beautiful face
to her breasts; I offer this flaming camphor to her
to her hands
with the beauty of lotuses, to her exquisite hair
like a swarm of bees,
to her loveliness
I offer this jewelled camphor

Here is the camphor flame offering to Shri Maha Lakshmi
Daughter of the Milk Ocean, sitting enthroned in the lotus

To her tender feet, her thighs smooth and shining
like the stem of a banana tree, sincerely offering
camphor from a pearl-studded box;
to her navel and her hips
offering with ardent love
this many-splendoured camphor flame

Here is the camphor flame offering to Shri Maha Lakshmi
Daughter of the Milk Ocean, sitting enthroned in the lotus

I offer this white flaming camphor
to the queen of glorious Lord Venkatesha
and her many-splendoured charms
I offer this burning camphor here, auspicious light,
to the most beautiful Alamelumanga
source of all the beauty in this world

Here is the camphor flame offering to Shri Maha Lakshmi
Daughter of the Milk Ocean, sitting enthroned in the lotus

Madhava bhavatu   (attributed to Annamacharya, BR pp. 24–5)

Glory be to Madhava
auspicious glory
to the killer of demons Madhu and Mura

Auspicious glory to the lotus-eyed
Lord who removes all sins
and is worshipped by gods

Auspicious glory to the son
of the emperor, on whose banner is
the serpent-eater, sapphire blue Lord

Auspicious glory to the son of Nanda
thief of butter and curds
lifter of Mandara mountain

Auspicious glory to the immortal Lord
whose teeth are like jasmine
with jingling anklets and beautiful face

Auspicious glory to the butter–thief
who sports with the cowherd girls
killer of demons Madhu and Kaitabha

Auspicious glory to the Lord who plays
in Brindavan with cowgirls, protector of devotees
wearer of the great *tulasi* garland
Vijayagopala Child Krishna

Rama Govinda Rama Rama Govinda Rama
Rama Govinda Rama Raghava
Rama Govinda Rama Rama Kalyana Rama
Rama crowned as king Raghava

Govinda Madhava Gopala Keshava
Narasimha Achyuta Narayana

Son of Dasharatha, Consort of Sita
Killer of demons, Ocean of mercy

Rama Raghava lotus-eyed Lord
Giver of boons, elephant saver

Krishna Keshava lotus-eyed Lord
Grantor of our wishes, Lord of the Yadu dynasty

Manujudai putti (SVBPM no. 2; also AS no. 41, p. 46)

Having been born as a mortal
why achieve nothing but misery
by always serving some other mere mortal?

Arriving at some dismal site
for the sake of your hungry belly
you beg some nobody
for your share of pathetic mush
with grief in your heart you approach
the place you started from
—why go on with this suffering?

Having been born as a mortal
why achieve nothing but misery
by always serving some other mere mortal?

Born in everyone, dwelling in all
God assumes the various forms
why don't you win the priceless bliss
worshipping the glorious Lord
of Venkata hill

Having been born as a mortal
why achieve nothing but mortification
by always serving some other mere mortal?

Molla lele naku tanne (SRP)

What are these jasmine flowers for?
Tell him to wear them himself
For what am I but a tribal girl *(chenchu)*
my hairstyle has fragrance naturally

What would I do with this silk sari
Shiny green leaves are good enough for me
Give it back; tell him that he can wind it
as a sash around his waist—I'm a tribal

What do I want with a bed with a canopy
Tell him to keep it and sleep on it
What am I but a chenchu girl who'd really
Rather roll around on the earth beneath a tree

Muddugare Yashoda (SAS no. 8, p. 8)

The son of Devaki, child of ineffable glory
  he is a pearl to beautiful Yashoda

He is a ruby in the palms of the gopis' hands
He is the vajra—diamond hard to obstinate Kamsa
His lustre is like emerald to his beloved ones
  in all the three worlds
This little Krishna so near and dear to all

The son of Devaki, child of ineffable glory
  he is a pearl to Yashoda of great beauty

His red lips are like coral to Rukmini, who enjoys
His sweet loveplay; to Govardana hill he's the gem
    of four colours
In between the conch and the discus he shines
    bright as lapis lazuli
The lotus-eyed one who saves when we take refuge in him

The son of Devaki, child of untellable glory
    he is a pearl to Yashoda of great beauty

He is pure topaz to Kalinga on whose head he dances
He is the sapphire reigning atop Venkata hill, he is
The divine gem remaining forever in the ocean of milk
The Lord Padmanabha who roams around like a little boy

The son of Devaki, child of ineffable glory
    he is a pearl to beautiful Yashoda

Murahara nagadhara (BR p. 20)

Killer of the demon Mura
Lifter of the mountain
Mukunda Madhava
Lord seated on Garuda
Lord from whose navel
the lotus of creation grows
Lord Narasimha, man–lion
namo namo
Narayana worshipped by
the great Narada
namo namo

Sleeping on the great milk ocean
having sun and moon as eyes
Lord whose feet are worshipped
by Brahma, Lord who put Bali down
lover of the gopis
namo namo to you
Lord from whose navel
the lotus of creation grows
Narayana . . .

Lord with the Shrivatsa
mark on your chest
wearing the cloth of gold
son of Devaki, ocean of compassion
protector of cowherds,
lifter of Govardhana hill
Lord fond of cowherds
namo namo
Narayana . . .

Son of Kaushalya
generous giver of all we need
ocean of compassion
effulgent one
son of Dasharatha
death-god to demons
father of Kusha and Lava
namo namo to you
Narayana . . .

Killer of Vali
born in the solar dynasty
Lord whose feet are worshipped
by ascetics, Lord who slew Maricha
worshipped by Hanuman
Lord who built the bridge
over the ocean
namo namo
Narayana . . .

Supreme Lord
worshipped by all the scriptures
member of the Yadava clan
Lord with the beautiful body
Lord who lifts up the Vedas
Shri Venkata Nayaka
beloved of Radha
namo namo to you
Narayana worshipped by great Narada
namo namo to you

Nanati baduku (SVBPM no. 8)

All that transpires in this world is but a drama
Kaivalya—salvation—is arriving beyond it

For sure once you're born death is certain
and in between the whole thing is a drama
This world stands here spread out before us
but Kaivalya lies beyond traumas and tortures

All that transpires in the world is a drama
Kaivalya—salvation—is reaching beyond it

Whatever food is eaten, whatever clothes are worn
All the world's a stage, the people in it, players
But beyond all the actions, both good and bad
beyond wealth inherited or won with sweat is Kaivalya

All that transpires in this world is but a drama
Kaivalya—the saving—is being beyond it

Sin is a constant, good deeds live on and on
It's an endless drama, in which time giggles
Salvation is otherwise—beyond this—in the skies
where Lord Venkateshvara lives, up on his hill

All that transpires here on earth is a drama
Kaivalya—removal—is arriving beyond it

Paluku tenela talli (SAS no. 5, p. 5)

Our mother, whose words are sweet as honey,
    is taking her rest
This woman, who spent the whole night
    in love-play with the Lord

With her hair rippling across her shining face
She sleeps until broad daylight
because she was up until dawn;
with unending inventiveness
held the heart of the Lord of the world enthralled

The edge of her sari has slipped down charmingly revealing
the goddess' breasts, as she sleeps in a golden mansion,
her lovely eyes are like the pink lily—red because she's exhausted
from all the intimate exertions she enjoyed with the Lord,
father of the love-god . . . so she's taking her rest.

In elegant style she sleeps on a pearl-strung bed, still fatigued!
She embraced Lord Venkatesha so long that her face, exquisite as a
half-blossomed flower, is covered with a fine dew of sweat drops

> Our mother whose words are sweet as honey
> is taking her rest
> This woman who spent the whole night
> in love-play with the Lord

Sandehamu (AAS Vol. II, p. 244; also AC p. 5)

Doubt has vanished, now I feel satisfaction
Now I've attained holy bliss—*brahmananda*

Since you've put the words of sweet songs in my mouth
I believe that you really will protect me
Because you accepted me in my youth
I am convinced you will save me, surely

Doubt has vanished, now I feel satisfaction
Now I've attained holy bliss—brahmananda

Ever since your form, O consort of Lakshmi
Came into my mind I am certain you are mine
I am known as your servant, near you in this world
I know you'll protect me without being asked twice

Doubt has vanished, now I feel satisfaction
Now I've attained holy bliss—brahmananda

You became accessible, gave me orders in a dream,
Lord Venkatesha, now I believe you're with me always
Now I always am before you, and that is the way
I've become purified and how I attained fame

Doubt has vanished, now I feel satisfaction
Now I've attained holy bliss—brahmananda

Sharanu sharanu (BR p. 18; also AC p. 67, 'Waking song')

We surrender, we surrender,
Lord worshipped by Indra
We surrender, Lord of earth mother
Bhudevi, we surrender,
Lord who squashed
the pride of demons
We surrender, Lord Venkatanayaka

Gods who never wink, sages,
regents of the eight directions
immortals, *kinnaras, siddhas,* glorious
celestial nymphs of Indra's court—
all of them wait upon you
with worshipful anticipation . . . We surrender . . .

Shiva the Lord holding the deer,
Lotus-born Brahma, and the sun god
who opens lotuses, and
the moon god who closes lotuses—
all thrilled with anticipation
they are awaiting the moment
of your holy presence . . . We surrender . . .

Vaikuntha Govinda Madhava
Lord from whose navel a lotus grows
Janardhana Lord Vishnu
Upholder of earth, rider of Garuda
Smasher of the pride of titan Bali . . . We surrender . . .

Well-known devotees like Prahlada
have come to worship you
Listen to our appeals O Lord
Lord of Venkata hill
Victorious Venkatanayaka
Svami Raghunayaka . . . We surrender . . .

We surrender, we surrender
Lord worshipped by Indra
We surrender, Lord of the earth mother
we surrender Lord who squashed
the pride of demons
We surrender Lord Venkatanayaka

Shriman Narayana (AK no. 47; also SVBPM no.1)

Shriman Narayana, Shriman Narayana Shriman
    Narayana I surrender to your lotus feet

You are the sunshine on the lotus face of Lakshmi
    Beloved of Kamala, your eyes are lotus-like
You're beneficent to Brahma sitting in the lotus
    Garuda is your vehicle. O lotus-navelled Lord
Your feet are my refuge.

You're the good fortune of the most excellent yogis
    Ultimate Lord, Supreme Being
Spirit pervading all, you're the infinite in
    sub-atomic particles, Shri Tiruvenkatagiri,
        Lord of the Seven Hills

Shriman Narayana, Shriman Narayana, Shriman
Narayana I surrender to your lotus feet

Suvvi suvvi suvvi (AK no. 45, pp. 46–7, 'Rice-pounding song')

'Suvvi suvvi suvvi . . .'
    singing like this (at the temple festival)
        pearly-teeth girls with lovely smiles pound,
            using the glances of their lotus eyes as pestles
                (to mash rice in the mortar stone)

Like this the women become centred in their minds
repeating 'Ola! ola!' with joy, immersed in their love
The girls pound out the sound, again and again
using the glances of their lotus eyes as pestles: 'Ola!'
    Suvvi suvvi suvvi . . .

The golden lacy borders of their silk saris sway when
they pound the rice this way saying 'Suvvi!'
the dangling silk rhythmically sways as they have fun
pounding together as a group in joyous unison 'Ola!'
    Suvvi suvvi suvvi . . .

Their loose long hair is swaying, and dangling garlands
swing from their abundant bouncing breasts
and the pretty women like half-blossomed flowers
are overflowing with beauty and they are pounding 'Ola!'
    Suvvi suvvi suvvi . . .

The tinkling of their bangles makes a *ghalghal* sound
the women with hands soft as new leaves say 'Ola!'
their midriffs are pretty and their hips rock back and forth
the women pound using their glances as pestles, 'Ola!'
    Suvvi suvvi suvvi . . . .

The girls have an aura of the fragrance of camphor
and sweet flowers decorate this festival place
they sing praise of the Lord of the temple pool,
in love with him, full of desire for his love-play 'Ola!'
    Suvvi suvvi suvvi . . .
        singing like this (at the temple festival)
            pearly-teeth girls with lovely smiles
                pound, using their glances as pestles
                    smashing rice in the mortar stone

Tan-da-na-naahi (SAS no. 21, p. 2; also AK no. 48, pp. 50–1)

Tan-da-na-naahi
    God is only one, the Supreme Being is only one
        the Supreme Lord is only one, the Supreme is one

Distinction between high and low is not part of oneness
Hari alone is the inner Self of all
all beings in this world are therefore the same
for Shri Hari is the indweller in every being—
    God is only one . . .

Fulfilling the sex urge is the same for the gods
    as it is for worms and animals—and the very same
    days and nights in the final analysis are there
    whether you're a rich man or poor
        God is only one, the Supreme Being is only one
            the Supreme Lord is only one, the Supreme is one

Valevalenani (Deshi Suladi) (DS)

'I want you, I need you!' Seeking
his love like that
am I not caught inside his net?
So, for my mere wants,
or just because he gets angry
why should I ever quarrel with my husband?

There may be other women in his life
but I know that I'm his permanent wife;
a bee may hover and wander many fields
but he comes home to his favourite honey petals.

Please won't you go tell him these words for me:
when I behave so modestly
is it right that Lord Venkatesha should get so angry?

The other day I calmly watched him
talking with another woman—did I make a big to-do?
Did I waste even a precious word
in criticism or suspicion? Still
the Lord has not let up in his trickery
Please . . .

Let him think over
the words he might have said
and you can swear by the breath of these two breasts
to the Lord of the temple pool on his holy hill
Please . . .

Well, from now on I won't go in
for sarcastic remarks—I'm just a bashful woman
yearning for the Lord of the hill Seshachala
Please . . .

Working up a sweat, fuming and fussing
will never win over
the Lord of the hills
but I will melt his heart
with my coy glances
Please . . .

I'll go to him myself
and find out his response—
where there is love, enjoyment develops
but first of all go
ask the love-god's father Vishnu for his ring
Please . . .

When he came to my house
misunderstandings and stubbornness went away
Why say more?
I bow to Venkataraya
Please . . .

With love flowering forth in passion
he caressed me O friends
and we joined together in ecstasy
Please . . .

Purandaradasa's Life

Purandaradasa,[1] who lived from 1485 to 1565, is one of the best known, best loved and well remembered composers who ever left a deep impression on the hearts and minds of the people of south India.

Purandaradasa was in the prime of his life during the heyday of the Vijayanagara empire, when Krishnadevaraya was bringing a golden age into existence, building on what went before, and expanding. When Krishnadevaraya died in 1530, Purandaradasa was in his early middle age. The fall of the Vijayanagara empire in 1565 led to many problems in society and some of Purandaradasa's songs reflect the loss and bewilderment of a turbulent land crying out for help.

Purandaradasa's death coincides with the battle of Tallikota in 1565, which opened a six-month spree of looting and pillage, desecration and vandalism in the capital by the forces of Adil Shah and Ibrahim Kutub. Much of what had been associated with the old order changed at that time.

Earlier signs of good fortune show us that Purandaradasa's family enjoyed the blessings of the king. A copper plate inscription[2] dated 24 Feburary 1526 records that Krishnadevaraya handed over Vyasamudra village, also known as Bettakonda village, to the guru of the dasas, Vyasaraya (also known as Vyasatirtha). In turn Vyasaraya passed it on to 308 scholars including three sons of Purandaradasa; Lakshmanadasa, Hevanadasa and Madhvapati. They belonged to Vashistha *gotra yajusa shaka* subsect, and are described as *vidvans* or scholars.

Annamacharya's grandson Tallapakka Chinna Tiruvenkatanath in his essay *Dvipada prabandha* refers to Purandaradasa arriving in Tirupati one morning when his grandfather Annamacharya was already an old man. Watching Annamayya the Telugu composer at his worship, the youthful fellow-Vaishnava Purandaradasa 'felt as if the Lord himself was present'. The elderly singer invited the young man to his home, and asked him to sing, and Purandaradasa accepted. Annamacharya is said to have felt as if Lord Purandara Vithala himself were present at the sacred occasion.

A song by Purandaradasa in tribute to the greatness of his wife speaks of transformation from worldliness to spirituality.[3] He praises his wife as instrumental in this change: 'May my wife's family increase a thousandfold—because of her I've come to hold the staff, the Haridasa's *tambura*'. Vijayadasa echoes this, saying that Purandaradasa was not spiritual in the first part of his life, and then became a great devotee overnight and sang appreciatively of his helping wife.

Two famous stories are often told of Purandaradasa—one about his wife's nose ring, and another about a *devadasi* and a bracelet. Both are seriously disputed by historians but happily remembered by villagers. Both have to do with jewellery and both illustrate man's rigidity and God's fluidity. God's grace melts even the most hardened heart, bringing an ego-breaking awakening to more love, to a spirit of expansiveness and an expansiveness of spirit. The popularity of these stories may indicate more about the love of this theme among tellers of saints' lives than about actual events, but it is poetry dynamic with bhakti meaning nevertheless.

The first story runs like this. Once Purandaradasa wanted water to drink while at the Pandarpur temple of Vithoba. Since there was no companion or disciple around, God came disguised as a fellow devotee and graciously gave Purandaradasa water. However, instead of feeling grateful, the preoccupied Purandaradasa lost his temper because the water had not been brought immediately and so threw the pot at the tardy 'fellow devotee' who made a quick exit.

That night God, who loves to play trickster lilas with his devotees, assumed the form of Purandaradasa, and visited a devadasi, giving her a bracelet from the divine image in the temple. Next day the temple priest discovered a bracelet missing from the wrist of the image and raised an alarm. Word spread and the devadasi revealed that she had been given the bracelet by Purandaradasa. Temple officials arrested the baffled suspect Purandaradasa, tying him to a pillar and interrogating him.

Then the voice of God was heard: 'Purandaradasa is innocent, leave him alone', and the other bracelet fell jingling from the image as a sign.

This is the gist of some words in a song beginning *Muyike*, attributed to Purandaradasa: 'Krishna brought water in a golden pot; I didn't know who he was and I beat him up . . . Lord, you gave a devadasi your golden bracelet making me look guilty, and I was beaten up . . . Then you saved me.'

The other story revolves around a poor brahman trying to arrange the money needed for his son's thread ceremony. Purandara the miserly jeweller shooed him away when the brahman asked him for help. The brahman then asked Purandara's wife, who was compassionate and gave him her nose ring. However when the brahman tried to sell the nose ring to Purandara, he recognized it and was furious, and berated his wife so much for her generosity that she became depressed and decided to end her life. She put poison in a cup of milk and was about to drink it when the nose ring miraculously fell into the cup. Realizing this miracle was a sign, Purandara changed his life; he left the tightwad's life of devotion to gold to become a dasa, an inspired devotee, a singer of Lord Vishnu's praise.

That Purandaradasa spent time in Hampi is a fact supported by ancient texts, as well as songs. In one *suladi* (literally, 'easy path', a medley type composition), Purandaradasa says, 'I don't know how, but thanks to the *punya* of many previous lifetimes, I found Vyasaraya's lotus feet. I became a member of a holy order, able to worship Shrisha.' There is another reference to his guru Vyasaraya in the same suladi, in which Purandaradasa says he received his name from him: 'A song without 'Purandara Vithala' doesn't shine; Vyasaraya gave me this signature'. Vyasaraya composed a song honouring his disciple, Purandara:

> 'Dasa' means Purandaradasa
> If you want to know what true devotion is
> Watch Purandaradasa pouring forth his love
> Worshipping Vasudeva Krishna—that's it

> The hypocrite, having no food to eat at home,
> Puts on a garland and goes out and begs
> Without self-nausea he pesters folks for food
> Collects some coins, pretending to be a dasa
> Can you call such a huckster a haridasa? No
>   'Dasa' means Purandaradasa
>   Want to know what real devotion is?
>   Watch Purandaradasa worship—that's it

Pretending to pray the Lord's name in public
With gusto he takes all the good food he wants
Not understanding the scriptures of Lord Vishnu
Holding a tambura in his hand—do you think
One becomes a haridasa just by strumming strings?
   'Dasa' means Purandaradasa
   If you want to know what devotion is . . .

Wandering around, receiving alms, is this all
It takes to make a haridasa? The true haridasa
Goes around, comes home and shares all his alms
The false one stuffs himself without sharing
Is a singer attached to worldly pleasures a dasa?
   'Dasa' means Purandaradasa . . .

Repeating songs by rote, chirping them like a parrot
Entertaining an audience of motley illiterates
Applying the *nama* mark on people's bodies, busying
Himself in the deception of bestowing his blessings
If one does all this is he really a haridasa?
   'Dasa' means Purandaradasa . . .

Knowing well the scriptural code of conduct, dasas
Realize God. Lord Vishnu, ever present within
Hanuman, the devotee worshipping Lord Krishna with
Wonderful songs and dance, yes, this is truly it—
The sincere Purandaradasa is that true haridasa
   'Dasa' means Purandaradasa
   Want to know what true devotion is?
   Watch Purandaradasa pouring forth his love
   Worshipping Vasudeva Krishna—that's it.[4]

Records show that Vijayanagara kings supported various religious creeds; Krishnadevaraya had regard for Tatacharya, who was a Shrivaishnava, and also for Vyasaraya, who was a Madhva Vaishnava. According to oral tradition and folk–memory Vyasaraya was an incarnation of Prahlada. He was said to have been trusted by all in Vijayanagara, and was able temporarily to take the throne, to be a stand-in when astrologically it had been diagnosed to be a bad time for the king and disasters were expected. Several Purandaradasa songs praise Vyasaraya who died in 1539.

According to Vijayadasa's song, Purandaradasa stayed with Vyasaraya and received initiation. Jagannathadasa, Vijayadasa's disciple, said that after his initiation, Purandaradasa began composing kirtanas, and he did not spend all his time in Hampi, but travelled to many places, promoting spiritual values with his songs.

Purandaradasa came into contact with Kanakadasa in Hampi where they met and became friends. According to many accounts, Kanakadasa received *diksha* (initiation into teachings) from Vyasaraya. It seems that Kanakadasa was already with Vyasaraya and had become known as a poet before Purandaradasa came to Hampi. Purandaradasa is said to have held Kanakadasa in high esteem. Kanakadasa does not refer to Purandaradasa in his songs. It is thought that Kanakadasa may have been older than Purandaradasa, and that when Kanakadasa was composing songs, Purandaradasa was not yet famous as a composer.

Purandaradasa wrote a song with a refrain which asks: 'When Vyasamuni shows such high regard for Kanakadasa, why are his followers in the *matha* (monastery) so mean-spirited and full of scorn?'[5]

Purandaradasa is said to have often gone to Tirupati, writing many songs to the Lord enshrined there, who was his ishtadevata or his favourite form of God. Where Purandaradasa was born, the Lord of Tirupati was already popular, and in Vijayanagara, the kings went to Tirupati to worship too. Purandaradasa went to other pilgrimage sites as well, and some of his songs reflect his prayers at these places of worship. Before he died he returned to Hampi and one song by his son Madhvapati says he breathed his last in Hampi *(Virupaksha kshetra)* near the temple of Vithala.[6]

After Vyasaraya died, Purandaradasa became a prominent leader of the *dasakuta*, but after Purandaradasa the movement was rather dormant. Purandaradasa in one of his songs says he composed 475,000 songs, and that this prolific output was inspired by his beloved guru Vyasaraya. Vijayadasa said Purandaradasa composed half a million songs. The huge number is probably meant to indicate 'a large number'. We have about 1,500 Purandaradasa songs now (probably 1000 to 1300 authentic ones, according to modern musicologists) and one cannot say how many were lost.

Purandaradasa, as far as we know, never wrote his lyrics on paper systematically. It is not known if followers of his were able to do that for him either. But the songs have a vivid quality; they clicked in the folk mind and lodged in people's memories. They survived and thrived on their own, echoing in devoted minds. Children learned them by heart, singing them with family members, repeating them to friends.

Purandaradasa was a prominent dasa. The Dasakuta was a forum of dasas, a school of 'servants' of Vishnu organized by Vyasaraya. It was the dasas who probably memorized, taught, compiled and kept Purandaradasa's songs intact. Purandaradasa for some time was the central point of this forum or *kuta* coming together. Then others collected the songs too, and later wrote them down. In the Dasakuta forum his songs were sung again and again. In this fashion Purandaradasa remained popular even after he passed away. Wandering dasas circulated the songs in towns and villages.

In 1565, Vijayanagara was invaded, and for six months the enemy soldiers ruined buildings, looted and plundered. At that point what was the fate of the dasas? It would seem that they scattered; ragas were lost and bhakti traditions fell into disuse in the time of crisis and in the struggle for survival. After the fall of the capital, Purandaradasa's songs were strewn about here and there but eventually the Dasakuta revived. Vijayadasa over a century later dreamed and yearned to be part of that line of devotion, and, inspired by the beckoning image of the great musician–saint Purandaradasa, sang some version of the dasa tradition back into existence.

It is uncertain just how intact and faithful to the original versions the songs, as we have them today, are; since it was an oral tradition, the form could have changed during the intervening five centuries. We cannot say if today's versions are the only ones, or how many may have ·been lost. It is likely that the Haridasas who preserved them may have interpolated some elements here and there, raga, *tala,* words; it happens, just as episodes in stories told to wonder-loving people take on different aspects when often retold. And some Haridasas who were composers in their own right, when rendering Purandaradasa songs might have changed them. Most lovers of Purandaradasa's songs admit their inability to know whether all songs with his signature are really by him. The songs are not always uniform; most likely some Haridasas put in their own words when they forgot the original ones, since that is a natural process. At present there are about eight hundred Purandaradasa songs available from the Dasakuta tradition.

Purandaradasa composed in a variety of forms. The pada is a simple song which even those without training are often able to sing after hearing it a few times. The *suladi* form, of which Purandaradasa was a master, is a medley of verses which uses a variety of talas. In his compositions Purandaradasa used about thirty ragas and primarily two talas: *Jhampe,* and *Chapu.* He wrote 140 ugabhogas, which are short pithy verses. He composed some songs on the spur of the moment while encountering events in his travels; some in ecstasy of devotion, others in dejection, or happiness. Some he sang when reflectively meditating. He sang easy-on-the-ear lyrics with colloquial phrases. He mocked hypocrisy, upheld dharmic values, encouraged striving for the highest spiritual ideals, and spread the joy of heartfelt devotion in songs that people could not forget. His lyrics depended more on images from *Puranas* and *Itihasa* material than on words from the *dharmashastras* (law books).

The history of the publication of Purandaradasa songs is sketchy. His songs were preserved by people who loved them so that future generations could enjoy them. The first collection was compiled at the time Vijayadasa lived—over a century after Purandaradasa died. By that time the dasa forum was no longer in existence, but individual dasas kept the songs in writing or orally. Vijayadasa was active in collecting and writing them down; publicizing and popularizing them, thus beginning a revival of Purandaradasa songs, a process through which scattered songs were culled and classified.[7]

There are perhaps as many as 1,300 songs, if one considers the contents of all the collections, which many musicologists, linguists and religious studies scholars feel confident are by Purandaradasa. Some songs in which the Madhva creed is stridently pushed as the exclusively best path may not have been sung by the broad-minded saint in his maturity. Then again, enthusiasm sometimes generates statements which later seem excessive. Autobiographical references may have sometimes been inserted by imaginative dasas of later times, to 'help out' their beloved tradition with augmentation, giving people what they wanted and expected.

In any case, Purandaradasa has a unique place in Karnatic music and Kannada literature. Though lyricists Tyagaraja and Annamacharya were denied a place in Telugu literature for a long time, even though they were valued as saints and musicians, Purandaradasa's poetry is considered to be full of vitality, vividness and euphony by the people of Karnataka. Purandaradasa is highly esteemed for musical compositions but more than that, he won many hearts in Karnataka with his poetic abilities.[8]

The songs in the following chapter have been selected from his many works to suggest the range of his lyrics.

Notes

1. In the following points of biographical information about Purandaradasa, I rely almost entirely on the Kannada introduction to Volume I, *Purandara Sahitya Darshana* (PSD) in 4 volumes, S.K. Ramachandra Rao, ed., Bangalore: The Directorate of Kannada and Culture, Government of Karnataka, 1985. This definitive work is the 500th Birthday Celebration commemorative edition of Purandaradasa's songs. Narayana Bhat and Yashoda Bhat, who are Kannada speakers and writers, graciously worked through this Kannada writing during several sessions with me in their New Delhi home in July 1992. I took copious notes, and I have selected points of interest from Rao's discussion, rephrasing some of his conclusions here in English.

2. Cited by Professor Desai Kamalapura Bellari, *Epigraphia Indica*, vol. 21, p. 139. The plots are numbers 175, 291, 292, respectively.

3. 'Adadella olitye ayitu', PSD Vol. I, p. 161, song no. 49.

4. 'Dasarendare Purandaradasa' by Vyasaraya, PSD Vol. I, song no. 1, p. 59.

5. Purandaradasa's song 'Kanakadasa namela', PSD Vol. I, no. 54, p. 171.

6. A carving at the entrance to the Vithala temple compound is said to be a likeness of Purandaradasa. A many-pillared stone mantapam on the Tungabhadra river is said to have been given to the saint by the king.

7. In 1850 there was a collection edited by Mangalore Holekallu Narasimhayya, which was later re-published by a British officer, J. Garrett, functionary in the Mysore government. It contained 173 kirtanas by Purandaradasa and other dasas. Two years later in Madras a similar collection came out. In 1894 Balakrishna Rao of Madakashira brought out a Telugu script collection entitled *Purandaradasuluvaru Padina Kirtanalu.*

Abaji Ramachandra Savant of Belgaum published a similar collection in Devanagari script, in four volumes between 1880 and 1894. He published the suladis in 1908. In 1914 T.N. Krishnayya Shetty of Bangalore brought out 802 Purandaradasa songs. In Udipi, Pavanje Guru Rao brought out in five volumes 1,050 songs of Purandaradasa from the library, Shrimadhva Siddhanta Granthavali. In the last volume 144 ugabhogas were included. The first volume appeared in 1912, the last in 1932. In 1925 Suboda Rama Rao published the first volume of the series *Hari Dasa Kirtana*

Tarangini, and two more volumes in 1926. There were 543 padas, 128 ugabhogas. In *Udayaraga* on 'Sunrise melody' pieces on Draupadi's disrobing and the *Gajendra moksha* episode of the *Bhagavata Purana* were featured, as well as fifteen suladis and one prose piece.

In 1940 *Panayadi Lakshmi Narayana Upadhyaya* by Venkata Tamanacharya Laksmi Narayana Adiga came out, a collection published by Tulu Nadu press, in four volumes. In 1944 in Lingasuguru, Gorabala Hanumantha Rao brought out another edition published by Varadendra Haridasa Sahitya Mandal. In 1957 there was a collection published which consisted of fifty-five suladis composed by Purandaradasa.

In many collections like these at the grass roots level—often in paperback books of about 600 songs, the kirtanas of Purandaradasa stayed alive among Kannada speakers. Then the Kannada Sahitya Parishatu Akademi in Bangalore commissioned R.S. Panchamukhi of Dharwar to compile an authoritative volume on Haridasa literature with critical annotations, and to write a biography of Purandaradasa. In 1956 it was published by Purandaradasa Seva Mandala in Hospet near Hampi. In 1959 in Hubli at Tulu Nadu Press S.S. Karan published 656 padas and 36 suladis.

The approach of the 400th year celebration of Purandaradasa passing in 1963–4 found celebration committees in Bangalore and Dharwar publishing major volumes. Under S.K. Ramachandra Rao one hundred songs with notation were published. The Dharwar commemorative celebration committee brought out six volumes, 901 compositions under Burli Bindu Madhavacharya, published by Minchina Balli Prakashana, Dharwar, edited by Betegiri Krishnasharma and Bengeri Hutchchu Rao. The first volume of *Pujatattva*, 'Principles of worship' came out in 1963; the second volume in 1964, *Arthabhava*, 'Calling out in emotion'; the third volume in 1964, *Mahatmyajnana* 'Wisdom of greatness of self'; the fourth volume in 1965, *Krishnalile*; the fifth volume in 1964, *Lokaniti*, 'Conduct in the world'; and the sixth volume in 1965, *Sankirna sangraha*, miscellany. This is a very useful Kannada edition, with anecdotes, comments, meanings and glossary. Kalamdani Guru Rao collected 800 songs; A.M. Karodhi 600 and Upadhyaya Publishers in Bangalore in 1954, 250; B.G. Sankeshwa of Gadag collected 626, all in vogue. The list of popular inexpensive paperback collections available in Kannada is also extensive.

8. Here we bring to a close information gathered largely from *Purandara Sahitya Darshana*, the four-volume commemorative collection published in 1985, introduction by S.K. Ramachandra Rao. For further information, see, V. Sitaramiah, *Purandaradasa*, New Delhi: National Book Trust, 1971,

1981; Sadguru Sant Keshavadas, *Lord Panduranga and Mystic Minstrels of India*, Rajahmundry: Saraswathi Press, 1973; D.B. Mokashi, *Palkhi: An Indian Pilgrimage*, Albany: SUNY, 1987; T.S. Parthasarathy, *Music Composers of India*, Madras: C.P. Ramaswami Aiyar Foundation, 1982; M.V. Krishna Rao, *Purandara and the Haridasa Movement*, Dharwar: Karnataka University, 1966; G. Srinivasan, *The Haridasas of Karnataka*, Belgaum: Academy of Comparative Philosophy and Religion, 1972; R.D. Ranade, *Pathways in Kannada Mysticism;* P.S. Srinivasa, *A Comparative Study of Sarana and Dasa Literature*, Madras: University of Madras, 1981; M. Mariappa Bhatt, 'Purandara Dasa (1480–1564)', *Journal of the Music Academy of Madras*, Vol. XIV, 1943, pp. 72–8. Recently the National Book Trust of India published a three-volume anthology, *Masterpieces of Indian Literature*. Among the Kannada entries (over two dozen examples drawn from the sixth century to the twentieth) Purandaradasa is given a place of honour.

Purandaradasa's Songs

Adaddella (PSD Vol. 1, no. 11, p. 89)

Whatever has happened all has been for the best
It's become a rich opportunity for serving further, Shridhara

Once I was ashamed of holding the staff
May my wife's family increase a thousandfold
—because of her I've come to hold the *sadhu* staff

Whatever has happened all has been for the best

I used to be so proud feeling like a big man
I wouldn't hold a vessel for collecting alms of rice
my wife caused me to take it—may she live long

Whatever has happened all has been for the best

Before, I felt I was a king, why should I
wear the tulasi necklace? Lord Purandara caused me
to put it on (initiating me to the dedicated life)

Whatever has happened all has been for the best

Ambiga (PSD Vol. II, no. 202, p. 403, 'Boatman song')

Yo Boatman, Boatman!
I'm counting on you—
Lord of mother earth
My trust is in you!

Yo Boatman, the boat rocks
In the flooding river;
Boatman this is a boat
with nine holes in it
O Boatman please steer
carefully this frail craft
guide it with fervour
always mindful of the goal—Yo Boatman!

The river's overflowing!
Do you see how full it is?
Karma's current runs—
It's so swift, and it's so deep!
I'm caught, I'm drowning
I'm down in this whirlpool!
Pull me from this treachery!
Boatman rescue me please!—Yo Boatman!

Boatman, look there, see
the six waves are coming!
They rise up, higher
and higher—am I a goner?
Boatman there is no one else
to help me overcome them—
Only you, my Boatman,
are able to take me across. Yo Boatman . . .

Now the sun has set, O Boatman,
Now the five senses dim . . .
Go—row full force—now
This is the time to take me!
No, Boatman, don't linger!
Don't wait, this is my chance!
Take me all the way over
to the realm of the ultimate! O Boatman . . .

Row, Boatman, row, with
your oars of supramental bhakti
And we'll wend our way
along the path of righteousness.
Take me, my dear Boatman
right to the *mantapa* of *mukti*
granted by the sweet grace of
Lord Purandara Vithala—O Boatman . . .[1]

Anjike yatakayya (BR p. 678)

What is there to worry virtuous men
what can make them fear
If you practise remembering Hanuman
what is there to fear?

If you are afflicted with grief
if your mind is disturbed by nightmares
when you remember Hanuman
these evils will all disappear

What is there to worry decent people
what can make them fear
If you lock your mind on to Hanuman
all your troubles disappear

If you remember epic hero Bhima
(an incarnation of Hanuman)
the man who revealed a million
lingas at the root of each hair
all your sins will disappear

What is there for decent folks to fear
Remembering Hanuman worries disappear

If you remember the guru Madhvacharya
(Avatar of Hanuman) who worships
Lord Purandara Vithala
there is no more reason to fear

What can there be for good people to fear
When remembering Hanuman makes fears disappear

Atatunatadare (PSD Vol. 1, no. 49, p. 161)

For him who takes God's holy name
humiliation is most welcome

To one who takes God's holy name
to be insulted is not to be shunned

Ego is built on respect others give you
your tapas is lost when you're given respect
egoistic Duryodhana was ruined
but there's no doubt about one who can take
 respect and humiliation with equanimity
  for one who says God's holy name humiliation is welcome

Through humiliation one's sadhana flourishes
One's good deeds become fruitful when you're humbled
because of trying tribulations and humiliations
Lord Vishnu came to save the child Prahlada
 for him who takes the holy name humiliation is welcome

  Where will I go, and what will I do?
  As long as you are there O Vithala, Lord
  of forest-dwelling yogis, protector of the poor
  I don't want for anything—except humiliation
   —with humiliation I'm able to get you
   so for him who takes God's holy name
   humiliation is most welcome

Barida (PSD Vol. III, no. 60, p. 177)

Time has passed and I've gone nowhere
time has passed away, I haven't progressed

I used to feel this human existence
was a permanent condition, O Ranga

This desire is tormenting me, O Seshasayi
O Hari, I am wounded, without remembering
you, O Vasudeva, my existence is ruined
I've become a useless fool
and I am deceived, O Krishna, for

Time has passed and I've gotten nothing
time has passed away and what have I achieved

Under the illusion that 'this is my wife,
these are my children' I became foolish.
O imperishable Lord, through constant enjoyment
I am ruined, my mind has lost its purpose
I'm off the path, O Highest of all, Lakshmipati

Time has passed and I've nothing to show for it
Time has passed away leaving me without a gain

I served others, spent my days praising them;
lost in folly I became a scatterbrain.
Now I believe in you, and seek your refuge—
Kindly show mercy, and protect me
O Purandara Vithala, you are all I need

Time has passed and what does it all mean?
Time has passed and what have I achieved?

Bevu bella dolida lenu phala (PSD Vol. III, no. 86, p.163)

What's the point of leaving a bitter neem leaf
    in sweet brown sugar (spoiling the taste)?

What's the use of feeding milk
    to a poisonous serpent?
Unless one gives up crooked ways
    what's the use of chanting the name?

Phonies addicted to telling lies—
    if they go on pretending, what's the point?
If someone who puts his parents through hell
    then goes on a pilgrimage—what does it prove?

Merely reading stories of piety
    and morality is a useless exercise;
if you don't also give up
    all your sneaking duplicity—what's the point . . .

What good is it if a woman keeps her *vrata* vows
    but constantly carps about her husband?
When guests come to your home if you treat some
    as lesser should you expect to find salvation?

Without giving up meanness
      if you take a dip in the Ganges
Or if you observe silence
      and never chant Purandara's name
What's the point . . .

Bhagyada Lakshmi (PSD Vol. 2, no. 66, p. 181)

Welcome to you, Goddess of fortune,
      please come in, dear Mother
You are Lakshmi, the gist of good fortune, welcome, welcome

Step by step, slowly coming our way, your anklets jingling
      approaching the people who are eager to worship you
      how did you arrive? Like butter emerging from milk
      being churned, welcome to you, Goddess of fortune . . .

You come showering on us a rain of gold, you show us
      what our aspirations are—may they be fulfilled.
      You come bright as the glittering million-rayed sun,
      you who took birth as Sita—welcome to you, Goddess . . .

Giving us wealth without end, come to us
with the bracelets on your wrists turning 'round
an auspicious vermilion mark on your forehead
O proud wife of lotus-eyed Venkatarama, welcome to you . . .

Without moving hither and thither (wavering?) in the house
      of devotees, let there be festivals every day;
      auspiciously you are always revealing yourself as truth
      in the minds of saints, decorated like a beautiful doll . . .
      welcome . . .

Come to our puja on Friday, O Consort of Purandara
      Vithala, at the time when canals of sugar and ghee are
      overflowing, come to us O queen of Alagiri Ranga
      (in Andhra Pradesh), welcome to you, Goddess of fortune . . .

Baiyiro baiyiro (PSD Vol. III, no. 94, p. 117)

Go ahead, help yourself, harass me to your heart's content
You're really giving me blessings by giving your carping vent

I can't be bothered by this one's scowl
or respond with meanness to that one's abuse;
in fact you take on all my faults
among yourselves when you put me down
     so go ahead . . .

I've taken the lives of many ants and flies
I'm also guilty of speaking ill of others
I've made a lot of mistakes in my life, so
measure, generously share them among yourselves
     go ahead and help yourself . . .

The sin of abusing my father-in-law
The sin of abusing my mother-in-law
being a drag, nagging my elders—and worse
the sin of forgetting Lord Purandara Vithala—so
     go ahead, help yourself
          abuse me to your heart's content
     you're really giving me blessings
          by giving your carping free vent

Dariya   (PSD Vol. I, no. 22, p.115)

Which way is the way to Vaikuntha
Kindly show me the way to go
What is the way, please show me
O Lord, the very form of my support,
what is the way to reach you?

I've had enough experience of this earth
I'm shivering groping in the dark
I suffered and wandered this way and that
without finding the way, so kindly
show me the radiant way, the way to God

Which way is the way to Vaikuntha . . .

For the sins I committed in the past
this karma's been smeared on my body
Now I am pleading, O Lord of Lakshmi
Bhupa Narayana
O Lord please protect me

Tell me the route to Vaikuntha . . .

After this I'll never take birth again
on this earth; I've become your slave now
Lord sleeping on the cosmic serpent
Shri Purandara Vithala, kindly won't you
see to it that I'm not born again
Lord Narayana please,
Which way is the way to Vaikuntha . . .

Dasana madiko (BR p. 350)

Make me your slave
why are you harassing me so much
Why are you cheating me, Lord Vishnu
 so full of mercy

Help me free myself from all bad intentions
Let me wear the protective armour
 called mercy of the Lord
Let me serve at your feet, and
Tie the flower
 of your hand signalling 'Don't fear'
 to my head
Make me your dasa
why are you harassing me so much
Why are you cheating me, Lord Vishnu
 so full of mercy

Pleading for staunch devotion to you
I will bow down at your feet every day
singing your praises
Give me a sidelong glance with your eyes
Let me meditate on you
 without interruptions
Make me your servant
why are you harassing me so much
Why are you cheating me, Lord Vishnu
 so full of mercy

They call you the Lord who protects
    those who make pitiable laments
So don't forget your title
    saviour of the downtrodden
dissolving all my sins
O guru Purandara Vithala
    save me
Make me your slave
why harass me so much
why cheat me, Lord Vishnu
    full of mercy

Dasayya (PSD Vol. IV, no. 10, p. 59, 'Invitation')

Hey there dasa, if you come to my village
    I hope you'll come to my neighbourhood

And dasa if you come to our neighbourhood
    please come to the cowherds' lane

O dasa wearing leaves from trees around your neck
    O dasa who has lifted the mountain
        with just your pinkie finger
    I'm crazy about you
        can't live without seeing you
            day and night—Hey there dasa . . .

You are black skinned, Dasayya
    You are Vishnu, father of the love-god
    If you come close to my mind, where I live
        hugging you tight
        I'll give you a dish
            of sweet rice—Hey there dasa . . .

What will you find if you go further that way?
    O dasayya, playing on your beautiful flute
    O dasayya don't go away like that
        dasayya come here
            I'll give you a golden ring—Hey there dasa . . .

You are a dasa
    with a small mark on your forehead;
    O dasa kindly come to our home, please
    If you come to my house
        I'll give you a beaded necklace
        Hey dasa, if you come to our village
            I insist that you come to the cowherds' lane

Don't be angry with me now
    You're the Lord Shri Purandara
    Vithala—no,
    Don't toss me aside
    I'm going to give you a round sweet
        made of tambiti gram flour
    Say there dasa, if you come to my village
        please come to my neighbourhood
            you can look me up in the lane of the cowherds

Dayamado dayamado (BR p. 376)

Show mercy, show mercy, let your mercy flow
    O Ranga
Show mercy, consider me your servant,
    your dasa

Give me enduring longing for your presence
    you must protect me,
O lotus-eyed Lord
Show mercy . . .

O Lord of Lakshmi you alone are reality here
    and hereafter, so why should I fear
when you are there, Lord fond of devotees
Show mercy . . .

Lord who gave boons to the elephant
    Father of cupid
Lord Purandara Vithala, virtuous Lord of all

Show mercy, show mercy, let your mercy flow
    O Ranga
Show mercy, consider me your servant,
    your dasa

Dhaniye (PSD Vol. I, no. 101, p. 284)

I feasted my eyes upon Lord Venkateshvara
    until my mind was fully satisfied

I saw the pure one with his hair tuft in a knot
    I feasted my eyes . . .

I saw the one who enjoys boiled rice
      and who uses
    wealth without giving up even a penny
    the one who causes folks to sell rice and *dosas*
    the one who dances joyfully in the company
      of dasas—I feasted my eyes . . .

I saw the one who wears an upper cloth with knots
      of pure gold
    the one who goes hunting, and enjoys
    the sound of bells, the one who declares
    with his right hand that this place is really
      heaven on earthly land—I feasted my eyes . . .

I saw the one who lives in the hills
    who is favourable to his devotees, the one who
    keeps his promises, the Lord of the universe,
    Purandara Vithala, I feasted my eyes
    upon Lord Venkateshvara
    until my mind was fully satisfied

Donku balada nayakare (PSD Vol. I, no. 40, p. 148, 'King Snoopy')

So what have you eaten today
O leader with a curled up tail?

You snooped your way into a kitchen
where a woman was trying to knead dough
she probably whacked you with a stick
now you're singing in the raga of 'Kuikui!'

So what else have you scarfed down today
King Snoopy with a curling tail?

You sniffed your way to a home
where another sweet dish was being prepared
and I' would take a guess the lady there
took her ladle and bonked you good and hard
and again you howl the raga of 'Kuikui!'

So what else did you scavenge or steal
to eat today O leader with a curled tail?

Roaming around on the big main road, sometimes
on your back rolling around in black ashes
without ever remembering Purandara Vithala
you aimlessly wander, fritter your days away

So what else did you scavenge or steal
to eat today King Snoopy with a curled tail?

> *Durdu*   (PSD Vol. IV, no. 55, p. 116)

But how is this? What's this now?
　　Are you complaining about our Ranga?

Would you really accuse him of thievery?

The Lord so dear to all the three worlds
Would you speak of him as a common thief?

How is this? What is this now . . .

The boy is playing on his flute
　　majestically leading the herds
　　in Nanda's Gokul—could you
　　speak ill of him? How could you?

How is this now? What is this about?
　　Are you complaining about our Ranga?

Sure, he may sneak into the homes
　　of all the cowherd girls, and maybe
　　when they raise a hue and a cry he
　　might give their cheeks a bite
　　but really, are you complaining?

What the . . . I mean how could this be?
　　Lodging complaints against Ranga to me?

I think you've got a desirous eye on
    my child—you're hot under the collar
    and in your brain, so you complain
    about the Lord Purandara Vithala

How is this? Just what is this now?
    Are you complaining against our Ranga?

Enayita (PSD Vol. III, no. 180, p. 297)

What's going on here?—what happened?
These people sunken in silence
    have forgotten their Lord

Did a thorn get stuck in their tongues
forcing them to keep quiet?
Are they possessed by demons?
Did their two lips grow together into one
Or did Death come and terrorize them?

Hey! What's going on here?

Did some deadly cobra strike
poisoning their poor brains?
Or did a butcher hack out their tongues?
Did they develop such wicked minds
that out of spite they refuse to say God's name?

Say, what's going on here?

Is there some danger that the heads
of those who repeat Lord Hari's name
will suddenly fall off and roll on the ground?
Is Hari's name not written on their foreheads,
so they're blank? Would lightning zap them
if they took Purandara Vithala's name

Just what's going on here—what took place?
That these people are sunken in silence
    cut off from auspicious sounds of God's name

Giliyu . (PSD Vol. I, no. 57, p. 180)

O Lord, the bird has flown away
leaving just this empty cage

O sister, I brought a parrot home
and I cared for it
but when I was away
a cat came and took it
Lord the bird has flown away
leaving just an empty cage

I lavished love on my parrot
made it a necklace of pearls
Now it's gone—disappeared
pearls and all, what to do?
Lord the bird has flown away
leaving me with an empty cage

Such a smart little green parrot
O so very bright
It lost its life—I've lost it
now I feel so desolate
Lord the bird has flown away
leaving just an empty cage

The soft-bodied parrot used to chant
'Rama, Rama'—the parrot of
this dasa who promotes
gandharva vidya—the wisdom of divine music
Lord the bird has flown away
leaving a mere empty cage

In the nine-doored house
jampacked and congested
the pillar fell and broke
the child flew up to the skies
Lord the bird has flown away
leaving a mere empty cage

Feeding it butter eternally fresh
giving it milk without fail, I watched
the parrot eat and drink with gusto
but it was all to no avail
for now, Lord, the bird's flown away
leaving behind an empty cage

The parrot would play in the palm
of my hand, perch on my wrist
cavort in Purandara's court
now that bird has vanished
Lord the bird has flown away
leaving just an empty cage

Gudasika (PSD Vol. I, no. 45, p. 154)

O I didn't find the nest
  or even know anything
    about the way to the nest

Both wives (Papam and Punyam) ran away
  the wall of maya just collapsed
    and there was an open abyss

I never woke up
  I was wild with pride
    My life was like a jaggery lump
  that fell in the fire
    sputter-danced like mad then vanished

I did not find the nest

I have arrived at old age
  but I have not enjoyed the *paiyasam* and ghee
    sweet porridge of Rama's name
      suddenly the pot of ghee
        topples and spills in the garbage heap

O I did not find the nest . . .

Yoga, my work, is gone now
 but I have never understood
  what is in store for me next
   I forgot Lord Purandara
    Nagasayana Lord reclining on the serpent coil
     and my mind is a barren land

No I didn't find the nest
 I didn't even have a clue
  about that ultimate place

Both wives ran away
 the wall collapsed
  and I was left with an abyss

Gudigudiyana (GISSI p. 24)

Try putting some of this in your pipe and smoking it:

Untie the binding cords of your personal faults
And open up your mind's stash-pouch—

Take out the leaves of your daily failings,
Shred them to bits—you can get high on them—
Just heat them up in the pipebowl of your body
Using the bright flame of contemplating God;

Yes, put some of this in your pipe and smoke it.

In this hookah, using the tube of *gurubhakti*
Pour the water of Lord Narayana's holy Name.
 Listen to me, ecstatic hubblebubble smoker,
This high will really make your mind float

So put some of this in your pipe and smoke it!

Dissolving your laziness and other hang-ups,
Wisdom will surely dawn upon you before too long
And Lord Purandara Vithala, Lord of guru Shri Madhva
Will even manifest himself before you—so

Try putting some of this in your pipe and toke on it.

Guru vina (PSD Vol. II, no. 9, p. 68)

O brother you will never find salvation
Until you become the servant of your guru

I've read so many scriptures and wasted all my time
Even if you read the six Shastras, and study the eighteen Puranas
Without seeking the company of good people
if you pose as a big man speaking to large numbers
    it's all futile

Brother you'll never be saved until you become the guru's slave

You might have a rosary strung round your neck
You can finger those beads and pray but it's useless
You can act like you're holy—but it has no effect
You can wander ash-smeared like a wild *avadhuta*

Brother you'll never be saved until you become the guru's slave

Until you fix your mind on Purandara Vithala
Who is praised by Narada, even if you give up all
Sexual pleasures and perform hard acts of penance
It's still no use, you will not achieve what you want

Brother you'll never be saved until you become the guru's slave

Harihari (PSD Vol. I, no. 52, p. 167)

There's no special exclusive hour
    for chanting the name of the Lord (Hari)
    O this whole human existence
        is just being wasted (in curry, worry and hurry)

In the midst of the Ekadashi vigil
    when you're up all night in the name of Hari
    you're mostly mentally rehearsing the feast
    you get to give yourself next day when it's over
When you're on your rounds accepting rice
    as a wandering Haridasa your mind
    is always busy fantasizing cooking vegetables
When you're engaged in activities you worry,
    when you perform religious practices you worry,
You refuse to show generosity, and your mind
    is always full of worry—There's no special time . . .

A person who is given a weapon
    begins to worry: 'Now who should I attack?'
One with a shield to protect himself
    worries 'Who shall I be on guard against?'
'Should we or shouldn't we do this?'—uncertainty
    like this also leads to anxiety
Acting with ignorant arrogance
    we're anxious to preserve our lives
There is no particular time for chanting the holy name . . .

While taking a bath in the sacred Ganges
    my mind frets about the small vessel
    I left on the bank;
Then another worry strikes:
    What if my companions leave without me?
Without fail if one worships Purandara Vithala
    the Lord reclining on the coil of the cosmic serpent
        one will enjoy a worry-free existence

No single point of time has been appointed as the best hour
    for chanting the name of Lord Hari
    The entirety of human life is going down the drain
    wasted (in curry, worry and hurry)

Harinamadaraginiyu (PSD Vol. III, no. 202, p.325)

In this world the parrot of Hari's name flies about
    the best of devotees cast their nets to capture it

The cat called Anger would swallow the parrot
    The tiger of burning anger would carry it away
    You can protect it by concealing it deep in your heart
    That dear parrot will come to your help in
        times of distress
    In this world the parrot of Hari's name flies about
    The *paramabhagavatas* cast their nets to capture it

When you move about on the road you won't have to
    worry about thieves
If a demoness or evil spirit comes the name
    will repel them
If the cruel messengers of Lord Death come, the parrot
    will strike with beak and wings
And this parrot will show the way of salvation, and
    lead you to the town where Krishna lives

In this world the parrot of Hari's name flies about
    the best of devotees fling their nets to capture it

How much shall I praise this dear parrot
    There are seven worlds inside the belly of this parrot
    Remembering again and again the Lord of the universe
    Contemplating the Lord and touching his feet
    Worship Lord Purandara Vithala and also the parrot

In this world the parrot of Hari's name is flying about
    The best devotees cast their nets and capture it

Harinarayana Harinarayana (PSD Vol. III, no. 201, p. 322)

O my mind chant the name of Harinarayana Harinarayana
    Harinarayana

The seed of 'Harinarayana' was planted in this world
    by the sage Narada

The young boy Dhruva was responsible for its sprouting
    The tendril grew further thanks to Prahlada
    And it kept expanding thanks to Rukumangada the king
    Thanks to Bhishma it blossomed into a flower
        O my mind chant the name . . .

Thanks to Arjuna's wife Draupadi it grew to an unripe nut
    Thanks to Gajendra elephant king it became a fruit
    Sukamuni was responsible for its ripening to maturity
    And Ajamila squeezed the juice of the fruit and savoured it
        O my mind chant the name . . .

When there is a name which grants you all boons
    Why bother with sacrificial fires, rites and tapas?
    Chant the lord Shri Purandara Vithala's holy name
    Remember it with sincere constancy, chant it, O mind
        O my mind chant the name of Harinarayana, Harinaryana

Hari smarane (PSD Vol. III, no. 1, p. 43)

Always remember the name of the Lord

This is the sole support to attainment

God is a lion to the elephant of sins
    prevailing, protecting those seeking refuge; always . . .

Lord, you protected Prahlada, and you
    are the one who tore Hiranyakashipu's belly; always . . .

When Draupadi in her distress appealed to you
    you granted her the boon of an endless sari; always . . .

Gajendra, tormented by fierce jaws, called you
    when he needed you; you came and saved him; always . . .

Worship the cosmos' Lord, Purandara Vithala
    Touch his holy feet, yes worship Shri's Lord

Always remember the name of Hari

Hasimayagutada (PSD Vol. IV, no. 80, p. 147, 'Yashoda and Krishna')

O ma I am so hungry
    please just give me rice flakes
    mixed with jaggery
        I'll take it and go

Because you're giving me hot rice my palm is
    getting burnt, so put that aside
    give me some rice flakes, I'm so hungry
        mix them with jaggery, I'll take it and go

No, don't give me the hot spicy *rasam*
    along with the hot rice, no please
    give me something sweet, then I'll gulp it down

Hey, no, O ma I'm so hungry . . .

Don't give me melted ghee now, please
    give me something solid—give me
    solidified ghee and I'll lap it up

    No, see, O ma I'm so hungry . . .

Don't give me thin buttermilk, flowing
    on the ground, but give me solid yogurt
    and I will gobble it right up

    But, please ma I'm so hungry . . .

'O Lord Krishna please get up and I'll wash
your cup and bowl and plate, and I will
give you the cream from boiling milk.'

    Hey come on, ma I'm so hungry . . .

My friends have come now—they're calling me
    Give me bananas with jaggery and
    I'll go play with my friends

    Really, ma look I'm so hungry . . .

O mother look my friends have come
    they call me—give me dried coconut
    with sugar I'll just take some and run

    Now listen, ma I'm so hungry . . .

Come to Brindavan and give me a doll
    a doll made of sandalwood, come
    to Brindavan with a doll for me

    O dear ma you know I'm hungry . . .

'Don't go outside now there's a tiger
    waiting out there for you, stay here,
    play right here inside your home.'

    Ma, don't you get it, I'm hungry . . .

'O Purandara Vithala do come in.
    There is a tiger crouching out there
    with a sheep's face, come here inside the house.'

O ma I am so hungry
      please just give me rice flakes
    mixed together with jaggery—
      I'll take it to go

Helabarada (PSD Vol. IV, no. 48, p. 109)

Could you not tell your child the right way to behave?
    he's like a bullock roaming free doing what he pleases

He goes from lane to lane with his companions
      disturbing each lane, all the girls of the cowherd families

On the first floor where the milk pots are hung
    he sticks his finger in one, then licks it with his tongue
We pleaded: Don't do that, it's a very bad habit!
    So what does he do? Gives me a kiss and says
      What's the problem?

Could you not teach your child rules of proper behaviour?
    he roams like a bullock without regulations

He came and sat near me while I churned the butter
    At the time I thought he was just an innocent little child
When he pressed my breast I patted him sweetly,
    So then he opens my sari cloth and presses my breast again
      then he ran away

Could you not properly teach your child some manners
    he's out of control reckless as a wandering bull

If he sees butter he won't let it be—poof! it's gone!
    When I call him, considering him to be a mere child
He always wins me over, enticing me, and I get tangled
    In his many games, with his charm and his tricky talk

Could you not teach your child some decent etiquette?
    he goes wherever he likes like a bull that's unhitched

Did you know he will take our clothes while we bathe
    Leave us there stranded in the nude? He'll say:
'I'll give you your saris back, just reach out your hands',
    And then when we protest he acts like we're old prudes!

Could you not teach your child the basics of good manners?
  He runs around free as a bullock who's never been tethered

O Yashoda, how much more of this do I have to tell you?
  Really, you seem to have no compassion for your neighbours!
What does it take, how much must we explain to you
  About Purandara Vithala, the Lord of the whole universe

Could you not give your child advice on how to treat people
  he does whatever he pleases wandering like a free bull

Hyange barandito (PSD Vol. I, no. 48, p. 160)

Earlier lives have written the lines
  which we must follow in subsequent lives

Like a bird alighting in a forlorn courtyard
  it settles then suddenly flies far away

Like weekly markets gathering from many paths
  arriving from different corners, suddenly gone

Like children who build palaces with care,
  then say 'Enough!' demolish them and run elsewhere

It's like a wanderer finding an inn for the night;
  early morning he gets up and soon is on his way

Lord Purandara Vithala, destroyer of demon Kamsa,
  Please come and free me from worldly life's bondage

Earlier lives have written the lines
  which we must follow in subsequent lives

Idu bhagya (PSD Vol. III, no. 23; also PSD Vol. IV, no. 23, p. 77)

This is happiness, this is joy, this is good fortune, Lord!
  Service at the feet of the lotus-navelled Lord is bliss

Live in the treacherous river of life in the world
  as if you were a solid rock
Live in the midst of the clever and powerful
  bending with humility
Learn to please and gently win the mind of Lord Madhava
Among relatives live like jaggery

This is good fortune . . .

Let us correct ourselves, body and mind
    Using our deeper wisdom
Approach sages and yogis with pure respect
    We should be a fish in the ocean of Madhva learning
Let our three *karanas*—body, speech and mind—
    enjoy purity

This is good fortune . . . happiness . . . bliss

We should burn up sensuality as if in a grassfire
    Night and day we should remember Lord Hari
Sing the holy name of Purandara Vithala
    And serve his ever-smiling devotees in this world

This is such good fortune, this is joy so sweet
    The bliss we enjoy, praising the Lord's feet

Indu nanenu (PSD Vol. I, no. 95, p. 273)

I don't know what good deed I've done
    Lord Venkata has come to my home
Famous for sacred auspiciousness, today
    Lord Venkateshvara has come to my home

Wearing a bracelet and golden ring
    seven pendants on the chain around his neck
        large lustrous pearls glowed in his necklace
Riding on the back of a buffalo
    Lord Venkateshvara has come to my home
        I don't know what good deed I've done . . .

Bells tinkling on his anklets, wearing
    wooden sandals, on his head a crown of nine
        auspicious gems, mouth red from chewing pan
            in his hand a small box holding camphor
        the Lord who lives atop the highest hill
            that Lord Venkateshvara has come to my home . . .

Shawl wrapped tightly around his body
    string of pearls around his neck, a smile
        playing on his lips, revealing a row
            of attractive teeth, wearing embroidered silk,
                a sword in the sash around his waist—
            That Lord of Yadugiri hill in Melukote
            Lord Venkateshvara has come to my home
                I don't know what good deed I must have done . . .

Forehead smeared with camphor, tilak mark
    red in the middle, they tried to cover the eyes
        His talk is juicy like nectar, he gazes
            through petal-like eyes; he is so handsome
                like a beautiful young man, this glorious
            Venkateshvara has really come to my home
                I don't know what good deed I've done
            but Lord Venkateshvara has come to my home

In the kali yuga he comes with the conch and chakra
    Fourteen worlds he holds inside his belly; he comes
        riding upon the falcon, and appearing this way
            how he enchants all three worlds—The Lord who is
        Purandara Vithala has come to my home
            what have I done to deserve such good fortune?
        Famous for his sacred auspiciousness,
            Lord Venkateshvara has come to my home today . . .

What have I done to deserve this good fortune
    Lord Venkateshvara has come to my home
        The Lord so auspicious has graced my home today

Innu daya barade (BR p. 326)

Still your pity doesn't come,
    your grace does not flow to your servant
    O Lord in repose on the cosmic serpent
    O supreme Lord Hari

I was well born in various wombs
in different regions at different times
then I fell into this hell
called 'I-me-mine'
and then I found you, my refuge—
but to this servant trusting in you

Still your grace doesn't come . . .

I'm a sinner full of blame
wrapped in thick darkness
of lust and the other six enemies of life
Lord who enchants the mind of Lakshmi
Lord who is the father of Cupid
your name is the only refuge
but to this servant trusting in you

Still your grace doesn't come . . .

I made an offering to you,
a sacrifice of all the acts I perform
with mind, speech and body
O killer of demons
How does it matter what I do
my soul is yours, Svami, Lord of Lakshmi
Purandara Vithala
to this servant

Still your grace doesn't come,
your compassion doesn't flow to me
your servant
O sleeper on the cosmic serpent
O supreme Lord Hari

Irabeku illadirabeku (PSD Vol. III, no. 29, p. 85)

The Haridasa should learn
to be in the world but not of the world

These men give up their virtuous wives
  then they give themselves to prostitutes.
  They keep company with drunks, lives wrecked,
  but assert that in this world they're the best.

Sometimes a woman will give up her husband
  and traipse around with the lover she keeps.
  I'm sorry to say that in today's world
  examples of such affairs have only increased.
    O all you people, listen, hear . . .

People whose polluting conduct is untouchable
  if they are rich are praised and brought home.
  They are given offerings of gold-threaded cloth
  and treated with courtesy as if it were owed.

But they will never come to aid a poor person—
  and it's no use asking, whatever be his merits.
  This is the time of the great super-idiots
  O my Lord Purandara Vithala listen to this:

O all you people, listen come listen,
  hear the way your fellow humans act

Kala (PSD Vol. I, no. 42, p. 151)

O I've wasted my time, life's gone,
  but knowledge has not come to me

What shall I tell Yama's emissaries
  when they come to take me away?

I was born and as a baby loved to suck
  on my mother's breasts; a baby in her arms,
  soon I was enjoying drinking buttermilk—
    O I've wasted . . .

As a boy I played with a ball and with
  a spinning top, I demanded good food and
  roved with cowherd boys in a group
    O I've wasted . . .

In the thick of my youth I was arrogant
    enjoying the company of pretty girls
    I cultivated a wicked temperament
        O I've wasted . . .

I had kids—now I'm dependent on them,
    helplessly attached with foolish fondness;
    agitated, I've lost my chance for knowledge
        O I've wasted . . .

Wearing out my hands' strength as I did
    I never worshipped Rama; wearing out my eyes
    I never had the darshan of Lord Purandara Vithala

O I've wasted my time, life's gone,
but knowledge has not come to me

Kallasakkare (PSD Vol. III, no. 194, p. 313, 'How sweet it is')

Have some sugar candy—only those
who have tasted it really know
    just how sweet it is

Lord Krishna is sugar candy
take his name, it's really good
this is none of your ordinary
everyday merchandise, it's not
stuff to be packed into gunnysacks
not some bullock cart cargo of cheap wares
you can take it anywhere
and never have to declare it
this most excellent commodity
which gives most benefit and profit

Have some . . .

When you take this item
you will never suffer losses
It's not perishable, this merchandise
won't go bad and smell
you can help yourself to all you like
it's free! the big black ants
won't line up to haul it away
this wonderful product is the best deal
in town—don't underestimate
its wonderful properties. Have some . . .

You don't have to waste time
going to some weekly market
It's not for sale in bustling bazaars
this item is forever to be found
on the lips of devotees, the Lord
Purandara Vithala's name is sugar candy
step right up and take some
roll it over your tongue

Have some of this sugar candy—
only those who have tried it know
just how sweet it really is

Kanakadasa namela (PSD Vol. I, no. 54, p. 171)

When Vyasamuni shows such high regard
    for Kanakadasa
    his followers in the matha are full of
        scorn and meanness

Every day when giving tirtha (puja holy water)
    Vyasamuni says 'Call Kanakadasa
    I want to give him tirtha'
    And the cunning scholars will say 'O yes,
    his attainment of *sannyasa* has
    now really become fruitful'
    and Vyasamuni gives a smile.

When Vyasamuni shows such high regard
    for Kanakadasa
    his followers in the matha are full of
        ridicule and meanness

Next day to test them, Vyasaraya
    summons all the so-called scholars,
    along with Kanakadasa;
    he passes out bananas
    and tells them 'Take these to a place
    where no one is present—
    eat them, and come back here'.

When Vyasamuni shows . . .

They all went off to different corners
   of the village, ate the bananas
   and returned. Only Kanakadasa
   came back with the fruit uneaten,
   saying 'I could not find a place
   where there is no one present.'

When Vyasamuni shows . . .

Kanakadasa then asked Vyasaraya
   'When so many entities
   exist within the body,
   how can I say I'm alone and eat—
   the five senses live such active lives
   there is really no privacy.'
   The people present were pleased.

When Vyasamuni shows . . .

It is like placing a choice diamond
   in the hand of a monkey,
   Like playing on a musical instrument
   for a buffalo, or like
   playing a flute for a deaf man,
   or trying to show a blind man
   his face in a mirror.

When Vyasamuni shows . . .

Can the ignoramus ever understand
   the real import of the discourse
   of Kanakadasa?
   They called him a buffoon.
   But you will not find another as wise
   if you search the length and breadth
   of the entire country.

When Vyasamuni shows . . .

Vyasamuni devised a test
    'Alright tell me, what's in my fist?'
    The pandits guessed with
    their own modes of thought
    but Kanakadasa said 'I find
    Lord Purandara Vithala
    there in your fist.'

When Vyasamuni was showing high regard
    for Kanakadasa
    his followers in the matha
    carped with meanness

Kanda beda (PSD Vol. IV, no. 72, pp. 138–9)

O my child don't eat mud
    my dear child don't eat mud
        it will give you a bellyache

Give up this playing in mud
    get up quickly
    the strange *jogi* is coming this way
    he will frighten you—O my dear child . . .

Child Krishna on hearing his mother
    took a pinch of mud and
    deliberately put it in his mouth
        'O my dear child don't eat mud . . .'

'I'm going to thrash you
    I'm losing my temper. Don't touch mud.
    I'll get you butter.
        O my dear child don't eat mud . . .'

'But mother there's no mud here—
    not in my mouth—honest—please
don't call the *bhogi* man—
    I'll behave, I promise.' 'O my dear child . . .'

The mother called and pleaded
    'O my child, come, come now',
she tried to search his mouth
    'O my dear child don't eat mud'

She saw a vision of all fourteen worlds
    there inside his little mouth
    forgetting her body she became
        totally entranced—'O my dear child'

She saw the entire *gokula* there
    and the cowherds also in the mouth
    of that little Krishna in her arms
        'O my dear child don't eat mud . . .'

She also saw the antics of the child
    Gopala Krishna in his own mouth
    he was making mischief in gopis' homes
        'O my dear child don't eat mud . . .'

She also saw the child eating mud
    and the mother cleaning it out
    right there inside his mouth
        'O my child don't eat mud . . .'

The mother then observed
    'O you're not a child—Lord Vishnu
    close your mouth.
        O my child don't eat mud . . .'

God of gods, son of Devaki
    Father of Manmatha (the god of love)
    Please come. Victory to Lord Krishna!
        O my child don't eat mud . . .

Victory to the circle of
    his devotees—Victory
    to all his people everywhere!
    O my child don't eat mud . . .

Lord fond of divine play,
    the one who is dear to Rukmini and who
        showed all a miracle that day—
the divine child (don't eat mud) and
    the father, Purandara Vithala

Kande kande (PSD Vol. I, no. 146, p. 373)

I saw! saw him! gazed and gazed
    till my eyes were weary and dazed
        by the auspicious form
            of Krishna of Manaru

I saw him wearing the golden *pitambara*
    and a diamond studded shirt—I saw! saw him . . .

I saw the churning rod of Krishna of Manaru
    Dvaraka of the south, I saw! saw him!
    gazed to my joyous heart's content,
Saw the gold waistband on the dear Lord of Manaru

I saw Devaki, saw the gopis rejoicing
    I saw Lord Krishna who slew his uncle Kamsa
I saw! saw him! gazed and gazed
    till my eyes were weary and dazed

I saw Gopala Krishna who was tending cows
    The resident of Vaikuntha, Manaru Krishna
I saw! saw him! gazed and gazed
    till my eyes were weary and dazed

I saw the thousand-named Lord reclining on the bed
    Of the coiled cosmic serpent, Lord of Lakshmi
        Purandara Vithala, Lord Krishna

I saw! saw him! caught him in my gaze
    looked till my eyes were weary and dazed
    enjoying the auspicious form
        of Krishna of Manaru

Kande karunanidhi (PSD Vol. I, no. 160, p. 411)

I saw the ocean of mercy
    the one who carries Ganges on his head

I saw the garland of skulls Shiva wears
    the Lord Shiva

The one with red eyes, the one with
    a fiery eye in his forehead
I saw the dark-throated Shiva
    who drank the poison
I saw the friend of Vishnu who is father
    of Manmatha
The one who destroyed the Triple City.
    the one who is praised by *munis*
I saw the Lord ornamented by serpents

I saw the one who smears himself
    with ashes as decoration
I saw the Lord who is ever in
    the hands of devotees
I saw the Lord Pashupati
    in this world he
Is the one who is always seen
    with the crescent moon
Coolly glowing on his head

Lord Shiva who grants the fruits
    of people's desires
The one who protects with love
    all his devotees
I saw the one who takes the name
    of Lord Rama,
Husband of Rathi,
    the destroyer of Manmatha
I saw Lord Shiva

The one residing in the holy place
    known as the Kashi of the south
The one residing in Purapampa
    in holy Hampi
Teaching the saving Rama mantra
    the *taraka mantra*
O Lord Purandara Vithala
    protector of your devotees
I saw Lord Shiva

Kandu kandu ni (PSD Vol. I, no. 163, p. 421)

Seeing me again and again would you just
 let me down or would you drop me
  O Pundarika Purushottama Hare

I don't have relations, no happiness in daily life
I am pained by attacks and criticism, O lotus-eyed
you are both my father and mother also my relations
I'm always deeply devoted to you O Krishna

Your providential eye on me ever and anon
Would you now drop me and let me down?

One minute seems like an age, my fate is as lowly
as a grass-blade's, I've suffered countless miseries
You are revered by Sanaka and other great sages
Father of Brahma, Lord reclining on the coiled serpent
One who has taken a liking to Prahlada, O Shri Krishna

You've watched so well, looking out for me
Would you now let go of me?

Now that you have earned the title 'Dear to devotees'
Shouldn't you now heed your devotees
You're the one who grants liberation
You are the resident of the golden town Honupuram
capable guru Purandara

After you've looked out for me time after time
would you now just let go of my hand?

Karunakaraka (PSD Vol. II, no. 228, p. 453)

I really don't know why you're called 'Merciful One'
Seeing how you gave this human existence different forms
Again and again you make us weep, melting our hearts
 in various ways, I'm really not so sure
  why you're called the 'Merciful One'

They say you're the one who saved them all: Elephant–king,
Dhruva, Bali, Draupadi, Ahalya
When we carefully examine these stories
They begin to sound like fiction—I really don't know . . .

If you're really the merciful one, if it is so,
Immediately take me by the hand, lift me up
and protect me, O lotus-eyed one—if you really are
    so merciful why do all these worries and problems torment me?

You were pleased with Ajamila at the time of his death
You are Vishnu, Lord of the Garuda banner; if you
really have to justify your high-sounding titles
you must immediately come to my rescue, Purandara Vithala

I really don't know why you're called 'Merciful One'
Seeing how you gave this human existence all its aspects
always making us weep, melting our hearts
I wonder why you're called 'Merciful One'

Kattabeku (PSD Vol. III, no. 203, p. 325)

Tether the rebellious buffalo cow and enjoy her milk
    Milk her as much as you desire, and enjoy the taste

Your feeling of pride is the buffalo
    chanting the name is the rope
        and the goad to control the ego
    milk this buffalo and offer to Brahma daily—Tether . . .

Grind your mischievousness into cattlefeed
    transforming your stubbornness into grain
        turn your harsh behaviour into a bundle of grass
            then milk the name of Panduranga
        and enjoy in your heart the milk—Tether . . .

Care well for your buffalo, removing illusion
    in your consciousness
        This buffalo which few can know
        is found at the farmhouse
        of Lord Purandara Vithala—Tether . . .

Kurudunayi (MSDM)

It is said a blind dog
    came to the fair—
Why do you suppose
    he came there?

He doesn't like sugar candy
    he likes to bite flesh
He is fond of abducting children
      no one was there to stop him
why did he come?

He ran into a shop suddenly
    the owners beat the dog
with a stick trying
    to get rid of him

He never read Vedas or Shastras
    making them his own
He went astray, became
      the prey of death-god Yama

He has taken many births—
    was born as a human being
Roamed from jungle to jungle
    always forgetting himself

He lost every chance like
    a monkey with a diamond
right there in his hand,
      forgetting Purandara Vithala

A blind dog came to a fair
    why do you think he came there?

Kusu (PSD Vol. I, no. 138, p. 355)

Have you seen the adorable child, Lord Krishna Gopala?
    He wears leaf-shaped silver ornaments
      on his head and feet

The child with a bracelet on his wrist
    wearing a chain ornament on his hand
    this child must have passed through this courtyard
    Have you seen him? the adorable child, Lord Krishna . . .

A child with little tinkling bells on his anklets
    wearing a golden chain around his neck
    wearing a shirt with frills, the child was
    inside the house, but then he went out
    Have you seen the adorable child, Lord Krishna Gopala?

A child wearing a good-luck necklace of tiger-claws
 he has a ring on his finger, square-shaped
  ornaments on his ears
 He's not where he was sitting before, any chance
  you've seen him? Have you seen . . .

The child who is blue like a rain cloud,
 wearing a blue ear-ring too; he was sitting near
 the water's edge—now he's gone far from there
 Have you seen him, Gopala Krishna . . .

The child who was living in Pandarpur
 the child who protected the five Pandava brothers
 the child who roams in the cosmic egg Brahmanda
 mighty Purandara Vithala as a child

Have you seen the adorable child, Lord Krishna Gopala
 he wears silver ornaments with a peepul tree-leaf pattern
  on his head and feet

Kuttavaru (PSD Vol. I, no. 47, p. 158)

It's all one, the two are the same
The one who denied us, the one who gave
The one who gives also receives
something which sometimes gives him conceit

To the ones who take their refuge in
The destroyer of demons, the Lord of Lakshmi
Givers and non-givers are both alike
It's all one, the two are the same . . .

For us (dasas) the king and the beggar
are the same, and the one who speaks sweetly
and the one who speaks bitterly are the same
For those always praising Narahari's lotus feet

It's all one, the two are the same . . .

Won't the Lord who created us give us food?
Devoted dasas who have faith in Lord Purandara
Lord of Tirumalai hills, have well understood:

It's all one, the two are the same
The one who denied us, the one who gave
The one who gives also receives
something which might give him conceit

Madhvamathadolate   (PSD Vol. II, no. 19, p. 87)

The best matha is Madhva matha
The puja worshipping Raghupati
is the purest holiest faith

This matha believing in chanting
        the name of Narayana
    This faith conducive to the study
        of scripture, Vedaparayana
    This faith which gives joy
        to the brahmins who after careful
    study of scriptures uphold the
    shruti, smriti and itihasa
        and then conclude that

The best matha is Madhva matha . . .

This faith is an ornament of diamonds
    worn by the one without blemish, Lord Hari
    This faith is the best matha for the whole country
    This faith gives distinction to the ones not guilty
        of crookedness—Shuka, Sanaka
            and other saints, superior sages
    and in turn all their actions show their greatness

Yes the best matha is Madhva matha . . .

Enlightenment, good-natured truth, harmony, goodness
    This faith is replete with these
    This faith is conducive to the *guru–sishya* relationship
    This matha is the faith advocated by pandits
        who criticize and reject other faiths
    This faith of Purandara Vithala, Hanuman matha

The best matha is Madhva matha . . .

Madi madi yendu (PDH 'Holier than thou')

Where do you get this madi you talk about
You say 'madi'—ritually clean cloth, pure white
    and try to keep three furlongs away
Where do you get this 'madi', you parasite?

For all your talk of 'madi', unholiness is also yours
You are the impure as well as the pure
So stick your 'madi' in the flames and let it burn
you poor beggar

A bag of bones, you happily stand
in a pit of piss and shit
are you enjoying it?
Beggar, you fell
into this body of nine exits
containing so much filth
so where do you get
this 'madi' you always talk about?

When you are born there is *sutaka*
—several 'impure' days
and when you die there is 'sutaka'
—inauspicious, ritually impure days of mourning
Do you think you can be pure in the days between?
If you incessantly dip and dip
in the holy Kaveri river
do you think you'll give impurities the slip?
where do you get this 'madi'?

If you scrub your skin do you think
your karma will also be washed?
O beggar you do not understand the meaning
of this subtle mystery
Take Lord Purandara's holy name
and lead a pure life—

Where do you get this purity you prate
saying 'madi' this, 'madi' that
ritually pure cloth so white
you try to stay three furlongs away
where is this 'madi' coming from, you parasite?

Mangala jaya mangala   (PSD Vol. II, no. 109)

Auspicious, let the auspicious prevail

Victory
to the fish who rescued the Vedas
    Matsyavatar
to the tortoise who held up the
    cosmic mountain
to Varaha who held the world and
    carried her to safety
to Narasimha who protected
    the good child
Auspicious, let the auspicious prevail

Victory
to Vamana who asked for the grant
    of land
to the One who has conquered
    the great king
to the Lord called
    Ramachandra
to Gopala Krishna, consort of
    Satyabhama
Auspicious, let the auspicious prevail

Victory
to Buddha who stood there
    naked
to Kalki riding on his
    excellent horse
to Purandara Vithala who protected
    devotees in ten incarnations

Marula madi   (PSD Vol. II, no. 68)

O Lakshmi Goddess of illusion
you have bewildered somebody

How incessantly, both day and night
Lord Vishnu is after you

Wise people daily give up food
and meditate in various ways
on Lord Vishnu, and Lord Vishnu
successfully avoids them, but
he is always after you

O Lakshmi Goddess of illusion
you have bewildered someone

Incessantly, both day and night
Lord Vishnu is after you

Giving up all company,
becoming a monk, a *sannyasin*
Vishnu, even then, keeps you
all the time in his heart

O Lakshmi Goddess of illusion . . .
Lord Vishnu is after you

At the time of deluge, reclining
on the leaf of a banyan tree
ornaments washed away by water
you cleverly enticed him
O Lakshmi Goddess of illusion . . .

You made Lord Ranga your mate
You are 'Young lady on a flower',
he is 'Alamelumanga'-Pati
of Serpent hill. Yes, you made
Venkateshvara of Tirumalai
accept you as his dear bride

O Lakshmi Goddess of illusion . . .

You thought if you had a child
in the usual way your beauty
would vanish, and so your child
was born through the navel instead

O Lakshmi Goddess of illusion . . .

Left side there's Bhumi, earth;
Right side Shri; in front Durga;
on Vishnu's lap you are Lakshmi—
so all the time God fondles you

O Lakshmi Goddess of illusion
you've made him foolishly confused
Day and night non-stop Lord Vishnu
is bewildered because of you

I'll never forget you because
with joy you bring to the world
our Lord Purandara Vithala
who is under your control

O Lakshmi Goddess of illusion
you've obsessed him, he's confused
Day and night, night and day
Vishnu's bothered, obsessed with you

Muttu kolliro (PSD Vol. III, no. 197, p. 317)

Pearls for sale! Come one and all, buy pearls!
The best pearl of all is here right now
the pearl called being—awareness—bliss

The divine pearl is strung
    on the thread of spiritual knowledge
and you can possess it by becoming wise
    Even the poorest devotee can afford to own it
        once he is enlightened
Pearls for sale! Come one and all, buy pearls . . .

You can't wear this pearl on your nose
you can't use it for a status symbol
to evil people this pearl is invisible
    This holy pearl is also known as Krishna
Pearls for sale!

Your hand can't grab this intangible pearl
    yet it is truly a priceless gem
This genuine pearl known as
    Lord Purandara Vithala, Lord of the universe

Pearls for sale! Come one come all, buy pearls!
The very best pearl is here now
the pearl called being—awareness—bliss

Mulama (PSD Vol. III, no. 77, p. 153)

Some people may know how to wash away dirt
    but not how to clean their minds

What's the use of dipping
    in many sacred waters
muttering mantras to yourself

Enjoying the fruit of *bhoga* and *vishaya*
            pleasure and material goods
    Intoxicated by emotion and greed
    going around showing off—
    Do we call such people 'fortunate men'?
    Strutting around like roosters, acting
            like holy yogis, many people
    like you go dip in the sacred waters
            like crows having a wash—
    will you receive the spiritual fruit
            of actions done in a holy hour?

You harbour bad feelings toward others
            and wish them ill
    You pine for other women, thinking this
            will bring you supreme bliss
    Like one observing silence
            with firm determination on the outside
            but unable to control yourself within
    you embody hypocrisy on this earth
    What if you sit on the bank of a river
            like a crane meditating—so what?

Some people know how to wash away dirt
            but not how to clean their minds and hearts

So you go about calling yourself a Haridasa
            for the purpose of collecting coins
        Going from region to region, enduring sufferings,
        ending up in Banaras without giving up your ties
    You don't relinquish attachments
            so your mind is repulsed and attracted
    You pretend to be desireless, your senses
            burn with craving
    Will such a man receive the rewards of
            a true pilgrim to Banaras? Some people know . . .

When your poor parents were wandering around
      begging for food did you bother about them?
During that time your main concern
      was enjoying the company of women.
Then when your father died you called in
      a hundred priests and fed them well
And each of them exclaimed to you:
      'Your father's soul is happy now.'
Ignorant folks behave like this. Some people know . . .

What is the use—all the shruti you hear
      and all the smriti you read—
Unless you take to Lord Achyuta
      wisdom's light won't shine
What's the use of observing silence,
      doing all those rites
      when you've become low-minded
Will Shrinivasa Vithala approve
      of your conduct? He can see
      right through you, fool

Some folks know how to scrub away dirt
      but not how to purify mind and heart

Muyyakke muyya (PSD Vol. I, no. 53, p. 169)

Tit for tat O Lord of the universe
Lord who helps devotees win ultimate victory

I thought 'he's just a small boy' so I asked him to get water
but this Krishna who stole butter he brought water in a golden pot
I didn't know what was up,
I threw things at the boy, I even beat him up—Tit for tat . . .

O Lord you gave a bracelet to the prostitute
and made me responsible for that
you caused me to get beaten up—
now the accounts are settled—Tit for tat O Lord of the universe
Lord who helps devotees win ultimate victory

O God, if you have to be called *bhaktavatsala*,
'dear to devotees', shouldn't you be
attentive to their pleas? Never have I seen
any other deity who was such a cunning tease
Lord of Mukti, Purandara Vithala, Lord Pandari
Tit for tat . . .

If you want the title 'Lord fond of devotees' then please
throw away your second bracelet. I find no other
only you can grant salvation. I was tied to a pillar,
Lord, and because of you now I'm free

Tit for tat O Lord of the universe
Lord who helps devotees gain their ultimate victory

Na donkadareno   (PSD Vol. IV, no. 17, p. 70)

What if I'm crooked, is your name crooked, O Vithala?

O Vithala if the river is winding is the water curved?

If the sugarcane is bent is the sweet juice twisted?

What if the flower is bent, will the fragrance be awry?

What if the cow is crippled, will the milk be lame?

If the bow's bent does it mean the arrow's not straight?

I may be an untouchable but will your name get polluted?

So what if I'm an ignorant man, you're all-knowing, Lord
    Purandara Vithala, protect me
What if I'm off kilter, is your name off-kilter, O Vithala?

Nageyu baruthide   (PDK p. 9; also IIJ no. 3, p. 5)

It makes me want to laugh and laugh
when I see the so-called intelligent people
    of the world
stumbling around in such a muddle
caught up in the puppet show of folly

I just can't stop myself from laughing

Men who take up with someone else's wife
then take a dip in the holy flowing water
and go on counting the beads with their fingers
I just feel like laughing
when I see these 'people in the know'
taken in by some street show . . .

Or a woman who's given up the company
of her own husband, preferring some other man,
but still she keeps observing religious rites,
ritual bathing, and the like
I can't help but laugh when I see such folk
supposedly intelligent
wandering in foolish confusion . . .

Keeping low qualities in one's mind
a person becomes a festering nucleus
        where all life's toxins multiply
yet he still keeps on chanting the holy name
of Purandara Vithala, always present
        silently in the devotee's mind

It makes me want to laugh when I see smart folks
lost without a clue in the world's hullabaloo
I can't seem to keep myself from laughing
as if someone's playing a joke

Na madida karma (PSD Vol. III, no. 169, p. 285)

If the deeds I've already done
        in the past are so forceful
what can you do about it O Lord?

        I haven't fed the birds
        I had the company of other women
        I'm ignorant, foolish,
                I was enticed to sin
        What is the way out for me
        Lord who rides on Garuda?
                If deeds I've done recoil with such force
                what can you do about it O Lord?

Like a dog I said 'my house' 'my home'
I didn't remember you
and perform the normal rites
 When a man's deeds are so bad
 what can you do O Lord?

Kindly arrange for me to have the company
of your dasas, oblige me from now on
kindly show your mercy
I have no one to take care of me
Purandara Vithala, help me from now on
 If the deeds I've done are so forceful
 what can you do about it O Lord?

Nambiketava (PSD Vol. II, no. 118, p. 275)

Those who have faith in Lord Rangayya have never gone astray
 If they do not believe in him they may go astray
  and if they go astray let them go astray

Vishnu Lord of the whole universe unequalled, Adi Purusha

When Dhruva sat with joy on the lap of his father
 His foolish mother Suruchi pushed him away
 Have faith in Murari who gave an eternal throne
 to Dhruva (as a star in the heavens)—remember
 Those with faith in Lord Rangayya have never lost their way
 Those who forget him have cause to repent
  but if they want to regret it let them

The father of the excellent boy devotee Prahlada
 Was tormenting him and Prahlada cried out
  'O Lord you're my only refuge'
 With great love and affection God protected the child
 and he tore the villain Hiranyakashipu to pieces
 remember those who have faith in Lord Rangayya
  they have never lost their way . . .

He protected the king of the elephants, said
　　'Don't worry, be fearless'
Who said this to the Lord of elephants?
The Lord riding on the back of the Garuda
Without doubt have faith in the lotus feet
　　of Purandara Vithala—remember
Those with faith in Lord Rangayya have never lost their way
Those who have no faith in him are always going astray
　　and if they go astray let them go their own way

Namma deva nimma deva　(PSD Vol. II, no. 74, p. 199)

'My God', 'Your God', don't talk like that
There is only one God
for those devoted to the Supreme Being

In the beginning the elephant was caught
　　by the crocodile
When the elephant cried out in pain
　　'Adideva kindly protect me'
'This God' or 'That God' did not rescue him
Only Madhava came and saved the elephant

'My God', 'Your God', don't say such things
There is only one God
for those devoted to the Supreme Being

Hari (Vishnu), Hara (Shiva), Brahma—of these three
which should we consider supreme?
Bhrigu posed this question to gods and demons
and finally announced 'Vishnu is Supreme'—

Therefore 'My God' this and 'Your God' that
There is only one God
for those devoted to the ultimate

There is only one Vishnu, the Vedas say
through various mouths; there is only one: 'Vishnu is unique'
Give up your ignorance and with reverent care
worship Purandara Vithala husband of Shri

'My God' and 'Your God'—don't say such things
There's only one God
for those devoted to the Supreme Being

Naneke (PSD Vol. I, no. 66, p. 195)

Why should I feel forlorn
         why should I feel I'm poor
      O Hari Shrinidhi as long as you're
      with me why should I feel forlorn

You are my father my mother my friend
      you're everything to me, kith and kin
      you are the precious gem in the jewel-box
      as long as you're with me Shri Krishna, since
      all this is you there's no need to worry
         Why should I feel forlorn . . .

You are my brother you are the one
      who will take care of my belly
      you'll give me clothes you're the one
      who'll care for my wife and children
      as long as you're my benefactor
         Why should I feel forlorn . . .

You are the one who gives me knowledge
      you are the one who'll give me wisdom
      you're my saviour, my dear, as long as
      I remain here at your lotus feet, Lord
      Purandara Vithala why should I fear
         Why should I feel forlorn
      why should I feel poor
O Hari Shrinidhi as long as you're
      with me why should I feel forlorn?

Nanenu madideno (BR p. 342)

What have I done, O Lord Ranga
      shouldn't you save me

The honour or dishonour is ultimately yours
      it's not my concern
            O saviour of the downtrodden
Tirupati Venkataramana

When the elephant king Gajendra cried out—
When Draupadidevi made her appeal—
When Ahalya, having been turned to a stone,
    was then reinstated as a woman—
O Govinda, in all this world,
    aren't these the ones who know?

Well what have I done, O Lord Ranga
    shouldn't you save me too?

Listen, O killer of demons, wasn't
    Dhruva just a little boy?
Ajamila, guilty of committing sins,
    was he your sister's son—no!
O Govinda you took pity on him

What have I done, O Lord Ranga
    shouldn't you save me too?

Did you not shower abundance on Kuchela
    who approached you
        with just three handfuls of parched rice?
O Lord reclining on the serpent
    O Vithala of Purandara
O immeasurable Govinda

What have I done, O Lord Ranga
    shouldn't you save me too?

Narasimha (PSD Vol. II, no. 126, p. 286)

You would do well to worship the feet
    of Lord Narasimha
If you do this *padapuja* he will use
    his diamond-sharp weapon
And remove the mountain
    made of your sins

On hearing the cries of the child
eagerly he came, took the villain by the throat

When all the angels in heaven were trembling
When Lakshmi appealed to him
he burst from the great pillar

Shiva, Virinchi and others prayed
with their hands held high and he became
absolutely peaceful again, our Purandara Vithala

You would do well to worship the feet
of Lord Narasimha

Narayana anabarada (PSD Vol. III, no. 42, p. 101)

What's your problem, you can't say 'Narayana'
Some kind of thorn get stuck in your tongue?

Why haul yourself to far-off Banaras
and suffer so many pains while there
Why walk around balancing on your head
a water pitcher all of the time?
Why go wandering here and there
endlessly out trekking on your own?
Isn't the name of God the best
travelling companion you could have?
What's your problem . . . thorn in your craw,
you can't even say 'Narayana'?

Why observe daily fasts and suffer
and why shiver with cold
Dipping in the holy Ganges. Mechanically
why chant your circled beads?
Don't you think the name of the Lord
is the best practice for release?
What's your problem . . .

Why give up children and wife
and go to the forest where the *yatis* live
Why observe religious rites
and strict regulations, growing thin
With so much fasting—doesn't it suffice
to remember the name of Lord Purandara
Vithala with absolute devotion and fervour
What's the matter, you have some kind of problem
like a thorn stuck in your tongue
that you can't say the name just once?

Nayi bandadatta (PSD Vol. III, no. 206, p. 328)

Some kind of dog is trotting this way, my brother,
Here, let's play it safe and move off the road

This is not your ordinary dog—
it's the fallen state of man
the lowest form of human existence

This dog never gives back money he borrowed
This dog doesn't keep his promised word
This dog barks with vehement pride and ego
After he claws and climbs to the top of the heap
Some kind of dog is trotting this way . . .

If this dog gives a gift he boils with rage and regret
This dog teases and taunts you after donating food
This weird dog was born of a quite good mother's womb
Yet he grows to commit gruesomer acts than a dog would do
Some kind of dog is trotting this way . . .

This is a cur who abandons the wife he married
This is a cur who sniffs out abandoned wives
This is the weird dog now trotting this way
He never remembers Lord Purandara Vithala

Some kind of dog is trotting this way, my brother
Here, let's play it safe and move off the road

Ninya (PSD Vol. III, no. 11, p. 55)

Why do I want you, why do I seek your mercy?
I don't need you, or have to be concerned with you

It is enough if I have the power of your holy name

'Mara this and Mara that'—while Valmiki
was meditating like thus
he discovered the holy name Rama—
all he needed to protect him

When the woman in the assembly (Draupadi)
was assailed
By someone trying to pull off her sari
Balakrishna rescued her

When the messengers of Yama, god of death,
    came to take Ajamila
The holy name Narayana
    came to his rescue

When the elephant caught by the crocodile
    cried to you for help
The name Adimula came
    to the elephant's rescue

When Prahlada's father was troubling him
    the holy name
Narasimha came
    to Prahlada's rescue

When the boy Dhruva went into the forest
    he took the name
Vasudeva and that name came
    to the boy's rescue

Nothing is as great as your name
    O Lord, supreme
Shri Purandara Vithala, known
    for great deeds

Ragi tandira   (PSD Vol. I, no. 33, p. 136, 'Bless you')

O—have you brought *ragi* gruel?
Bless you—may your life be gracious
and not gruelling—may no one treat you cruelly

Bless you generous feeder of the poor,
giving up talk, except songs of God,
singing bhajans daily—have you brought ragi? . . .

May God's blessings be upon you
and the guru's compassion, know
the guru's deep intentions, remember
his feet and do good deeds—have you brought ragi?

Go on remembering Lord Shrinivasa
be the devotee of Lord Hanuman
rise above miserly ways
bless you, have you brought ragi gruel? may your life
    be gracious and not be gruelling,
        may no one treat you cruelly

Observe all the religious rites
Praise Lord Vishnu who rides Garuda
may there be no jealousy or other
upsets in your belly. Have you brought ragi gruel?

May you understand the Vedas
and Puranas, and be a ruler of the earth
a follower of the saints' faith
may you be spiritually wise—have you brought ragi?

May you be well-versed in the six paths
of yoga and the three *margas* of *vedanta*
give up evil company, and may you
attain the supreme *tattva* state. O—have you brought ragi?

Give up lust and greed
perform religious rites
attain enjoyment in the higher state
and dance with joy lovingly—have you brought ragi?

Remember always Lakshmi's Shri Ramana
may you realize your Self
try to get beyond pins-and-needles samsara
gravitate to Purandara Vithala—have you brought me ragi?
    you're giving me gruel today?
      Bless you, may your life not be gruelling,
        and may none treat you cruelly.

Ramanama payasa (PSD Vol. III, no. 193, p. 312, 'Old Dasa Recipe')

Add the sugar of Krishna nama
    To the tasty Ramanama pudding of rice

When this sweet pudding is served
    Add the melted butter called Vithala
      and smack your lips with delight

Bring the wheat of concentration
   grind it on the stone of vairagya
   with a good mind take out the cream of wheat
   and make it into slender noodles

Add the sugar of Krishna nama
   To the tasty Ramanama pudding of rice

The ingredients are all prepared
   the heart is the cooking vessel
   feeling is the water steaming
   stir with the spatula of wisdom
   knead, and serve on a shining tray

Add the sugar of Krishna nama
   To the tasty Ramanama pudding of rice

Ananda, ananda! that's what you burp
   after eating the delectable food
   Purandara Vithala embodies ananda
   remember him chanting his holy name

Add the sugar of Krishna nama
   To the tasty pudding of Ramanama rice
   When serving this pudding
   Add the melted butter called Vithala
   And smack your lips with delight

Ramanama ratnahara (PSD Vol. II, no. 128, p. 289)

I received the diamond necklace
designed around Rama's jewel name

As a result of previous good deeds

It has a diamond known as fish Matsya
set in the midst of a golden tortoise
Varaha the boar is the thread
   which runs through the golden beads
the rope of pearls is known as
   Narahari nama
I received this diamond necklace
designed around Rama's jewel name

On the string of the necklace
   which is named Vamana
the green emerald Parashu–Rama
   is strung, and the connecting
links of the chain of this necklace
   are formed of Krishna

I received this diamond necklace
designed around Rama's jewel name

In the chain the tiniest part
sesame-seed small is called 'Buddha'
the hook is known as 'Kalki'
and Lord Purandara Vithala's name
is the perfect string of pearls
   in the necklace of good fortune

I received this necklace of jewels
designed around Rama's precious name

In the chain the tiniest part
sesame-seed small is called 'Buddha'
the hook is known as 'Kalki'
and Lord Purandara Vithala's name
is the perfect string of pearls
in the necklace of good fortune

I received this necklace of jewels
   designed around Rama's precious name

Sadhusajjana   (PSD Vol. I, no. 82, p. 240)

To be in the presence of sages and saints
   is to savour a perpetual feast

To know the essence of Vedanta
   is to celebrate a great festival

To rise above prejudice
      is to relish an endless feast
   To splash and float in Bhagirathi river
      is to partake in a joyous festival
   To be in the presence of sages and saints . . .

To win what you've long aspired to win
    is to enjoy a sweet holiday
To be a yogi completely carefree
    is to enjoy festival moods everyday
To be in the presence . . .

For a householder who hasn't dug himself
    deeply into debt, worldly life is a feast
And the body that's sound, free from
    diseases, also is itself a festival
To be in the presence . . .

To gaze and gaze upon the holy City of Light,
    Kashi, is itself a feast for the eyes, and
To chant again and again in praise
    Padmanabha's holy name is a festival
To be in the presence . . .

In this world to live in Banaras
    is to partake in a continuous holiday
And worshipping Purandara Vithala
    is always and everywhere a sacred feast
To be in the presence of sages and saints
    is to savour a perpetual feast

Sakala graha bala nine   (DPS IV, pp. 34–5)

You alone are the power behind all the planets,
    O lotus-eyed Lord

Only you pervade everything
    O protector of the universe

The sun and moon and Mercury are you, just you
The two nodes, *rahu* and *ketu* are only you
Jupiter, Saturn, Mars are you, just you
day and night are you alone
all the nine planets are only you, just you
you are the medicine for curing
    the disease of existence

You alone are the power behind all planets . . .

You are the fortnights which make up the months
You alone are the auspicious weeks, yes you
You are the blessed periods of time
You rescued the honour of Draupadi
    to whom you gave the vessel of abundance
You are protector of the world, just you
You are the Lord who rides upon Garuda

You alone are the power behind all the planets . . .

You are the six seasons (*ritukalavu*)
You are the days of austerity (*vrata dinangalu*)
You are the sacrifice and prayers said
    at dawn and noon and dusk
You are my true path to the ultimate victory
    of liberation
You're the great glory which transcends
    all the scriptures

O Lord Purandara Vithala

You alone are the power behind all the planets
    O Lotus-eyed Lord, just you
Nobody else pervades everything—
    Protector of the universe, only you

Sanditayasa (PSD Vol. III, no. 57, p. 127)

I am old now and time is passing by

There was not a day that I was happy
    I'm worn out, bothered and harassed
    O Lord, father, protect me and
        free me from all these fetters

I spent three months in the womb of my father
    knowing nothing, spent nine months in mother's womb
    being roasted. A whole year I spent that way.
    O Indiresha, listen to my tale of woe.
    I'm always living in some kind of prison
    without seeing the way to reach liberation

I am old now and time is passing by

'I can't live in darkness,' so saying,
   I have sought refuge in you, approached you.
   In my childhood I daily spoiled my clothing
   with my own piss and shit. I spent my time on myself.
   At the age of sixteen I grew proud, roamed the world.
   Illusions of family ties attached themselves to me
   and I'm caught tight in the snare of worldly life

I am old now and time is passing by

I fell almost daily into Sin Ocean
   without taking care to see the other shore
   I burnt myself in grief, feeling agonies within
   I prayed to you 'Kindly put me on board the ship
   named Meditation' Lord, this is my request to you
   Take me to your feet without fail
   O Lord Purandara Vithala

I am old now and time is passing by . . .

Sharanu sharanu (STAJ p. 68, 'Song to Ganesha')

We surrender, we surrender, we surrender, Lord worshipped
   by Vishnu, we surrender, son of Parvati, Maruti, divine form
   we surrender O Siddhivinayaka (Ganapati)
   Refuge and Fulfiller of desires

Lord with a third eye on your forehead,
Son of Devi, dear son of Shiva who wears serpents,
your beautiful body brilliant as a lightning streak,
   wearing dangling ear-rings (*kundalas*) in your ears—
   we surrender . . .
You wear a fragrant garland and pendant of fine pearls,
you have four arms, and on those arms are golden armlets,
   and you hold the noosed rope, and the goad—
   we surrender . . .

You have a big pot-belly, you hold a bow of sugarcane
you are the true servant of Lord Purandara Vithala who
rides on the falcon Garuda—
   we surrender . . .

Smaranayonde   (PSD Vol. III, no. 3, p. 45)

Isn't remembrance enough,
isn't Govinda's name enough?
　　O supreme Lord,
when folks put their trust in you
is the trouble of their sins too much?

What if a man is a great fool
what if he commits bad deeds
what if he's low caste or a dullard
O Hari, protector of Prahlada
　　without fail
Isn't remembrance enough?

What if he is a person who has
　　committed great crimes
what if he killed everybody?
what if he became a sinner
　　in the excited heat of the moment
O Hari, saviour of Ajamila
　　with affection
Isn't remembrance enough,
isn't Govinda enough?

To get the good fruits of holy deeds
of going on pilgrimages to
　　all the sacred tirthas
with ceaseless devotion daily
　　the name of the renowned
Lord Purandara Vithala
　　Isn't remembrance of that enough?
　　Remembrance of Govinda's name
　　　　is enough
O *paramapurusha*
when folks put their trust in you
do the troubles of their sins
　　seem to be too much?

Summane baruvude (JC p. 68)

Will liberation come to you for nothing?

Without thinking with devotion
    of our endless Lord who never slips
Will liberation come to you for nothing

In your mind you must be firm
you should avoid contact with sinners
you must drop all your doubts
you have to decide to surrender all—
body, mind and wealth; otherwise

Will liberation come to you for nothing?

You've got to lose desire and anger
let go of your feelings of attraction
toward the women of others, and
immolate all your wishes for gold—
you have to chant the name of Hari

Will liberation come to you for nothing?

Without a mind brimming with devotion
    toward our endless Lord who never slips
Will liberation come for no good reason?

Tala beku (PP pp. 87–8)

There should be: good rhythm and suitable accompaniment
at an undisturbed time, with people who want to hear music

Yati and *prasa*, alliteration cycles, within the kept tempo
and the utmost love felt toward Cupid's father, Lord Vishnu
    There should be . . .

The singer must have a clear voice, knowing well the songs
The singer should lose any grief and have a pleasant face
    There should be . . .

There should be knowing people to listen and joy increasing
Purandara Vithala should be recognized as Supreme Being
    There should be . . .

There should be good rhythms and suitable accompaniment
at an undisturbed time, with people who want to hear music

Tambulava kollo   (DPS Vol. IV, p. 169)

Take these betel leaves,
O lotus-faced Lord who slew the demon

Having prepared them,
lotus-eyed Lakshmi is offering them

Offering jasmine flowers, distilled rose water,
a cup of sandalwood paste, camphor, saffron,
various scented oils, musk, sandalwood oil,
oil of champaka, champaka flowers to tie
    in your hair
Take these betel leaves . . .

Rukminidevi is offering crushed betel nuts,
cloves, cardamom, fragrant nuts,
    slivers of tasty nuts,
leaves of *jajikhai*,
lime made from pearls,
    and here is camphor
Take these betel leaves . . .

The bed has been made up
the garlands of jasmine have been tied
come forward, lie down here,
Rukmini with wandering eyes
is eagerly awaiting you
anticipating you,
    O father of the love-god
Purandara Vithala

Take these betel leaves
Lotus-faced Lord who slew the demon

Tandena   (PSD Vol. I, no. 77, p. 224)

I have seen Lord Krishna of Udipi, the greatest lover
in the whole universe—he can win anyone over

Before going to the temple I saw the great pool
     and bathed
          I went to the temple of Chandramolishvara—Shiva
          and prostrated
     Went to the temple of Ananteshvara, then to the temple
          of Hanuman
     Then I went to the temple of Lord Krishna, and

I have seen Lord Krishna of Udipi, the greatest lover
     in the whole universe—he can win anyone over

I saw the river flowing all around, I saw everywhere
          effulgence of the sun
     I saw the lake named Madhva *Sarovar*
     Saw the shrines of the eight great saints
          of the Madhva tradition
     And I saw the famous Lord Krishna of Udipi

I have seen Lord Krishna of Udipi, the greatest lover
in the whole universe—he can win anyone over

I saw the ring, the charming waistband
          he wears
     I saw his sash, and its jingling bell
     I saw the necklace of nine auspicious gems shining
          around his throat
     Saw Lord Krishna dancing—din din din!
     I saw the lotus feet of Lord Purandara Vithala

Yes I have seen Lord Krishna of Udipi, the greatest lover
     in the whole universe—he can win anyone over

Taraka bindye (PSD Vol. I, no. 85, p. 242)

Please dear sister
     fetch me the pitcher
used for bringing
     water from the river

If this pitcher
     happens to shatter
it costs just a penny
     so bring it hither . . . Please . . .

Please bring the pitcher
    used to fetch the
Rama nama water
    fresh and delicious

I want to spend time
    with the water fetchers
the women who carry this
    water in pitchers . . . so please . . .

Please bring the pitcher
    which is used to carry
the water known as
    great Govinda Hari

I'll pour ablutions
    on Lord Purandara
sitting on the hill-top
    Lord Bindu Madhava . . . so please

Udaravairagya (PSD Vol. I, no. 29, p.129)

This is just belly vairagya
    not real renunciation
        (Piety should be for soul not for show)

The hypocrite with rot in his heart
goes to the river and piously shivers
astounding all the people around him
but arrogance and envy are packed inside him
He is so holy—not! This is just belly vairagya!

Chanting the Name fingering rosary beads
you hang a veil down over your face
inwardly you unveil and enjoy that woman's face
you want to pose as a great renunciate
really you're mostly a great hypocrite
This is just belly vairagya . . .

Your display of copper and brass images
is as impressive as the workshop of a coppersmith
You place a variety of lamp-flames there
to make the images' surfaces glitter and glow
this is the way hypocrites perform worship.
This is just belly vairagya . . .

So deceptively to show off your devotion
You pretend you've no equal in piety
Like the *natakastri*—man playing a woman's part
You make an impression but there's no real woman there
this is merely a way to earn a living
This is just belly vairagya . . .

Hey lose that big ego, seek the company of the wise
Know that whatever happens is God's will
Yes everything is only due to God's grace
Unless you look to Lord Purandara Vithala
All you do is bogus, pure hypocrisy
It's all just the scheming of belly vairagya
    not real renunciation
       (piety is for soul, not for show)

Guna hinanige (PSD Vol. III, no. 96, p. 179)

Can a man who has no self-respect
expect to take any pride in himself?
Can a man unreceptive to wisdom's light
presume to receive the guru's teaching?

Why should a man wandering the jungles
want or need golden ornaments?
Why should a man accustomed to eating from
broken earthenware wish for a metal tray?
One who gives nothing to mendicants—
should he be puffed up feeling generous?
One who can't even carry a tune—should
he feel haughty about his musical knowledge?
Can a man who has no self-respect
expect to take any pride in himself?

Should one accustomed to rice-water meals
expect to taste nectar-sweet food?
One who gets by in an old blanket—
should he covet ritually pure cloth?
A man who indulges in street acrobatics—
what business has he with majestic conduct?
Someone who retains material desires—
what need has he for the holy name of God?
Can a man with no self-respect
expect to take any pride in himself?

Does the murderer of brahmins have the right
to make a display of excessive piety?
Should one who breaks the word he gives
be considered worthy of much trust?
When agony disturbs your mind
what good will going on pilgrimage do?
If one does not give up desire
what good is public renunciation?
Can a man who has a low self-image
feel that he's worthy of honour's privilege?

That man who acts with recklessness—
why should he observe religious rites?
A man who is afraid of his own wife—
how can he claim to have any valour?
If you don't have a pure mind to begin with
what good is mantra, tantra and such?
Does a person heedless of consequences
have any credentials for brahminhood?
Can a man who has no self-respect
be expected to be proud of himself?

Why should an ordinary person
feel the need for sovereignty?
What is the use of having relatives
if they have no love for you?
Can the wretched lowly tamasic person
who never remembers Purandara Vithala
his Lord, expect to attain Kaivalya?

Can a man without self-respect expect
to take much pride in himself?
Can a man unreceptive to the light of wisdom
presume to get the guru's teaching?

Vyapara namagayitu (PSD Vol. I, no. 20, p. 111,
'Spiritual Chamber of Commerce')

We've gone into business—it's a service industry
    dedicated to the lotus feet—and this business keeps us busy

The mercy of Shri Hari has become the shirt I wear
the compassion of the guru has become my turban
What do I wear beneath my feet? The worst sinner called Kali
and treading on the chests of evil-souled people
    has become our commerce—we've gone into business . . .

The heart is like white paper, the tongue a pen
the mouth is the pen-holder, the stories of the names
of Lakshmi-enamoured Vishnu form our narratives, and we
gladly give this offering to the Lord after composing it
    that has become our commerce—we've gone into business . . .

The horrendous hassle of future lives—that fear is gone
forever. I've settled up my accounts: the accumulated burden
of my deeds, my debts—I've paid them off, torn up the IOU
and now I'm out of debt, paid off, completely debt-free
    we've gone into business—it's a service industry . . .

For every word tears of joy are shed and we feel the thrill.
That's reward enough—when your hand is inside the moneybag!
He gave me an irrevocable document and authorized the payment
of my salary in the form of sadhana leading to salvation
    this has become our business—it's a service industry . . .

I didn't prostrate shamelessly at the feet of all and sundry
whenever I would meet them. The Lord Purandara Vithala
had me fall at his feet and he blessed me, with welcoming
hospitality of areca nut and betel leaf he showed his regard for me
    We've gone into business—it's a service industry
        dedicated to the lotus feet—this business keeps us quite busy

Yadava ni ba (PSD Vol. IV, no. 4, p. 50)

Come to us, Yadava, dear to the Yadu clan
>   Madhava, Madusudana,
>   Slayer of your demonic uncle in Mathura
>   Come to us, son of Yashoda

With the jingling of your feet,
>   the sweet sound of your flute
>   playing a game of stick and ball
>   playing with a spinning top
>   along with your gang of cowherd pals
>   O Yadava dear to the Yadu clan, come to us . . .

In your hands: conch and shining chakra
>   proud little cowherd boy, please
>   come to us, child of spotless conduct,
primal Narayana, beloved favourite
of all the aspiring devotees O Yadava . . .

Come, Lord who rides the bird
>   King with the smiling face, come
>   I will proclaim your glorious feats
>   to the entire cosmos
>   O Purandara Vithala please come to us
>   Come to us, Yadava, dear to the Yadu clan
>   Madhava, Madusudana
>   Slayer of your demonic uncle in Mathura
>   Come to us, son of Yashoda

Yakenani (PSD Vol. I, no. 64, p. 192)

Lord why did you drag me to this kingdom?
If you can't feed me why did you create me?

I am a stranger here, knowing no one
and my body is weak
I have no inclination to follow
any particular path
I have no other go but to feel regretful
no one wishes me well here
only Vasudeva knows my plight—Lord why . . .

None of my relations or friends are here
There's no king here who can recognize me
my mind is not very happy here—no money
nobody to take care and help me
it's no good for me to stay here
Lord Indiresha knows this . . . Lord, why . . .

Nobody is here to call me, no one
to offer me help, no one to show compassion
I have no one but God
there is no cheer in my life now
my senses are all weakened
Lord Purandara Vithala knows all this

Lord why did you drag me to this kingdom?
If you can't feed me why did you create me?

Yarige (PSD Vol. I, no. 44, p. 153)

Who is there for whom?
This existence is a borrowed thing
The bubble on the water isn't real
Lord Sri Hari

I went to the well because I felt thirsty
there was no water, O Lord Hari
it has dried up

I went in search of shade from a tree
running away from the scorching wind
the tree fell on my head—O Lord Hari

I built a home in the forest
and tied a cradle in a tree
the child in the cradle disappeared, Sri Hari

O father, Lord Purandara Vithala
when I breathe my last
may you rescue me

Who is there for whom?
This existence is a borrowed thing
The bubble on the water isn't real
Lord Shri Hari

Yechcharita bhagyaledutu (IIJ no. 22, p. 28)

My Lord has made me a wandering fakir
    he gave me
the broken earthen pot of experience
    to use as a begging bowl
And my heart is my fakir's shoulder bag
    these two things he tucked under my arm
        and sent me on my way

The *dhoti* of temptation faced with calmness
    is wound around my waist
  What has he put in my hand?
    a tambura made of lacquer
    —*sadguru* made me a fakir . . .

He gave me a tambura to twang for the background drone
    and I thank him for the flower of enjoyment
He placed a knobbed cap on my head
    and gave me a distinctive style of preaching
He girded me up with the *lungi* of *amrita*
    and gave me the remedy of equality
sadguru thus made me a wandering fakir . . . .

He made me over into this person (the fakir I am now)
    he showed me the open space beyond
He put his hand on my head to bless me
    Lord Purandara Vithala rigged me up like this
        turning me into a wandering fakir
He is the one who equipped me like this
    sadguru turned me into a wandering fakir

Yellaru (PSD Vol. III, no. 186, p. 303)

Everyone does all this for the belly
    and for a piece of cloth
    But we worship Shri Vallabha for
    our salvation

Carrying a palanquin, grappling with wrestlers
    for the belly
    Barking lies is also for the belly
    But contemplating Vallabha is for liberation

Everyone does all this for the belly . . .

Reigning as king, mounting a black horse
   is done for one's livelihood
   Doing evil deeds, all just for the belly
   But for salvation we take the name of Shri Hari
Everyone does all this . . .

Carrying a load like a mountain: for the belly
   Shouting at the top of your lungs for the belly
   For liberation we take the name of Lord Purandara

Everyone does so many things for the belly
   and for a scrap of cloth
   But we worship Shri Vallabha for our salvation

Ugabhogas (PSD Vol. IV, 293–346)

1

Take the bitter neem tree seeds
dump jaggery over them in a heap
pour honey on to that like rain—
Have you removed the poison taste?

What's the good of the heaps you read
or the torrents of words you've heard
unless ignorance is all plucked out
your mind is a cobra blindly swaying
to the tune the piper's playing

O my Lord Shripati Purandara
Vithala, listen to me,
This is the way it is, O Lord

3

What good is a tree
which gives no shelter
what good is shade
if there isn't also water
what good is wealth
if one has no heart to give it
what good is mind
devoid of spiritual wisdom
what good is a life
lived without being
a menial worker labouring
for Lord Purandara Vithala

10

What's the use of chanting a mantra
if one has no purity of mind
What's the use of sipping holy tirtha water
if one has no cleanliness of body
What's the use of excessive bathing
in the water like a big or little fish
What's the use of standing still as a crow
in Shrisaila keeping your eye alert for food
outside you take a holy bath
inside you're not clean
Purandara Vithala saw phonies like these
and they made him start to laugh

15

If you have life there's no shortage of food
for the *jiva* there is no dearth of bodies
Birth and death—both are natural to this world
Throughout time one who has not heard
the auspicious qualities of the Lord
	his life is a waste
	O Lord Purandara Vithala

16

Sometimes you have me ride
	an elephant or horse
sometimes you make me walk barefoot
sometimes you give me a feast to enjoy
	other times you have me fast
you know your own greatness (*mahima*)
O Lord reclining on the serpent coil
Purandara Vithala

18

Should one keep a chicken in a golden cage
Would a shaven-headed widow need
white jasmine flowers to adorn her hair
Should a man who has no servants
fantasize becoming a king
Has a human being lived
if he has never served the Lord;
is his life not a waste?
O Purandara Vithala
please let me know

22

It's like going on a pilgrimage
to the sacred city of Banaras
carrying a dirty bundle under your arm
all the way.
Listen, man, if you can't drop ego and envy
What's the use of all you do?
It's just a waste
O foolish man, try if you can
to remember Lord Vithala

26

Saying 'A *holiya* (untouchable)
has just arrived outside'
you try to keep your God inside
you ring your ritual bell
what's the use

when your body flames with rage
isn't that inauspicious pollution
isn't mental duplicity
a kind of untouchability?
Keeping such untouchable impurities
inside yourself will never do

save us O Purandara Vithala

29

If we take birth as worm or insect
can we say 'I take refuge in God'?

If we take birth as lion or deer
can we say 'I take refuge in God'?

If we take birth as an ass or bear
can we say 'I take refuge in God'?

If we take birth as a pig or dog
can we say 'I take refuge in God'?

O mind of man, lest you forget it
your previous wrongdoings
        have been erased, and

you have taken birth now.
        in the prized human form

so make haste to recall
    Lord Purandara Vithala

30
O God, Lord Hari, if you are displeased
who will do anything for me
    even if they're friends of mine?
O Lord Hari, if you are pleased with me
who would do anything against me
    even if they frown despising me
O Purandara Vithala

35
For you, you are the infatuation
For you, you are the affection, love
For you, you are the devotee
For you, you are the enemy
For you, you are the enlightened
For you, you are the maker
For you, you are you alone Purandara Vithala

37
You are the Lord who protects
You are the Lord who takes life
You are Keshava, giver
    of the fruit of Kaivalya
I find this magnificence
    in no other form of God
O Killer of rapacious Ravana
Lord Purandara Vithala

39
Precarious
On your left side is a well
on your right, the lake
ahead of you this forest fire
the fire has spread
    wild flames in front of you
behind you the tiger
    comes creeping closer
Who is there for whom
    O Purandara Vithala?

69
To become a dasa
one should have done good deeds
    for many many births
You are radiant as one hundred thousand suns
Lord of Shri, full of virtues
You are indestructible, eternal
Please give me abundant opportunities
to serve your dasas
O Purandara Vithala

73
For the dasa it is good
for the *bhagavata*, riches
for traitors, poverty
for the dasa, fame
for the cruel, notoriety
victory to the godly
defeat goes to fools
loss for deceivers
profit to *mahatmas*
for slaves of Purandara Vithala, mukti
for demons blind darkness
There is no doubt about it

74
Teasing and teasing
    they applied *Harinama* on my forehead
Humiliating me they removed from me
    this gross craving
Terrifying, terrorizing me
    they rid me of lust and anger
Those who denigrate me behind my back
    are my real well-wishers, kith and kin,
O God I'm saved by the braggarts
    they were tormenting me so
        they harassed me
            right into eternal happiness *(kaivalya)*
They saw to it I didn't get a penny
    made me atone for my sins
They kept me apart, saying
    these belong to Hari.
Give me all your blessings
O my father Purandara Vithala
    Make me the dasa of your dasas' dasas

77
Your coming towards me is my responsibility
My business is to remember you all the time
You are responsible for my children and my wife
Through my dharmic action I must make you agree
It is your duty to feed and protect me
It is my work to fall at your feet
It's not my job to count my crimes and follies
It's not my way of life to live forgetful of you
Who else is there but you I can cry my pleas to?
Purandara Vithala

80
If you recline and sing his praise
    he will sit up, all ears
If you are sitting and singing his praise
    he will stand and listen enthralled
If you stand and sing his praise
    he will dance with joy to hear it
If you dance and sing his praise
Purandara Vithala will say
'Welcome to paradise!'

81
Kali *yuga* is the best yuga for man
In the Kali yuga if you take the name of God
all your sins are washed away
there is no yuga equal to the Kali yuga
Kaivalya is in your palm
        because with the lotus-eyed Purandara Vithala
            on your side your sins are washed away
                letting you enjoy a happy life

82
Men did tapas and meditated in the Krita yuga
    In the Treta yuga
        men cultivated spiritual wisdom (jnana)
    What shall I say about the Dvapara yuga
        the sacrificial fire was the sole means then
    In this Kali yuga singing the praise of God
        and chanting are all you need
Praise to Purandara Vithala

83
Who is a *haridasa?*

One who crosses the ocean of samsara
    strumming the tambura
one who keeps time with clappers
    and cymbals, beating out talas
one who has mingled with
    the immortals of heaven
one who has jingling bells
    tied to his ankles
one who has stepped on the chest
    of the villain Kala (Time)
one who has sung songs
one who has seen Purandara Vithala
seen the beautiful form of Hari
one who has made a beeline
    for Vaikuntha

89
I've been loading up
    the boat called body
        with the merchandise
called Hari nama

As I go about my business
    my senses block the way
        order me to pay the toll

so I show them the stamp
    of Lord Mukunda's emblem
        branded on me

I arrive at the presence
    of Lord Purandara Vithala
        and receive the profit
            from this enterprise:
liberation's bliss

91

By listening to the *Ramayana* we receive
   the boon of children
When we hear the *Mahabharata*
   all our sins are washed away
Even if you listen to a bit of *Vishnu Purana*
   you will become bright with wisdom
Grasping the real meaning of the *Bhagavata Purana*
   you get *dhyanabhaktivairagya*
      the detachment of devotion's meditation
If you do sankirtana
      singing Purandara Vithala's praise
         you get everything, including merging (*sayujya*)

98

What we seem likely to get at some future time
   let's get today
What we want to have today
   let's get it right now
What we are getting right now
   let's get it this very instant
Let's have the mercy of
   Lord Purandara Vithala

104

I can only stand if I'm holding your feet
   without that grasp I can't
I cry out beseeching you
   carrying your firebrand
I hold your umbrella, whisk,
      I sprinkle your tirtha water on my body
and evils are warded off

Never, no never, will I ever
give up your lotus feet
O Purandara Vithala I won't let go

107

As I get up
I greet Govinda
Opening my eyelids
I see Lord Hari
My tongue comes out
with a song
    'Narayana Nara Hari'
O Lord of the 16,000 gopis
Purandara Vithala
who rules over me

108

That *sandhya puja* is best
when you see a flood of star beams pulsing

That twilight prayer of connection is middling
if you see one or two stars

That *sandhya* meditation is worst
when you see not even distant stars

If you give up the stars
Purandara Vithala will give you up

117

Pray the holy name with one-finger *japa*

Ten-bead japa with jewels of wild olive wood

Hundred miniature conchshell-bead japa

Thousand little coral-bead japa

Ten thousand pearl-bead rosary japa

One hundred thousand gold-bead japa

Ten million *dharba* grass-knot japa

Innumerable tulasi-bead japa

    thus said Purandara Vithala

153
Today is an auspicious day
this week is an auspicious week
Today's star is an auspicious star
The yoga of what happens today
    is auspicious yoga
Today's cause (karana) is auspicious
Today's astrological moment (*laghna*)
    is an auspicious moment
Today because we have sung the praises of
    Lord Purandara Vithala
        it is an auspicious day

Jiva paratantra suladi (PSD Vol. IV, pp. 217–18)

My body and mind are at your mercy
My wealth and granary are at your mercy
My belongings and vehicles are also at your mercy
My sons and children, wife and friends,
all of these are at your mercy
My food and water are at your mercy
What is there at my mercy?
All is at your mercy
My desire also, Lord Purandara
    Vithala, is for everything to be at your mercy

Nothing moves—not even a grass blade
without your wind
God is smaller than an atom
and largest of the large
In a necklace the beads are joined by a string
Purandara Vithala is like that string
The smallest of the small, yet the support
    holding the whole cosmos
The universe is dependent on you

You hold my hand considering me as your own
I'll try to serve you to the best of my ability
For my attempt I need your support
Your support is within your control
For your effort you should help yourself
Everything is at your mercy O Purandara Vithala

Going along the path, *Smriti* is the guide
that brings us to you
O Lord do these ignorant people know
Do they know that you are responsible
that you are the cause of the universe
Do the rigidly orthodox (with their mechanical acts)
know the subtle living truth
All the realized souls know

O Lord Purandara Vithala you are all in all
for all the immortals of heaven
In all the main scriptures—*Shruti, Upanishads, Smriti,
Puranas, Itihasa, Pancharatra*—
the main topic is you and you alone

The rope with which we tie the bullocks is the Vedas
The cord through their noses is the Name
The bullocks are jivas
The implement for goading the animals is *bhaktirasa*
      the nectar of devotion
The load of this bullock cart is karma
Purandara Vithala is the merchant
      Owner of the cart

Lord Purandara is the one
who moves and is immobile
The one who goads all this universe of categories
is none other than Lord Purandara

Who is free in this universe?
Lord Purandara, who propels
this moving machine, is the
driver of this dynamic system (*yantravahaka*).

I seek refuge in you, I
seek refuge in you, I seek
refuge in you
Please protect me
Accept my appeal
O Lord Purandara Vithala

Srishti Suladi (PSD Vol. IV, pp. 181–2, 'Medley of Creation')

I bow before your fierce Rudra face
I bow before your creative Brahma face
I bow before your heaven-king Indra face
I bow before your moon face
I bow before your sun face
I bow before your fire face
I bow down before your changeless aspect
O Purandara Vithala
I bow to your changeful aspect
I bow to your universal aspect

The entire universe is a pavilion mantapa
The universal light inside
    is the flame waved in circles before you
Meru the cosmic mountain is your throne
Mandakini river is your ablution
The flowers of your garland are woven
from blossoms of the tree of paradise
    grown in Indra's courtyard

Child Krishna is found moving about in
    the golden cradle
hanging from the banyan tree
Balamukunda Purandara Vithala
    with his toe in his mouth

You created the world
You are living inside the world
Both inside and outside
you are complete
An outsider-insider who preserves
and protects the world
You are beyond the universe
    and are freedom incarnate
The only object of the universe
    is Purandara Vithala

You're the saviour of the universe
And you are in love with
your fascinating universe
You're the outsider, beyond the universe
Also the creator of the universe

You're protecting the universe
Although you are inside it
My dear Purandara Vithala
You're the Lord of the universe.

Jaya jaya Janardana
Purandara Vithala
Jaya jaya jaya
Victory over the delusions
of all the world's afflictions

Kanakadasa's Life

I fled Him, down the nights and down the days;
I fled Him, down the arches of the years . . .[1]

Listening to the songs and verses, and hearing about the life of singer–saint Kanakadasa, who lived in Karnataka during the height of the Vijayanagara empire in the 1500s, we are confronted with evidence of caste frictions and prejudices, birth status disadvantages and privileges, and we are moved to think about this poet–devotee's struggle for the dignity of being accepted as an equal among upper-caste Vaishnavas. Perhaps his literary urges were in part stimulated by his desire to prove to his critics that a Kuruba tribesman inspired by bhakti could be as eloquent as anyone else, or more so. His life story reveals that the recognition and respect he eventually won did not come easily.

His life began in Bada near Dharwar, in what is now the state of Karnataka. There, Birappa was a feudal chief[2] of a village of Kurubas, a herding and hunting clan. According to tradition he was the local revenue collector for the Vijayanagara ruler. His wife was named Bachchamma.

It is said that this pious Kuruba couple prayed to Lord Venkateshvara at the sacred pilgrimage shrine on Tirumala Hill, asking for a child to be born to them. This theme of parents-to-be praying for a child is found in the life stories of a number of saints of south India.

In time their prayers were answered and a baby was born to them, and after twelve days they performed the proper ceremony and put him in the cradle, naming him Timmappa. An energetic child, Timmappa grew up enjoying an active boyhood, running races, playing children's games, thriving on vigorous sports like swimming, and was soon quite strong.

It is said that in Tirupati Timmappa came into contact with the saintly teacher Tatacharya, an enthusiastic Vaishnava of the Ramanuja-charya school, and Timmappa learned Vishnu–bhakti from him.[3]

According to a legend Timmappa discovered a treasure of gold while digging a well once, and local people started calling him 'Kanaka Nayaka', meaning Golden Chief. Timmappa built a temple in the village of Kaginele (in what is now north Karnataka) to house the image of Lord Adikeshava, a form of Krishna, which he brought from a tumble-down temple in nearby Bada.[4] When Timmappa later took the name Kanakadasa, composing songs of devotion and philosophy, he would use the name appellation Kaginele Adikeshava as signature.[5]

Timmappa as a young man lived an active life in pursuit of *artha*, success and prosperity in life. Having taken over his father's duties he would go to Hampi sometimes in his official capacity as revenue collector. There he came into contact with the Vaishnava guru Vyasaraya, though at first it was from a distance.

An important theme in the traditional stories of Kanaka's life relates how he saw the Lord Chennakeshava in several dreams. Each time the holy presence, before vanishing, urged him to become a servant of God (the situation is like the one depicted in Francis Thompson's verses: 'Naught shelters thee, who wilt not shelter Me . . . Naught contents thee, who content'st not Me.')[6] Each time Timmappa resisted the call, saying he did not yet want to renounce the world, or did not yet need to follow so closely the divine taskmaster.[7] But the call kept coming back for Kanakadasa until at last he answered, and began a life of devoted service. The turning point at which it finally overwhelmed him is depicted as very dramatic indeed.

During a war in which Kanaka Nayaka was involved he was severely wounded, and he fell from his horse in battle. Losing blood, he was left for dead, but after hours of lying unconscious he recovered awareness. His rigid sense of self was defeated in this helpless state. He saw a dark form reaching for him, and heard the Voice around him 'like a bursting sea' ask 'Are you ready? Will you become my servant now?'[8] According to tradition, weary Kanaka answered: 'You again! Can't you see I'm dying?' The Voice said: 'I saved you from death, to be my dasa.' Kanaka asked: 'How is it you keep seeking me out? Isn't there anyone else to serve you?' The Voice said:

We have a special relationship. In past lives you were my dear servant, and you took this birth to serve me, too—can't you remember? Now all things fly away from you because you fly away from me . . . You drove love from yourself when you drove me away.

Kanaka wondered: 'If you saved me from the realm of death, could you put an end to my suffering as well?' The Voice responded: 'If with my touch I heal your wounds, will you believe and serve me then?' Kanaka said he would.

The name Krishna is often associated with the Sanskrit root meaning 'to draw . . . pull . . . draw towards oneself, attract', and in Kanaka Nayaka's life it is as if a 'strange attractor', a divine phantom, a kind of insistent numinous voice kept calling on him to serve, to devote his life to Krishna. The recurrent request was ignored by the stubborn rigid man until he had been tenderized into a dependent childlike state—finally the 'hound of heaven'-like force could not be resisted. According to traditional stories it was as if a divine vortex in the midst of the battlefield havoc ordered him anew and set him on a different course, signalling a new beginning. In the margins between chaos and order during the near-death experience, a renewed personality was born, committing to Krishna the inmost core of his being in a destiny–determining embarkation. The new direction and orientation was one of Vishnu-seeking urgency, feeding on the bliss of the sacred attractor, desiring more of the same. The allurement became irresistible[9] and it transformed Kanaka.

When he agreed to serve he found that he was well, undamaged by the fray. Revived and enthused, energized and fervent with fresh faith, Kanaka 'came to the Lord'; he left the destruction of the battlefield and ran to the temple, only to find it locked. Then he looked at the sky and realized it was the middle of the night. In his intense mood of spiritual desire he pounded his head against the gate and wept at being kept from his Lord. A famous song of his is connected with this part of his story, for it is said that he cried out in spontaneous prayer: 'Open the gate, allow me to serve you, O Lord, why can't you hear my pleas? When . . . when . . . when . . . why not now?'—he was singing out these words.

Stories depict the great moment when the gate burst open, bells rang in the sky, and mysterious brilliant puja lights waved spontaneously before the sacred image. This inspiring vision was an experience of the radiance of God; Kanaka Nayaka wept, his hair standing on end, his heart thrilled with love and reverent awe. The Voice asked: 'Kanaka, will you become my servant now?' and he exclaimed: 'Yes', and in his mood of surrender sang a song praising the holy feet of Lord Krishna. And Lord Krishna accepted him as a dasa and then Kanaka sang some more, according to the legends.

Kanaka had been pursued for years by the Lord directly, but he had not yet been initiated by a guru. In Hindu tradition it is usual for seekers to be in contact with a guru to attain a vision of the divine; Kanaka was rather unique in this respect.[10]

After having been inspired by the vision Kanaka went to the guru he had seen in Hampi, capital of the Vijayanagara empire. The guru's name was Vyasaraya. Emboldened by his vision, and despite the fact that he was a Kuruba and such people were normally not given initiation by royal gurus, Kanaka asked him for a *mantra*.

Vyasaraya, the famous sage, knowing nothing of Kanaka's vision, and surrounded by high caste devotees, in the habit of thinking in stereotypes about social classes, sarcastically told the chief of herdsmen: 'You can have a mantra—just repeat the buffalo mantra "Water buffalo, water buffalo . . .".'

The sincere Kanaka gladly took the insult of the high-born guru as a literal instruction, and went off to recite his 'buffalo mantra' religiously. As was the case with some other Hindu saints and ascetics whose faith was greater than that of their teachers, Kanaka's singular fervency in practice helped him develop his spirituality far beyond what anyone could have predicted, and he acquired inward strength and outward powers. His faith was such that he was able to move a big boulder which was blocking a spring.[11] (There is a place called Kanaka Jubu in Andhra Pradesh which people still associate with this incident.) When Vyasaraya saw this he knew that such intense bhakti could accomplish many things, and so he stopped fooling around with the sincere devotee. Giving Kanaka a real initiation, he welcomed him to the community of dasas. The guru's other followers were less than welcoming; some nicknaming him Kunidasa ('Dog–servant'), others Kurubadasa ('Herdsman–servant'). To show the jealous disciples their own limitations Vyasaraya is said to have given each dasa a plantain, saying 'Eat this plantain unseen by anyone'. They all scurried off to secret nooks; Kanaka alone was successful when he said, 'Mission impossible; because God sees all it's impossible to do anything "unseen". I admit my failure.'

Perhaps the most famous story told of Kanaka recounts how as a low-caste man Kanaka was not free to go inside the Krishna temple at Udipi. He stood by a chink in the wall to look in, and so intense was his fervency that he provoked the image of Krishna to turn around on the pedestal. Originally facing east, the charming statue turned to face west,. just to gaze toward this faithful servant. Temple priests left it just as it was, according to legends, as if to say 'Such is the power of devotion, and such is the greatness of the merciful Lord's grace.' A small window in the rear of the Udipi temple is called *Kanakana khindi* yet today.

Kanaka was said to have lived to the ripe age of ninety-eight. It was a belief among dasas that sage Vidura of the 'Mahabharata' story was reborn as the devotee Kanakadasa in the present age of discord, the *kali yuga*.

In addition to composing many songs, Kanakadasa is also known for his four poetic works; *Mohana Tarangini*—The River Waves of the Enchanting Krishna; *Ramadhyana Charitra*—The Story of the Ragi blessed by Rama; *Nala Charitra*—a Kannada recitative piece about Nala and Damayanti, with the theme of suffering for a worthy cause (this was his most popular work in verse, and it is the only version of this story known by most Kannada speakers) and *Hari Bhakti Sara*—one hundred devotional and philosophical verses dedicated to Krishna.

The lyrics in the following chapter are culled from Kanakadasa's many golden songs.

Notes

1. Francis Thompson, *The Hound of Heaven*, London: Phoenix, 1996.

2. Birappa was a Palegar and military chief, a shepherd leader and revenue collector, and Bacchamma was his wife in stories of Kanakadasa's life.

3. According to D. Javare Gouda, former vice-chancellor of Karnataka University, who wrote of Kanakadasa characterizing him as 'Vishvamanava', universal man, Everyman, on the occasion of the 500th year celebration of Kanakadasa. *Janapriya Kanaka Samputa: A Commemorative Volume to mark the 500th Birthday Celebrations of Sri Kanakadasa*, Bangalore: Directorate of Kannada and Culture, 1989; *Isabeku Iddu Jaisabeku: An Anthology of Kannada Kirthanas by Various Dasas*, edited by Shyamsunder Bidarakundi. Gadag: Alochana Prakashana, 1989. Also see: *Compositions*

of the Haridasas, Gouri Kuppuswamy and M. Hariharan; *Mystical Teachings of the Haridasas,* Karmarkar; *Pathways to God in Kannada Literature,* R.D. Ranade, Bombay: Bharatiya Vidya Bhavan, 1989. Sadguru Sant Keshavadas also wrote with admiration of Kanakadasa's accomplishments in *Lord Panduranga and His Minstrels,* Bombay: Bharatiya Vidya Bhavan, 1977, pp. 87–95.

4. As with many practices of Hinduism, the activities at this temple may not conform to simplistic expectations of outsiders; the *archakas*, priests offering praise there are *lingayats*, and have been for generations. Since this is a temple to a form of Vishnu, most would expect a non-Shaivite to officiate there. History's complexities are dynamical more than linear.

5. For songs which he composed in Belur, Kanaka is said to have used Velapuri Keshava as signature.

6. From Francis Thompson's 'The Hound of Heaven'.

7. In the western world St Augustine is known for his reluctance to change his life, and Francis Thompson's *The Hound of Heaven* is also an archetypal account of such a situation in western poetry.

8. Keshavadas, *Lord Panduranga and Mystic Minstrels of India,*

9. For thoughts on chaos and repentance, conversion, etc., see David Breed's forthcoming book *Theology of Chaos.*

10. Perhaps a western counterpart would be Sojourner Truth, who said that without any previous teachings, she encountered what she felt was the presence of Jesus.

11. Some say it was the 'buffalo' vehicle of Yamadharmaraja which came and moved the stone.

Kanakadasa's Songs

Adigeyanu madabekanna (KK no. 151, p. 135,
'Housework')

Ah my brother I have to do some cooking
   with the process of wisdom

I need to do some cooking, bend down the spine
   of arrogance, and scrub this house
      with the utmost enthusiasm, as my guru says

Ah brother . . .

I need to remember my guru, scrub the stain
of obsession with my body, a condition marked
by feelings of differentiation
I have to pound it with the pestle, grind it
with knowledge, sift and serve that essence
with care and polite etiquette
and wipe away and remove any blemishes
(such as the foes like anger, greed, envy and lust)

Ah brother . . .

I need to scrub the big tub of tattva
and hold to the truth, and grind the grain of love
and place the sawdust of mind in the oven
and lift up the sense of 'mine' which is burning
and wipe out its very name

Ah yes brother . . .

I must cook up the condiment of birth
heat the butter named 'body', and
have truth stand for me, be established as truth
Being the servant of Adikeshava whose abode
is the Tirumala Hills, I must eat the feast
thus prepared—the essence named bliss
and relish with zest as he tells me to

Ah my brother we've got some cooking to do
the process of wisdom will change me and you

Ajnanigala   (IIJ no. 45, p. 56)

Better to be at odds with the wise and good
than be buddy-buddy with great big fools

I'd rather beg and eat in an affluent berg
than stay in a court where the king's tight
     with food and clothes
Instead of craving for gossip and wasting your time
rather listen to dasas who remember Hari's holy name

Rather you should struggle and fight with the wise and good
than be on intimate terms with those who are fools

Instead of enjoying food donated by taunters
better to drink some water and say 'I'm on my way'
Rather than endless quarrels with in-laws
it's better to spend your days in the woods incognito

Rather you should fight hand to hand with the wise
Than hang around with fools, seeing eye to eye

Better to stay in a ruined temple than live
in a neighbourhood where envy's always on the anvil
being honed; O lotus-eyed Kaginele Adikeshava
better to accept spiritual servitude in this world
     Better to fight with the wise
        than be on intimate terms with fools

Arigadaru   (KK no. 51, p. 43)

It won't spare anybody
No matter who they are
Karma will have its way
even pestering Brahma and Shiva

Virabhairava has to go naked
Violent deities Mari and Masani
had to wander and beg;
the sun and moon are harassed by Rahu
And Shiva with his five heads
had to hold a skull in his hands

It won't give anybody a break
No matter who they may be
Karma will exact its take
Even Brahma and Shiva aren't free

Noble king Harischandra
had to eat on cremation grounds
Brahma the maker lost a head;
the guards of the eight directions
were liable to be put in jail
and ferocious Indra had eyes
placed all over his body

It won't hold back from acting
no matter who it is
Karma will cause its effect
even pestering Brahma and Shiva

The hero Duryodhana with a huge army
of Akshohinis had his thigh bones broken
out on the field of combat;
The Lotus-eyed Lord of wealth had to beg
from Bali; Dharmaraja's mother had to beg
for food to get something to eat
It won't spare anyone . . .

Dharmaraja the righteous ruler
turned into Kankabhatta; Powerful Bhima
turned into a cook. Brave Arjuna
wore dancer's bangles on his wrists, and
youthful Nakula and Sahadeva became cowherds
It won't let any off easy . . . .

Nandi, Shiva's bull has to chomp on grass
Brahma's swan must chew on lotuses
Vishnu's vehicle Garuda eats snakes
And above these karmic relationships
Adikeshava who holds the whole
is the thief of butter.

Aru hitavaru (JKS p. 12)

Don't be fooled and think 'That man wishes me well'
When tragedy hits nobody is your friend

In days gone by did the father wish the son well?
Prahlada's enraged father was violently hostile.
Shall we say the mother's always the protector?
What about Kunti, who wasn't true to Karna?
Don't be fooled . . .

Shall we say the son is servant to his parents?
Kamsa kept his own father locked up in jail.
The world says brother has affection for brother
Sugriva caused his brother Vali to be killed.
Don't be fooled . . .
You shouldn't assume all your blood relations
really wish you well; in fact, only he
who believes in the ever-merciful Adikeshava
of Kaginele will be safe and always happy

Aruballaru Hariharadigala (KK no. 166, p. 149)

Who could ever comprehend how great Shiva and Vishnu are?
That is beyond even the creator, and Indra and all others!

Shiva got the Narayanastra weapon as a boon won by penance
At that momentous time when he vanquished the three citadels
Vishnu won his powerful discus weapon, *sudarshana,*
After he had worshipped Shiva with great devotion.

Achyuta waited at the door of Bali the great *rakshasa* emperor,
Satisfied with his devotion; in a rather similar vein
Shiva gave a boon to Bana the rakshasa with hefty shoulders
and waited at his door like a close companion

So who could know the greatness of Adikeshava of Kaginele
With the celestial cosmic serpent, the Lord of Speech,
Who serves as both Shiva's ornament and Vishnu's couch,
who is responsible for creation, sustenance and destruction
In the cycles of the cosmos, and who is of the nature
Of *karana, karya* and *karma*—cause, effect and action

Badukidenu (JKS p. 81)

I am saved now I am saved
    my worldly existence is finished

I received the grace
    of Lord Padmanabha's feet

I received the prasad offering and the
    tirtha water—my tongue tasted them
    My ears received the nectar of Hari nama
    Haridasas have become my kith and kin
    The Vaishnava emblem branded in my skin
    during initiation—that's my ornament
    I am saved . . .
One hundred and one generations of
    my ancestors have won liberation, and I
    have become fit for *muktimarga.* My mind
    has become finely tuned in devotion
    to Shri Hari; Rukmini's Lord, Krishna has
    become accessible, possession of him
    is in my palm—I am saved . . .

Today my life, my very soul, is blessed
  with all fulfilments and prosperity, today
 my future life has become fruitful
 My father, Lord Adikeshava, today has been
  installed in the shrine of my heart
 This is the day all has come to fruition

 I am saved now I am saved
  my worldly existence is finished

Bagilanu (JKS p. 23)

Kindly open the door and give me your darshan

What, Narahari, didn't you hear me
 even though I've been shouting?

When you were with Lakshmi, reclining on Adisesha
 in supreme Vaikunta, the lord of elephants, Gajendra
 was in great pain—he chanted the name Adimula, Adimula
 and immediately you came and helped him
  Kindly open the door for me . . .

The villain full of rage, his sword in his hand
 yelled 'Where's your Lord—show me!' He banged the pillar
 and the child with firm determination went on remembering
 to chant your name, and you came out of the pillar
  Kindly open the door, bless me, let me gaze upon you

To the queen of Yudishthira, son of Yama, you gave
 the boon of limitless cloth, and in the time of need
 you protected Ajamila. Do you work only bankers' hours?
 O Lord fond of devotees, lotus-eyed Keshava, O please
  Kindly open the door and give me your darshan

Bandevayya (JKS p. 49)

O money-lender we have come, O Govinda Shetti

We have come, hearing about the tirtha water
 and trays full of prasad sweets, waiting for us
  so we have come

The many dishes given to devotees—'appu' sweets,
    atirasa rice, ghee, milk with sugar and cardamom,
        heaps and stacks of these rare dishes made available
        for sale by you, Govinda Merchant—a variety of
    sweet dishes for the 56 regions of this land
O money-lender . . .

You brought a broken red earth jar, you pounded it
        to powder for vermilion marks, and you're offering
    that for sale, and from whatever surplus rice there is
    you make a profit to buy your ornaments, like a miser
O money lender . . .

You're living in Seshagiri, and you're known all over
        the country as 'Shetti'. You're receiving interest
    on every single penny. You're known as Adikeshava
        Tirupati Tima Shetti
O money-lender we have come, O Govinda Shetti!

    Bhajisi badukelo   (BR p. 596)

    Listen, people, get a life
        worshipping with all your heart
            the Lord Shri Hari—
    Brahma, Indra and the other gods
        have worshipped his feet
            from the very beginning

    The feet which pressed down Bali
        in answer to Indra's prayer,
        the foot which killed Kaku Shakatashura
        the wheel-demon with one kick,
    the foot which conquered Shiva
        and received his worship,
        the feet from which Ganga,
            the world-purifier flowed—Listen

The foot which turned the woman
who'd been transformed to a stone
into a beautiful woman again,
the feet which walked on earth
to save Arjuna, and the feet which
caused the downfall of the Kauravas
the feet which danced on the mighty
serpent Kalinga, taming him—Listen

The feet carried by Garuda and Sesha
the feet which measured the universe
by taking two steps, the feet which Lakshmi
places on her lap and venerates
the feet of the great Lord
Adikeshava of Kaginele—Listen, people
get a life, worshipping with all your hearts
the Lord Shri Hari . . .

Bombeyatavanadiside (KK no. 74, p. 63)

While Brahma and Shiva and other deities observed
you staged the *Mahabharata* puppet show

You built the royal road called Kurukshetra
and erected the fivefold curtain of maya
You used earthly kings as human characters, and
held the horses' reins of Arjuna's chariot
you staged the whole *Mahabharata* drama; while Brahma . . .

Narada is the singer, Shiva accompanies him
and Badaranya narrates the tale.
Death who relieves earth of her burdens
makes the people laugh, generates *hasyarasa,* so
with the essence of scripture praising your glory
you played the game, *Mahabharata* puppet epic; while Brahma . . .

Collecting the fierce armies of eighteen Akshohinis
having them dance their violent battles eighteen days
saving only five, relieving the earth of her burden
fulfilling the bowl Shiva carries with joyous satisfaction
You put on the *Mahabharata* puppet show; while Brahma . . .

Glorifying the epic as the world's fifth Veda
making the divine assembly of Indra happy
Consoling Janamejaya who listened to the story
known as the string-puller of the whole drama
You played the puppet game called the *Mahabharata*; while Brahma . . .

Thus circulating through different realms
and displaying many playful manifestations
delightfully protecting the noble family of Bharata
O Adikeshava of Kaginele, praised by Vedanta
you staged the big puppet play *Mahabharata*;

> While Brahma, Shiva and others observed the display
> you staged the whole *Mahabharata* puppet play

Dasadasara (JKS p.13)

I'm the son of a servant woman—my mother served
    the servants of the servants of the Lord

I'm the son of a *dasi* at the house of Ranga
    The Lord celebrated with the *sahasranama*
        (the thousand names of God)

I'm just a foolish dasa of Shankudas's home
    And I happen to be the doorkeeper dasa
    serving the devotees who worship God
        I'm the son of a servant . . .

I'm the lowly poet in the house
    of the master poet Kalidasa
The weeping dasa in the house of Shiva's friend Vishnu
I'm the dasa you'll find at the feet
    of other dasas
I'm the son of a servant . . .

I'm the lowest of the low of all the houses
    of the dasas, the holiya or pariah
    in the house of worshippers
    devoted to you Adikeshava at Kaginele
    O God, my Krishna protect me!
        I'm the servant of a servant woman
            my mother served
        the servants of the servants of the Lord

Dasanagabeku sadashivana (KK no. 4, p.4)

Be a servant of Sadashiva
really you ought to be a servant
killing off the fivefold tortures
refusing to let your mind lose itself to desires
Knowing God is omnipresent in the cosmos
and crossing the hard border of delusion
    you know you really ought to
    be a servant of Sadashiva

Knowing the body is temporary
envision Lord Shiva in your heart
and know the greatness of his supreme magic
and give up attachment to degrading samsara
    you know you really ought to
    be a servant of Sadashiva

And you ought to know the Indivisible
radiating in the six chakras
and three strands of nature
Become the servant of Adikeshava of Kaginele
who is beyond the six, the three, the sixteen

Dhareya bhogavanu * (KK no. 213, pp. 201–2)

Be careful, man, don't get so engrossed
in your worldly pleasures
that you bring ruin to yourself—Listen—
worldly pleasures pass just like a dream.

Once a beggar sleeping in an old pilgrim shelter
just outside of town
had a dream. In it a ruler of a certain kingdom
died without leaving a son to succeed him. Be careful . . .

So an elephant was given a garland and was allowed
to wander; whomever the elephant placed
the garland upon would be crowned the next king
The beggar saw the elephant garlanding him
and was joyous in mind, thinking the he'd been made king
    Be careful, man . . .

*Sometimes attributed to Muppina Shadakshari

When the beggar was consecrated king, the nayakas
offered him tribute, and he ruled the kingdom well
in his dreams. He was joyous in his mind at the queen
by his side and soon they were the parents of children
girls and boys—watch out! Don't get lost in the
worldly joys you see, or you'll ruin yourself—
　　Listen! Worldly pleasures pass just like a dream

While in his royal court with children playing
on his lap, he watched his fourfold army with enjoyment
and soon he saw his daughters grow up, and
eagerly he planned their futures, speaking
with his ministers about arrangements for marriage
　　Be careful, man!

He requested the ministers to seek out the right grooms
and they went out and came back saying 'O king
we have found just the right grooms!' The king
commanded them to build a great hall for the weddings
and there they held the celebration with utmost pomp
and all the nearby rulers were grateful to be invited
　　Watch out!

Puffed up with pride at his own wealth and wife
arrogant to have such children and such a kingdom
the beggar was overjoyed. In the meanwhile
a growing number of foes got together and stormed
the palace in his dream. And his eyes went wide
　　with terror—watch out!

The beggar realized that the shining wealth
had all been lost, and he was too self-conscious to beg
anymore. O listen—wealth is just like a dream—
knowing this if you worship Adikeshava with pure love
he will give you bliss which never ends, so
　　Watch out—don't get so engrossed
　　in your worldly pleasures to such an extreme
　　that you bring ruin to yourself—Listen—
　　worldly pleasures all pass just like a dream.

Eke nadugide (KK no. 127, p. 114)

O lovely lady Mother Earth, Queen of the Lord
Supremely auspicious one, why did you tremble
in the middle of the night?

Did you shake with wrath at half-baked folk
who despise their own elders and gurus
who don't live up to their vows, and
won't fall at the feet of the Lord? Are you
showing they won't get special treatment—
that they will perish when trees fall on them?

O lovely lady Mother Earth, Queen of the Lord
Supremely auspicious one, why did you tremble
in the middle of the night?

Did you rumble unable to take it any more—
the howling human curs who push their own parents around?
Did you quake with the weight of most disgusting humans
who will give no credit to relatives though it is due?
    O lovely lady . . .

Did you shake when you couldn't take the weight
of the pariahs who don't remember the Lord
who rid the world of Mura in the Kali yuga,
never poring over inspiring scripture
but always just gawking at the girls?
    O lovely lady . . .

O guru please hear me—Adikeshava of Tirumala hills
the one who likes gold, stopped this trembling
even though villains increase on earth, and
some have learned to write degenerate poetry . . .
    O lovely lady . . . . Why did you tremble at midnight?

Ellaru maduvudu   (JKS p. 17)

The things people do for their bellies! for a yard of cloth
    and a scrap of dough!

We read scriptures, then we preach—for the sake of the
    belly and a little bit of cloth!

Valiant soldiers march, swords and shields in hand, off to
  kill the enemy—for what?
   the belly and a bit of cloth

Traders open shops, give quick sales pitches, take such pains
  to earn money—
   for the belly and a bit of cloth

The farmer yokes the necks of bullocks, ploughs the furrows,
  works his land—for what
  for his belly and a little cloth

If a man speaks honey-sweetly he will entice everyone—the
  fool just barks lies—then he enjoys
  filling his belly and wrapping himself in cloth

Pounding rice with a mortar, carrying logs for fuel,
  all your endless travails
  are for belly and cloth to wear

Accompanied by musicians with cymbals, tambura, shruti and
  such, dancing like a seductive hooker
  all for belly and cloth

Assuming various forms—sannyasin, mendicant, wrestler,
  stubborn boor
  all for the sake of belly, cloth and dough

Hiding in a flowing stream, holding a stone and rod in your
  hand, ambushing and robbing
  all for the sake of belly and cloth

Only one thing is untainted: meditating with perfect focus
  on exalted Lord Adikeshava Kaginele
   that finds liberation, bliss
  The rest is all just things folks do for their bellies,
   for a yard of cloth, for a mere scrap of dough

Enandu kondare (JKS p. 8)

How shall I praise you, and what shall I say about you
  O Lord, what do I know about the greatness of your lila

You're Hari, Mukunda, I'm a worm with a human form
  You're the supreme being, I'm an ordinary person
  You're the rider of Garuda, I'm a foolish sinner
  You're the ultimate light, I'm just a poor beggar—How . . .

Merciful Lord you are the one who reclines on the ocean
  I am short-tempered, lustful, leading a sinful life
  You, O beautiful person, are omnipresent in six or seven
  Worlds. I'm a wretched man who accuses you off and on. How . . .

You are fully present in each blade of grass, and inside
  the smallest atoms. I indulge in bad acts all the time.
  You're Vaikuntapati who created the creator Brahma
  I'm just like a doll with an ephemeral existence . . . How . . .

You're *anandamurti*, form of bliss who sprang from the pillar
  I'm a worldly man without any faith. You are the friend
  of Akrura who is fond of Ambaresha. I'm a hypocrite who
  does pretentious deeds. You are the absolute, invincible.

You're Venkatesha living in Tirupati, I live by remembering
  your holy name. You're the one who is known by many titles
  I'm the one who has come seeking refuge from you
  You are Shri Adikeshava of Kaginele, what do I know of you

How shall I praise you, and what shall I say about you
  Lord, what do I know about the vastness of your lila

Enna kanda halliya Hanuma (KK no. 12, p. 9)

Hey little kid, village Hanuman,
is Lakshmana the divine hero alright?

In days gone by Rama relished ghee
and the five nectars
but now he eats wild roots.
In those days he chewed betel-nut,
fragrant and tasty; now he eats
black dew from the cinders.
Then he slept on soft bedding and pillows;
now he's stretched out on a straw bed

So is Raghava, the Lord of Lady Prosperity alright?
Hey little kid, village Hanuman,
is divine hero Lakshmana well?

In those days he wore the finest of clothes;
now he keeps covered with bark and rough fibres.
Then he had a flower-sweet fresh head of hair;
now his locks are all matted. Then
he wore perfume and musk; now he smears himself
with earth's dust—is Rama doing alright

Hey little kid, village Hanuman,
Is Lakshmana the divine hero alright?

Once he went around in golden chariots
shaded by royal parasols,
with attendants waving the chowries;
now he walks barefoot in the blazing sun
O Adikeshava served by Sanaka and other sages
Are Hanuman and Rama alright? Hey

Little kid—village Hanuman
Is Lakshmana the divine hero alright?

Enu illada dinada (KK no. 36, p. 30)

Life lasts only a couple of days
Nobody knows what it means.

Be wise and be kind
be good, do acts of charity.

Feed the hungry who come to you
feed the child with butter and milk
give to the worthy arable land
don't lie to people you converse with

Samsara lasts a couple of days
but it doesn't really add up to anything
Wise to this open your heart
do good, and be gracious and giving

Don't steal just to eke out a living
don't crookedly sit around unemployed
In an assembly don't try being sneaky
don't gloat saying I have lots of gold'

Worldly life is a two-day affair
ultimately as empty as air . . .

Don't speak ill when you get power
and don't strut selfishly when riches come
be happy, take refuge at the feet
of the truly rich Lord Adikeshava

Life is only a two-day affair
The meaning of which is never too clear
Enlightened to the way things are
better be generous and give with care

Huva karuvara (JKS p. 19)

Me, I bring grass to the house of my betters
  who offer their flowers to our Lord

Deva, Chinmaya, Lord you protect me
  in every conceivable way

I've been a dasa in all my six or seven previous lives
  I've joined the service of your devotees, O Narasimha
Show compassion to me, please dry up the ocean of my sins.
  I bring grass to the house of my betters
  who offer their flowers to our Lord . . .

Lord Ranganatha I'm your humble servant, have it announced
  With attention-getting drumbeats in public thoroughfares.
Father of Ganga, kindly protect me; take pity on your
  devotees; I touch your feet. Without disturbing your order
    of things, please accept me among your devotees
  I bring grass to those who offer flowers . . .

Whatever I may do I happen to be your soldier
  I'm the son of a dasa by birth, orphan of a born dasa
Lord of the universe Keshava Kaginele, don't let go
  Of my hand—I swear by the name of Haridasas
  I bring grass to the house of my betters
  who offer their flowers to our Lord

Hyange ni dasanadi (IIJ no. 31)

How, O animal, did you become a dasa?

Like a monkey suffering humiliations
    in this material world
    what turned you into a dasa, O creature?

You couldn't give up greed for more
    though you had accumulated so much wealth
you became the object of accusations
    you also rolled around in filth—how, O animal
        did you become a dasa?

'This body is mine' you boldly claimed
    and you also seemed to really believe
'My son and wife, come whatever may,
    will always be there to take care of me'—how,
        O animal, did you become a dasa?

Are the emissaries of Yama, Lord of Death,
    kindhearted folks? O hypocrite you blew it
wasting all sorts of time and breath
    and lost your chance, now you're ruined

You begged from lowly people to fill your gut
    you put away your pride and self-respect
what wouldn't you do for self-aggrandizement
    how low can you go humiliating yourself?

Denigrating elders you built yourself up
    calling yourself a Haridasa most devout
you paraded up all the main streets in town
    went down the byways begging for a hand-out

You tied bells to jingle down around your ankles
    went around clapping the cymbals in your hands
you made an imposing impression pretending
    praising God's excellences was your sole intent

You danced around cavorting before an image
    of the supreme Lord, then bowed down at the feet
of good people, without seeking true attainment
    what have you won you contemptible creep?

You went around approaching perfect strangers
　　wheedling and whining with folded hands, kept
begging for scraps of food, a mean sort of person
　　without even an ounce of decent self-respect

However long you live, death is bound to come
　　but you have lived only for little copper coins
and for worldly things, you've made no effort
　　to swim across the ocean, to reach the other shore

Without worshipping continuously the Lord
　　inside your own body, he whose bright face
is the very incarnation of auspiciousness
　　without contemplating his feet in your mind

The river has run dry—water's become scarce
　　without cultivating the land by doing hard work
without planting the right seeds do you expect
　　a good crop to grow just because you loudly weep?

Your passionate lust just grew and grew, and you
　　never lost your greed for golden ornaments
you kept offering tulasi leaves to Shri Ranga
　　while clinging tight to everything mundane

Now you have the great worry of darkness
　　all around you; on top of that dimness
you're under the illusion of terrible fear
　　without finding the way to reach Lord Vishnu

After putting on a big act for the sake
　　of outer appearances, and accumulating loads
of sin inside yourself, if now you begin to pine
　　for support who is going to be there for you?

Without praising or appreciating the excellences
　　of Lord Vishnu, rider of Garuda, you spend your days
begging for rice; how peculiar your behaviour is!
　　It gives us a reason to feel baffled and amazed

Without remembering Kaginele Adikeshava
　　Without worshipping him, the supreme Lord
who reclines on the world stage and enjoys
　　without feeling great devotion to the Lord

How, O animal, did you ever become a dasa?

Ishtudina (JKS p. 20)

I used to think and say 'Vaikuntha is far far away'
    Then I saw with my own two eyes
        The Lord of the universe
           reclining Ranga Sai

First I lost eight bad habits, including pride
and I got rid of seven different kinds of vice.
I subdued the five senses and I put down Mischievous Mind.
So I'm allowed to come to you as your servant, O Ranga
    I used to think and say Vaikuntha is far away . . .

Surrounded by the green forest, and surrounded by the garden,
surrounded by deep lakes, surrounded by golden domes,
O Ranga Sai you are resplendent
    I used to think 'Vaikuntha is far' but then I saw . . .

I saw the roofbeams made of Vajravaidurya—diamonds and
precious stones, I saw the magnificent gate shining like the sun,
I saw old beings who are ageless, O destroyer of evil people,
O Shri Ranga Sai—I used to think Vaikuntha far . . .

I saw groups of *apsaras* like Urvasi and Rambai clustered,
saw Narada with his tambura; I saw many Rudras
emerging from the lotus, O Ranga Sai, father of Manmatha . . .
    I used to think Vaikuntha is far away, then I saw . . .

I saw the handsome form reclining on the serpent coil,
I saw Shiva who is the pride and gem of the enjoyers
I saw the assembly of the *bhagavatars*, and I saw you,
O Ranga Sai, Lord Kaginele Adikeshava
    I used to think and say 'Vaikuntha is far away'
        then I saw with my own two eyes
           The reclining Ranga Sai
           Lord of the universe

Japava madidarenu (KK no. 105, p. 93)

So what if you say a mantra and do austerities?
If you go astray with perversity and hypocrisies?

So what if believers in the doctrine of difference
who engage in debates, but don't know the supreme teacher
wander restlessly here there everywhere, recite aloud
Vedas and Shastras, but fail to know the right way? So what . . .

So what if they fail to do good deeds and give gifts,
their words will be about as effective as a reservoir
of water in a forest that is withering up.
They earn wealth and nice clothes for wives and kids
and then at last they are snared in Yama's helpers' net
    So what if they chant their mantra and perform austerities?

O mind of mine, don't be in such a turmoil, don't
get so anxious and tired out, waking up in the dark
as cold rain falls, immersing yourself in the river
saying your mantra and doing tapas—Remember to focus
on lotus-eyed Adikeshava, because
    what does it matter if you chant and do tapas
    if in perverse hypocrisies you get yourself lost?

Kande na tandatandada   (JKS p. 45)

I saw the gods assembled in the heavens
    I saw the mighty foe
        fierce and valiant Narasimha

I heard the cracking of lightning, rumbling in the pillar
    and saw sparks fly out. The assembled onlookers
    were all stunned—their hips shook, and they held
    the tops of their heads and they were terrified
        I saw the gods assembled in the heavens . . .

The Lord held the enemy's chest and tore open his abdomen
    easily he pierced it, ripped off the skin this way and that
    he tore out veins and bones, the blood was spurting forth
    and he garlanded himself with the foe's intestines
        I saw the gods . . .

Townspeople shrieked in shock, gods tossed a rain of flowers
    musical instruments played. 'We take refuge in you, Hari',
    they chanted; child Prahlada glowed jubilantly, praising
    the name of the mericful Lord Adikeshava of Kaginele
I saw the gods assembled in the heavens
    I saw the mighty foe
        fierce and valiant Narasimha

Kattava (JKS p. 50)

Even if you go to all sorts of trouble
    still you will not win
even if you're worried sick, you won't win
unless it's written as fate on your forehead
    O wretched lost man you will not win.

Even if you study hard an excess of books
Even if your best friend's a rich man
And if you are cunning as a fox
and if you pine and pout for this and that
    Even if you take immense pains you won't get it
    generate anxieties, you still won't win
    unless this fate is written on your forehead
    don't you get it, lost man, you cannot win

Even if you carry tales and tell them—no
Even if you stab someone in the back,
    acting like the hardest rogue
Even if you laugh your head off at others, you won't—
Even if . . .

Even if you're born brave or super wise
It is impossible, might as well forget it
Even if you move massive mountains, only if
Lord of the Universe Keshava gives it, then you get it

Kelirai shivasharanaru (KK no. 203, p. 185)

I'm afraid to say it to you, O Shivasharanas,
    you devotees surrendered to Shiva,
but please hear me out—you votaries
of the Lord with an eye on his forehead,
please investigate this issue for yourselves:

Though there are already three lingas obviously
displayed in a person's own being
foolish ritualists go out and buy yet another linga
they hold it on their palms, make flower and water offerings
and then tell their minds: 'There, now I've worshipped Shiva!'

I'm almost afraid to say this, O Shivasharanas
but please listen to me—you devotees
of the Lord with an eye on his forehead
look into it and see what you think for yourselves

Though the linga is already present, pervading oneself
these bound selves play around with outward lingas
Can drunken fools without the real experience
of the Self become devotees of Shiva? I'm afraid to say it . . .

If *nagalinga* is at play in one's very self
then why hunt around for other kinds of lingas?
Unless you realize he's none other than Adikeshava
of Kaginele, who has the *naga* for his couch
you run around in vain trying to find him

I hesitate to say it O Shivasharanas
but please hear me out—you devotees
of the Lord with an eye on his forehead ·
investigate this issue for yourselves

Kula kula kulavendu (JKS p. 26)

Don't break your clan into warring factions
    do you know how your clan began?

Everyone who was ever born came through the same passage
    from the womb they pass through the vagina
    There is no earth that has not been stepped on by humans
    Almost nothing exists that hasn't been cooked and eaten.
    There is no higher or lower—remember the Lord—
    and don't break up your clan into fighting factions

Isn't the water the mother of all communities?
    Do you know the origin of the community of water?
    Like a water bubble the human body is ephemeral.
    Try to find the real abode, offer your praise
        chant and meditate, O mortal,
        and don't break your clan into warring factions
        do you even understand how your clan began . . .

Hari is the highest of all, Hari is everyone's Lord
    Everything is full of Hari; the one who knows this
    and contemplates the lotus feet of Kaginele Adikeshava
    —he alone is born in an 'upper caste'
        don't break up your community into
        clashing factions—do you know how your clan began

> *Kula kula kulavennu* (JKS p. 25)
>
> People often speak of 'Our community'
> but to what community do they belong who
> are ever blissful knowing eternal truth?
>
> Though the lotus is rooted in the mud
> was it not offered to Lord Vishnu?
> Milk comes from the flesh of the cow
> but is it not enjoyed by Brahmins?
>
> People talk so much about 'Our community'
> but to which community do they belong who
> are ever blissful knowing eternal truth?
>
> The kasturi musk fragrance is a secretion
> from the impure navel of an animal, and yet
> don't Brahmins apply it to their foreheads?
> How does that apply to their community?

People always talk about 'Our community . . .'

Lord Narayana from his birth belongs
to which community? And also Lord Shiva—
to which community does he belong?
Can you tell us the answer to the riddle?

People talk and talk of 'Our community . . .'

The soul of life belongs to what clan?
Kindly tell me what is the caste
of the senses perceiving the truth—
The *tattva indriyas*—I want to hear your view

People talk so much about 'Our community . . .'

When Lord Adikeshava is pleased with us—
only then will we belong to a community
Dwelling in Lord Keshava, then we have caste
Before that, what use is talk of community

People have a lot to say about 'Our community'
but to what community do they belong who
are blissful knowing eternal truth?
The soul of life belongs to which clan?

Maganinda gatiyunte (KK no. 76, p. 66)

Can you really get release by having a son
Without deep search into Vedic meaning?

If people who've parched the deep urges
Through endless blissful immersion in the Supreme
Beyond the three strands of nature—
if they are sonless so what

If male and female attracted to each other by lust
couple and their sperm and blood come together
so the lump of flesh drops to earth
in accord with past karma—can this
lump then really save them and please the ancestors

Can you really get release by having a son
Without deep search into Vedic meaning?

Can you get release with a son who turns out
to be hideous, a slacker at doing his dharma,
a guru-abuser, nasty to elders and pious folk
who fools around with people from other castes
and with women, and in so doing shoves
his forefathers down into hell?

Can you really get release by having a son
Without deep search into Vedic meaning?

Truthfulness is a good son; serenity is another;
stopping negative tendencies is yet another son,
And peace of mind is also a fine son.
When you have four noble sons like these
so what if you don't have a biological one

Can you really obtain release through offspring
Without deep searching into Vedic meaning?

The made-up scripture which proclaims
that a man without a son has no refuge
is meant for worldly people—but is there not
release in this world for the one
who worships Adikeshava of Kaginele,
Lord of the universe—

Can you really get release by having a son
Without deep search into Vedic meaning?

Mumana   (IIJ no. 48, p. 59)

Will intelligent folk lodge in the father-in-law's house?

We might catch a serpent, might give up life
We might swallow bitter fire—but would it be wise
to stay in the father-in-law's house? Better we should die
    with self-respect
Will intelligent folk lodge in the father-in-law's house?

Each month interactions worsen, cumbersome, and more shameful
First month, the way you're treated is alright
Then they start trying to run your life with their advice
Then more and more often their strong words bite
O those who are householders know what I mean alright

Will intelligent folk lodge in the father-in-law's house?

No, this way of life, this eating arrangement
Cannot be good for the son-in-law—better to beg for alms
If you have no dignity, no vestige of self-respect
Become the servant of Shripati then worship Kaginele Adikeshava

Will intelligent folk ever lodge in the father-in-law's house?

Mutta bandide (JKS p. 86)

A precious pearl has come to our lane
    Listen, people, listen
Tie up this pearl in the corner of your sari
    If you have devotion

This lustrous pearl, this lotus-eyed pearl
    It destroys a mountain of sin
      The sacred pearl with the name Bala Rama
        brother of Krishna
      The pearl protects those who love and worship
        cutting away all sins
A precious pearl has come to our lane
    Listen, people, listen

This pearl strikes terror in the men
      who are usually fearless
    This pearl wipes out for good
      all varieties of sins
    This pearl enshrined in the heart
      of Sanjivaraya
    This pearl which Brahma and other gods
      carry on their heads
A precious pearl has come . . .

This pearl you can string together with
      the cord of spiritual knowledge
    This pearl shining in the minds of the enlightened
    This pearl which befits the mind
      of Lord Madhvacharya
    This pearl called the treasure of Lakshmi
      Adikeshava of Kaginele
A precious pearl has arrived in our lane
    listen, people, listen to me
If you have devotion you will be able
    to tie this pearl in the corner of your sari

Nandinda   (JKS p. 74, 'Whose fault?')

I've come to this earth just because of you
   So why hold me responsible?
   O God, did I emerge from myself?

O God, whose is the folly, yours or mine?

For nine months in my mother's womb
   you were my protector, and when
   I was reluctant to leave her womb
   Vishnu, didn't you goad me out then? I've come . . .

The guide who is helping the blind man along
   puts a stick in his hand to assist him
   If then he leads him into a deep pit
   Leader or blind man—whose mistake was it? I've come . . .

The mother stops fondling her child;
   the child toddles to the well, peeping down . . .
   If the mother fails to rush up and grab it
   Who is to blame—the mother or the kid? I've come . . .
The burden is yours, so is the complaint
   Wife, kids, body, mind—all are yours, Lord;
   You immerse me in water, you dip me in milk
   I've surrendered all so why demand a toll from me?
      I've come . . .

Is it a case of justice or injustice?
   Whose folly is this, who will tell me?
   Vishnu Kaginele Adikeshava, the love-god's father,
   Protect me, pay no mind to my foibles, O Lord.

I've come to this earth just because of you
   so why hold me responsible?
      O God did I emerge from myself?

Nannavva kalla bide (KK no. 229, p. 213)

Mama let me use the stone a while
so I can pound and clean this cloth completely

The *dhotra* cloth has to be made ready for the grace
of the divine child Keshava
so all the sins I did will be rinsed away

The dhotra worn so long is faded
from the five demons of the mind
I have to beat it hard against the stone
and rinse it in the water so the sins and woes will flow

Mama move over, let me use the flat stone
so I can smack and whack all the dirt from this cloth

I have to immerse myself in the Veda and free myself
from the divisions which the mind causes. I must
come to realize deeply with great fervour
and firm up my conviction so my anger
and the results of my sinful acts will wash out

Mama let me use that flat stone awhile
So I can pound clean this cloth completely

I've got to become a guardsman,
holding a sceptre in service to the divine child Keshava
of Velapura (Beluru village) without delay—right away
O mother with dark blue hair
move aside and let me use the stone

Mama let me use the stone awhile
so I can pound and clean this cloth completely

Narayana emba namada (JKS p. 76)

The seed is 'Narayana'
    plant it on your tongue
        after drawing furrows in it

You must use your heart like a field
Use the body as your plough
For the two bullocks yoke breath and energy
Make wisdom (jnana) the yoke
and the rope to tie the bullocks' neck
Take the grain (*dhanya*) called mind
and plant your crop—the seed is 'Narayana' . . .

Pull with care the weeds of lust and rage
remove the brush of envy and pride
put up a scarecrow of the five senses
to drive away the pests of temptation
and scare off birds of frailty
    The seed is 'Narayana'
        plant it on your tongue
            after drawing furrows in it

Measure your whole life out
carefully in piles of grain,
forming two portions—dusk and dawn
If you do all this with utmost care
and always remember Kaginele Adikeshava
you will lead a happy life
    The seed is 'Narayana'
draw furrows in your tongue
    and then plant it
        and raise a good crop

Navu kurubaru nannu (JKS p. 30)

We are the Kuruba shepherd folk,
our God is valiant Birayya
That whole herd of sheep, humanity,
is protected by Grandpa Aja

There are eight well-fed rams and
the goat named 'Drishtijivatma'
and there's a sacrificial sheep called
'Famous throughout the cosmos'
—our grandfather goads these animals
with his stick and he ties them up.
    We are the Kuruba shepherd folk . . .

Our grandfather takes care of
the sheep-herding watchdogs named
Veda, Shastra and Purana as they
work amidst the various herds.
After we have lost our way,
crying out, famished, thirsty,
finally we just fall down prostrate,
and our grandfather takes care of us,
giving us *umbali* rice gruel water
    We are the Kuruba . . .

Little lambs named 'Enlightenment'
frisk about gambolling in the herd,
and when the herds grow absent-minded
a wolf named Death sneaks in,
and Death blocks their way in the dark,
a marauder attacking them mercilessly,
and even though grandpa knows
all about this he seems to look
the other way, not seeing what's happening . . .
    We are the Kuruba . . .

There is no beginning to birth,
no end to death after death,
but our grandpa knows the way
beyond birth and death. Our grandpa
prepares so much rice gruel water
for so many different creatures
and our grandfather feeds us all
so much our bellies swell quite full . . . .
    We are the Kuruba . . .

Grandfather is the chief of the Kali yuga,
he's the companion along the way,
and he is the chief minister (mantri),.
he is also the son, and he has forgotten
about many Kali yugas already.
After pleasing the lotus-eyed Kaginele
Adikeshava, this mad shepherd
is the one who is worshipping him . . .
    We are the Kuruba . . . .

Ni vayiyilaga (JKS p. 24, 'Breath of my breath:
A meditation on mutuality')

Are you inside illusion or is illusion inside you?

Are you inside the body or is the body inside you?

Is the open space in the house, or
  is the house in the open space, or
    are both in the eyes beholding them?
  Is the eye inside the buddhi, or
  is the buddhi inside the eye, or
    are both inside you Lord Hari

Is the sweetness in the sugar, or
  is the sugar in the sweetness, or
    are both on the tasting tongue?
  Is the tongue inside the mind, or
  the mind inside the tongue, or
    are both inside you Lord Hari?

Is the fragrance in the flower, or
  is the flower in the fragrance, or
    are both inside the sense of smell?
  Unique Lord Keshava of Kaginele,
  life-breath is not just deep within me
    it is deep within you too.

Prachina karmavada (KK no. 71, p. 60)

Man O man if past acts don't stop
why worry and wear yourself out?

Hari couldn't lovingly relieve
Hanuman of wearing his loincloth
when he flew to Lanka, and helped build
the bridge and helped kill Ravana
and rescued Sita, handing her over to Rama

Man O man if past acts don't stop
why worry and wear yourself out?

The chariot of the sun had to traverse
the universe with a single wheel and
seven horses hitched; driver Aruna
who roamed all around the cosmos
was deprived of his feet by Lord Hari

Man O man if past acts don't stop
why worry and wear yourself out?

Adikeshava who has a thousand names
would not straighten Garuda's curved beak
—Garuda, his own vehicle, transporting
the Lord tirelessly on his shoulders
throughout the vast skyway. So see

Man O man if your karma won't quit
why worry and wear yourself out over it?

Ramanujare namo namo (BKP no. 33, p. 42)

O Ramanuja, incarnation of Lakshmana in person
again and again I offer my regards to you

O Master, holding the sacred staff, wrapped in ochre
so agreeable looking with claypaste marks on your forehead
with your long tuft of hair, wearing the sacred thread
with the twelve paste markings *pundrams* on your body
I offer my regards to you

O certain unfailing refuge of all who remember
the holy form of the Lord with the lotus stemming
from his navel, who vanquished *charvakas* (materialists)
and established the Vedic tradition,
O Pranava embodied my regards to you

O male bee hovering humming at the lotus feet of Keshava
Conqueror of heretics, Ornament of great teachers,
O incarnation of Sesha worshipped by greatest sages
O embodiment of Adikeshava—again and again
I offer my worshipful regards to you
O Ramanuja, Incarnation of Lakshmana in person
I offer my regards to you again and again

Sadhu sajjana satyagunakidirunte   (KK no. 73, p. 62)

What could prevail against folks with devotion
who steadily hold fast to truth?
Who is as great as Adikeshava?

For those who hold on to truth
can there be any fear of death?
For those without mental purification
can there be the other world?
For someone who loves his body too much
will there be liberation?
Is there any higher bhakti than knowing
the spiritual Self (*Atmanivedana*)? What could prevail . . .

What is of greater value
than begetting a son?
Can someone without intelligence
have any skill?
What service is higher
than a wife serving her husband?
Can someone be wealthy
if he doesn't have a wife? What could prevail . . .

Who is the untouchable
if not the mean miser?
Is there any charity on a par
with the gift of food?
Can a yogi who has mastered
his appetites know any fear?
Is a king who is a slave
to vices really happy? What could prevail . . .

Can there be anyone lower
than the one without wealth?
Do morals exist for hypocrites
cheating themselves?
Can one with the wisdom to honour
worthy souls ever be poor?
Will someone who is one of the humble
suffer humiliation? What could prevail . . .

What highest home exists for one
without devotion to Hari?
Is there any virtue beyond
pure harmonious balance?
What service could be greater
than service to the guru?
Is there any God other
than Adikeshava the generous? What could prevail . . .

Sahaja (IIJ no. 49, p. 60)

This statement is true—this is no lie

I'm giving now to you true words of good advice

The one who recites Vedas, Puranas and Shastras is a *Shudra*;
    The one who welcomes and honours guests is a miser;
He who observes the daily rites and prayers is a sinner;
    The wife who obeys her husband's wishes is a reprobate

This statement is true, it is no lie
    I'm giving you now true words, sound advice

One who refrains from charity is a religious person;
    The yogi is a man who cultivates egotistical pride;
He is a wise man who with violence hurts animals
    One who corrupts the poor but honest is a virtuous man

This word I give you is true—no lie
    I'm offering truth and good advice

He who builds waterworks for the commonweal is a traitor
    He who denigrates elders and gurus is a righteous man
He who remembers always the holy lotus feet of
    Kaginele Adikeshava is obviously an indiscreet fool

This statement is true—it is no lie
    I'm giving now to you true words of good advice

Saku saku (JKS p. 53)

Enough, enough of this serving fellow humans, O Ranga
    enough, enough, I'm weary of serving other people

Lord of the universe, Rangaraya, I want the worship
    of your holy feet

Rising early in the morning, hurrying somewhere
    scurrying, anticipating the whims of somebody,
    like a slave I run so many errands each day,
    but always I return home empty-handed
        Enough, enough of this serving fellow humans . . .

I left off ablutions, religious rites, the observance
    of silence, and daily sandhya prayers, became pitiable
    and low. I went to bad people, spent days like a dog.
    In my mind I boiled, harbouring all those evil greeds;
    happiness? I never found enough to fill up a sesame seed!
        Enough! Enough already! all this work for people . . .

Stuck like a fly fluttering hopelessly in a honeypot
    because of my hungers—O Vishnu—I too
    have my mouth wide open with greed—I'm stuck!
    Free me from the fetters of this bondage
    kindly give me the company of your devotees
    O Adikeshava of Kaginele, Lord of Venkatadri
    Madhava, Rangaraya!
        Enough! Too much! I've had about all I can handle
        Free me, O Ranga, I'm sick of serving other people
        I want to serve the Lord of the universe's holy feet

Satyavantara (JKS p. 35)

When you have the fine companionship
    of people who are truthful
Why do you feel the need to go far
    for ritually auspicious holy water
Why should you be worried when
    you've become a man of constant wisdom

Why do you crave this wealth you've built up
    When you don't even enjoy it
Unless you share it with others what's the use?
Why become a man who lives *sans* self-respect
Why live for a whole century without enlightenment
After you've given up your wife's company
Why do you still crave sensual pleasures?
        When you have such fine companionship
            of people who are true . . .
        What further good can seeking far-off
        tirtha water do for you

Why father children who arrogantly defy you?
Why would you want food sloppily
    plopped on your plate with no love?
Why keep an unruly guard who can't behave
    with proper manners?
What kind of man accepts defeat
    at the hands of a woman, fearing her?
        and who respects such a man?
        When you have the fine companionship
            of people who are true
        What further good can seeking far-off
            tirtha water do for you

Why do you want a wife who can't anticipate
    the needs of her husband?
Is there any good in serving a master who
    doesn't treat you with respect?
If I've given something away, and will never
    get it back, why keep craving it?
Why should I seek any Lord other
        than beautiful Kaginele Adikeshava
    When you have the fine companionship
        of people who are true
    What further good can seeking far-off
        tirtha water do for you

Shiva Shiva Shiva enniro (BR p. 586)

O people of the three worlds
why not say 'Shiva Shiva Shiva'?
This japa is the origin of
    Vedas and Vedanta
and it is the medicine to cure
    the root cause of your ailments

Being born of a human being
do not forget yourself
don't waste your body, mind and soul
don't forget your purpose

O people of the three worlds . . .

If you want to erase
a billion crimes and errors
this is the holy prayer, unknown
to those with ordinary knowledge

O people of the three worlds . . .

If you need to conquer afflictions
caused by the god of death
If you want to attain the true
perfect liberation

O people of the three worlds . . .

If you want to become strong
living here on this earth
If you want to attain high
spiritual status in this life

O people of the three worlds . . .

If you wish to know the true
gurus of the path of the Shiva linga
If you hope to realize
the supreme Self in all

O people of the three worlds . . .

In this world if you want to be
a true teacher of wisdom
If you want to merge with Tattvapati
Lord of Truth, Adikeshava

O people of the three worlds
why not sing 'Shiva Shiva Shiva'
This japa is the source
        of Vedas and Vedanta
This medicine will cure
        the root-cause of your disease

Tallanisadiru (JKS p. 14)

Wait a minute mind, don't get shook up, keep cool
The same Lord protecting all will also protect you

Who's provided water for the tree
    standing on top of the mountain?
The Lord who created it—he
    is responsible for taking care of us all
        don't doubt it

Wait a minute mind, don't get shook up, keep cool

Who's provided food for birds
    and animals living in the jungle?
Like a mother who gave birth
    to her child the Lord will take good care of us
        no doubt about it

Wait a minute mind, don't get shook up, keep cool

The frog who is found croaking
    inside a stone—who fed him?
That all-knowing Adikeshava of Kaginele
    certainly he will protect everyone—there is
        no doubt about it

Wait a minute mind, don't get shook up, don't lose your cool
The same Lord protecting all of us will also protect you

Tanu ninnadu (JKS p. 33)

It's all part of you—body and soul
    The joy and the sorrow—daily life as a whole

Yours is the sweet speech of Veda, Purana, Shastra
    to which we listen intently, the story the scriptures tell
        is your tale
    And fixed staring with great fascination
    at beautiful young girls, that gaze also is yours
        It's all part of you . . .

'Anointing the body with sandalwood paste
and kasturi musk and other fragrances—that's yours too,
Lord, and the tongue which rejoices in the food
of the six-flavour feast—that also is yours
It's all part of you . . .

This body of five senses caught up in the net
of illusory bondage—it is also yours O Ranga
O father of the love-god, Vishnu Adi Keshavaraya
are human beings ever independent of you, apart?
Our body and soul, our life, it's all part of you . . .
the joys and the sorrows, daily life as a whole

Varakavigala (JKS p. 90)

The mediocre man should never show off
his talent for doggerel
in the presence of gifted born-poets;
And one should not bow down
and say 'I take refuge' to a piece of stone

Don't display beautiful objects of art
in the presence of sinners and scofflaws
Don't hold serious spiritual discussions
with short-fused intolerant folk

Don't use a glue-patched earthen pot
when you need to boil some water
Don't go to your relations
when you're troubled with poverty

Don't put down Lord Vishnu and extol Shiva
unless you want a short cut to hell
Don't go astray denigrating others
and become one more sinner in hell

Don't quarrel with your neighbours merely
because your wife tells you to
Don't set up housekeeping in a place
full of mean and vicious gossip

Don't mix with backbiters
who flatter you to your face
Most of all, never stop thinking
of our father Adi Keshava

Varava (JKS p. 3)

Bless me to be in your good graces
Grant me your lotus feet
O Sarasvati, Goddess of speech

Our Lady of Virtues, girl with the perfect teeth
with your gentle smile, radiant moonlike face
on your earlobes pearldrop jewels sparkle
Lotus-eyed Goddess, please reside in my heart

Charming melodious-voiced Goddess with moon-bright face
your red apsara's lips and fine nose so angelic
You are an exquisite doll full of holy power
and you stun people, making them feel drunk
bewildered by the love-god's arrows. Our Lady
resplendent with gold champak flowers in your hair
O Sharadambe bless me . . . Grant me your lotus feet . . .

You have the brilliance of one hundred million suns
you are the one who dwells in pure lotus hearts
of hundreds of the highest calibre poets
Queen of Brahma, O daughter-in-law
of Adikeshava of famous Kaginele

Bless me to be in your good graces,
Grant me the boon of your lotus feet
O Sarasvati our divine Lady of Speech

Vishvalokesha vishvalokesha (KK no. 160, p. 143, 'The Cosmic Lord')

Lord of all the universe, only embodiment of pure consciousness
Uplifter of the cosmos, Lord illuminating the world
with your all-knowing form.
Lord, who else pulls the strings behind this vast puppet show
who else is all-pervasive of the inner and outer but you

In the crown adorning your head are Dhruvaloka and other worlds.
On your forehead bejewelled by nine gems there is the entire Veda
In your mouth shruti revelation exists, the Maruts are in your breath,
in your eyes are sun and moon, in your vision the stars
have their existence, in thy great tongue is Goddess Sarasvati.
In your immense ears Ashvin *devatas* abide, O Hari, in your being
every excellence abides.

Lord of the universe,
In your neck are countless guests and scholars; in your shoulders
and arms, kings shine with radiant glory.
In your chest Vishnu resides, and in your belly
Hara and Brahma. On your backside Manu and other sages,
On the front of you are the peaks of mountains.
In your joints are the gods of love. O Hari—you shine from the
pores of your hair, far extending. Lord of the universe

Lord of the universe,
In your back are the Vasus and in your member is Shiva.
In your navel the whole world has its being. In your palms
are the Vishvadevatas. In your thighs
the Vaishyas exist in all their vigour.
In you are rivers flowing, the power to enchant,
and Shudras are in your lotus feet. Thus, O gracious Adikeshava
of Kaginele, you have the whole universe in your body.

Lord of all the universe, only embodiment of pure consciousness
Uplifter of the cosmos, Lord illuminating the world
with your all-knowing form.
Lord, who else pulls the strings behind this vast puppet show
who else is all-pervasive of the inner and outer but you

Yadavaraya brindavanalola (KK no. 210, p. 192)

O Madusudana! Lord of the Yadavas!
You play the flute in Brindavan
attended by all the gopis and Radha!

You play the flute with graceful fingers
caressing the tones *sa re ga ma pa da ni,*
you sing, as shining ones and apsaras above
listen in groups, oblivious to all else.

You play the flute and sing while you tend
the cows, playing different melodies in
various styles, with Shiva and Brahma dancing
and Tumburu and Narada singing along . . . O Madusudana . . .

Dear Adikeshava with eyes like lotus petals!
You play the flute, petting the cows and
their calves, making them happy with your charm
your guiding them to where they must go never fails.

O Madusudana! Lord of the Yadavas!
You play the flute in Brindavan
attended by all the gopis and Radha!

Yake ninilli pavadiside (KK no. 80, p. 69)

O *Pashchima* Ranganatha! Lord Hari
Most well known Lord in the world
why are you reclining in repose here
what's the story?

Were you tired of fighting with demon Tama
tired of holding the mountain on your back
(as Kurma, Vishnu's tortoise incarnation)
and of holding up the Goddess Earth as Varaha?
Were you exhausted from ripping the guts
from the demon when you were the man-lion?
Were your lotus feet hurt when you measured earth
earth the embodiment of what endures?

What's the story, are you relaxing now,
after decimating, all by yourself, the whole
      royal–military complex
and then discarding your axe, as Parashurama?
Are you taking a rest after your big work-out when
you chopped off the wife-snatcher Ravana's heads?

Does your body feel bushed from annihilating
such a great foe as Vali, when you were Rama?
Did you get fatigued from all that tromping you did
on the head of the poisonous serpent Kali?
Did you bow your head and lie down here, being shy
when you stood naked travelling so far as the Buddha?

Finally you, holder of the four ages, have mounted
your horse and have arrived as the cleansing avatar
of the kali yuga. Did the long journey here
wear you out? Or did you recline here in your
auspicious form to fulfil with grace the boon
of the great sage Gautama?

O Adikeshava, Supreme Lord of Kaginele,
you whose abode is on beautiful Shrirangapattana;
I cannot see anyone waking you up, Lord,
no matter how long you recline on the world stage here.

O Pashchima Ranganatha! Lord Hari
Most well known Lord in the world
why are you reclining in repose here—
what's the story?

Yamadutarinnenu (KK no. 59, p. 49)

Lord of Lakshmi Lord Raghunatha
Please say—what damage can Yama's servants do
if a person has knowledge of you?

If some smalltown whore commits adultery
when her husband arranges it beforehand
O Hari—what has she got to fear
If the governor of the province finds it out
'arrests her and chastises her?
    What damage can Yama's servants do
       if a person has knowledge of you

If a thief who shares his loot with the king
should break into a house to rob it—O Hari!
What can the king's night-watchman do
if the thief is hauled before him and accused
of stealing the loot which is part the king's too?
    What damage can the god of death do
        if a person surrenders to you

I offer up the merit of my good deeds, and the sin
of which I am guilty in my language and my thinking
And therefore, Ocean of Compassion, Adikeshava of
Kaginele—what harm can anyone do to me?
Lord of Lakshmi Lord Raghunatha
    Won't you say, what damage can Yama's servants do
    if a person has knowledge of you?

Yelli nodidaralli (JKS p. 61)

Wherever I look I see Rama
    Those who know this secret know
        that in their own bodies they can see Rama

O my brother, in your body
    you can see Lord Rama

The eye itself is the seed of the god of lust, Manmatha,
    but you can see *mokshasamrajya*—kingdom of liberation
        through this very same eye
You can see God through your inner eye
    by closing down your outer eye
Wherever I look I see Rama . . .

The nose breathes in and exhales as well
    Through this nose you can find the yoga of renunciation
        through the subtle inner nose you can know
            the supernatural wonder
                which silent sages know
Wherever I look I see Rama . . .

The gate to karma is the ear
    You can hear *mokshasara* nectar of liberation
        through this ear
    This very ear is the axe of action, in the inner ear
        you can perceive the eternal vibration
        which is the root of existence
    Wherever I turn I find Rama . . .

But if you give up the body
    created by Lord Brahma
    and instead believe in the dummy made by Vishvakarma
    lost in endless pursuit of sense pleasures
    you are going to be lost
    Wherever I look I find Rama . . .

Ignorant people believe in superstitious customs
    be wise, don't have blind faith in wilderness stones
    All the futile little gods waver and falter
    Only our Badadakeshava truly knows
    Wherever I look I see Rama
        Those who know this secret know
            that in their own bodies they can see Rama

Bibliographic Code and References for Original Song Texts

AAS. V. Vijayaraghavacharya and G. Adinarayana Naidu (eds). *Adhyatma Sankirtanalu*. Madras: Tirupati Tirumalai Devasthanam, 1936.

AC. Sastri, V. Prabhakara (ed.). *Annamacarya Caritramu* (Life of Annamacharya) by Tallapaka China Tiruvengadanath. Tirupati: TTD, 1949.

AK. *Annamacaryula Kirtanalu*. Tirupati: TTD, 1977.

ARR. Rao, Adapa Ramakrishna. *Annamacarya*. Delhi: Sahitya Akademi, 1989.

AS. Setti,. Kanisitti Srinivasulu (ed.). *Annamacaryula Sankirtanalu*. Tirupati: TTD, 1977.

BKP. *Bhakta Kanakadasara Padagalu*. Bangalore: T.N. Krishnayya Shetty and Sons, 1975.

BR. Indrasaraswati, Anantananda (ed.). *Bhajana Ratnakara*. Madras: Sri K. Panchapagesa Iyer, 1972.

CH. Kuppuswami, Gowri and M. Hariharan, *Compositions of the Haridasas*. Trivandrum: College Book House, 1979.

DPS. *Dasara Padagala Sangrahavu* (Vol. I–IV). Belgaum: Sriramatattva Prakasa Printing Press, 1943, 1946, 1947, 1950.

DS. *Desi Suladi by Tallapaka Annamacharya 1408–1503 presented at the Annual Conference of the Music Academy*, Madras, on 28 December 1978. Madras, Tirupati: TTD, 1978.

GISSI. Raghavan, V. *The Great Integrators: The Saint Singers of India*. New Delhi: Publications Division, 1966. Ministry of Information and Broadcasting, Government of India, 1979.

IIJ. Bidarakundi, Shyamsunder (ed.). *Isabeku Iddu Jaisabeku: An*

Anthology of Kannada Kirthanas by Various Dasas. Gadag: Alochana Prakashana, 1989.

JC. Panchamukhi, Vidya Ratna Raghavendracharya. (Purandaradasa) *Jivana Charitre.* Hospet: Sri Purandaradasa Seva Mandala, 1956.

JKS. *Janapriya Kanaka Samputa.* Bangalore: Directorate of Kannada and Culture, 1989.

KK. Shastry, B. Shivanmurthy and K.M. Krishna Rao (eds.). *Kanakadasara Kirtanegalu.* Mysore: Government of Mysore, 1965.

MSDM. *Madhura Shri Dasa Manjari,* devotional songs sung by Sangeetha H. Katti, on a cassette produced by Madhuri Studios, Seshadripuram, Bangalore, n.d.

PDH. *Purandara Dasara Hadugalu.* Dharwar: Samaja Pustakalaya, n.d.

PDK. Rao, Pavanji Guru (ed.) *Purandara Dasara Keertane* Part I. Udupi: Sri Krishna Press, 1924.

PP. *Purandaradasara Padagalu,* n.d.

PSD. Rao, S.K. Ramachandra (ed.). *Purandara Sahitya Darshana* (in four volumes). Bangalore: The Directorate of Kannada and Culture, Government of Karnataka, 1985.

SAS. Rao, P. Venugopala (ed.). *Sri Annamacarya Sankirtanalu.* Madras: N.V. Gopal and Co., 1993.

SRP. Rao, Rajani Kanta. 'Some Raga Patterns of the 15th Century and Their Setting in Annamacharya's Lyrics', *Journal of the Madras Music Academy* Vol. LIV, parts 1–4, p. 186.

STAJ. *Sri Tallapakka Annamacaryulu Jivacaritramu.* 1978.

SVBPM. *Sri Venkateswara (Balaji) Pancharatna Mala:* Sri Annamacharya Samkirtanas Rendered by M.S. Subbulakshmi, Pamphlet accompanying 5 L.P. records of songs and *stotras* dedicated to the Lord of the Seven Hills.

WTP. Reddi, K. Sitarama. *Works of Tallapaka Poets,* Vol. II. Tirupati: 1936.